AIN'T NOBODY NOBODY

HEATHER HARPER ELLETT

Copyright © 2019 by Heather Harper Ellett
Cover and jacket design by Mimi Bark

ISBN 978-1-947993-70-9
eISBN: 978-1-947993-83-9
Library of Congress Control Number: tk

First hardcover edition September 2019 by Polis Books, LLC
221 River St., 9th Fl., #9070
Hoboken, NJ 07030
www.PolisBooks.com

POLIS BOOKS

To Mom first

And Bryan too

PART
ONE

CHAPTER ONE

Just before daybreak, in the Year of our Lord 1996, two of Randy Mayhill's hunting dogs cornered a wild hog, one dog backing it into a corner, one with his mouth clamped on its ear. Mayhill, still in his pajamas (boxer shorts, a holster), scrambled out of his tiny house to survey the commotion, and then stabbed the hog behind its shoulder, killing it before it could see another sunrise. Mayhill grabbed its hind legs, dragged it onto a tarp set aside just for this purpose, and shooed the dogs away so they wouldn't wreck his prize. Then he went to work immediately on the hog, skinning it with a hunting knife, occasionally tearing off scrap pieces and throwing them on the porch for the hero dogs because fair was fair, it was their kill. "Still," he said aloud to nobody, "they're my dogs."

Even as he gutted the hog—blood up to his arms, smiling like a televangelist—Mayhill was aware that most men would have preferred to trap the hog and shoot it point-blank, easy-peasy. Mayhill approached life like hand-to-hand combat. Van had said that once. At the time, Mayhill had choked out a thank you, touched that his best friend had known him so well, until he realized that Van hadn't meant it as a compliment.

But the hog plague was hand-to-hand combat. The feral hog. *Sus scrofa*. Destroyer of crops and canines. It was war, an unwinnable one at that, and lesser men snapped. Clet Boudreaux poisoned them with antifreeze, but it killed all his deer and squirrels. Rudy Lyons went bankrupt on a fancy German trap he bought off the computer. One night, after they uprooted his forest of pine seedlings, Jimmy Cason stood on his front porch—in full fatigues—and mowed down a bunch of hogs with an AK-47 he bought out of the trunk of a Honda Civic in Dallas. And Jimmy Cason was the game warden.

The hogs multiplied too fast: babies could have babies in six months, a plague of biblical proportions. And Snorty begat Prickly and Prickly begat Tusky and whatnot. The scientists called it "high reproductive potential," a condition that had never been a problem for Randy Mayhill personally, but to tell the truth, the hogs hadn't been much of a problem for him either. A man has to have something to lose something, and he didn't have anything.

Even though the dead hog was practically worthless, Mayhill was thankful because it instantly filled the abyss of his agenda. Most days, he drifted through his waking hours listening to the police scanner, waiting for something to happen. In the morning, the part of his day when he felt optimistic and the world was still intact, before the void of his schedule turned his stomach like a hangover, he fell into his routine. He drank his first breakfast Dr Pepper, read his books (Shakespeare and Larry McMurtry), fed his dogs (Boo, Atticus, and Pat Sajak the dachshund), and refreshed the hog trap bait (corn and strawberry Kool-Aid). He then stood on his front porch with a pair of 1970 Bushnell binoculars to check on his dead best friend's family, Birdie and Onie, to see if maybe, just maybe, today they needed him (they didn't). Then, for most of the afternoon, he settled into his chair, cleaned his collection of antique guns and handcuffs, all while lulled into a trance by the crackle of the police scanner.

Mayhill had mostly finished processing the hog when he noticed five buzzards circling high in the sky across the pasture toward the house where Onie and Birdie lived. He dashed to the front of the house and, without wiping his hands, picked up his binoculars. In the moons of the lenses, he saw Bradley the farmhand, and Birdie, his best friend's seventeen-year-old daughter, standing over a dead man folded over the barbed wire fence at the tree line. Four buzzards bring visitors, but five buzzards bring luck, the saying went, and something about the way the hair stood up on his blood-streaked arms told Mayhill that today, finally, he would be the lucky one.

He washed his hands, took a quick look in the mirror, and slicked down his thinning hair with his palm. He scrambled to find a shirt with buttons and a pair of jeans that fit, then slipped his gun in his shoulder holster. He hopped awkwardly to avoid his bad knee, pulled his jeans up in three yanks, inhaled to button them, and then shot out the door, forgetting his belt entirely.

Mayhill and Birdie had spoken only once or twice since her father's funeral a year ago, after which she retreated like a nun into Onie's and her cloister. Still, she and Mayhill had waved when they passed each other on the road. Or rather, he had waved. That was just fine because it was safer for Birdie to keep both hands on the wheel. Highway fatalities and whatnot.

But that was the past! Now, as Mayhill power-walked toward her in the pasture, he knew that Birdie needed him and would be thankful for him because, really, who better to call in such a situation if not Randy Mayhill? Certainly not Bradley. Had she called Bradley, the farmhand? A kid, just a few years older than her! *Bradley?*

The man on the fence had dark hair. He was dead—shot in the back, his body falling toward them, as if he had been running from something in the woods. He was folded over the fence like laundry, face down and arms splayed, and birds—three shrikes with brown crowns and black masks—flittered near his head. Then, one by one, the three birds perched on the fence as if the man were just another lizard or grasshopper they had impaled on the barbed wire prongs and waited to pick apart piece by piece.

Bradley and Birdie stood awkwardly at a distance from the body, facing away from it and from each other, and when they saw Mayhill approach, they turned like screws in their spots, only to look slightly in the other direction. Mayhill tipped his hat to Birdie, who did not prostrate herself at his boots and beg for his help. She stood frozen, indignant, arms crossed, her face a mixture of shock and rage that confused him. He had never known Birdie to be quiet.

"Bradley!" Mayhill shouted. "Get over here!"

Bradley startled and turned from the fence to look at him. He was dirty blond and big, almost as big as Mayhill, and had the vacant look of a Ken doll, a numb, open-mouthed expression not unlike the hog

Mayhill had just gutted. Mayhill had never entirely trusted him, though Van had trusted Bradley without question. Bradley walked closer but stood a curiously far distance away from Mayhill.

"Why you here, Bradley?" Mayhill asked. "Who is he? What happened?"

Bradley shook his head.

"You need to tell me, Bradley." Mayhill jabbed his finger in the air at him. "You need to tell me who he is and what happened."

"I don't know. I don't know." Bradley's eyes darted around the pasture. "I just showed up and—"

"You just showed up?"

"Wednesday," Bradley said. "I work at Birdie and Onie's every Wednesday."

This was true. Mayhill shaded his eyes and studied Bradley's face. Bradley's gaze was affixed to Mayhill's feet, his hands trembling. He had a long, dark bruise on his forearm, and body odor radiated from him, even ten feet away.

"You been in a fight?"

"No, sir."

"That's the bruise of a man who's been in an altercation." Mayhill pointed at Bradley's arm.

"No, sir," Bradley said again. "Accident at work."

Mayhill nodded slowly. Mayhill believed Bradley because young men like Bradley weren't built for lies. Lying required an intellect that Bradley simply did not possess.

Bradley glanced at Birdie. Birdie was tall and lanky like her father, Van, and had wild brown hair, which she tied up in a rat's nest of curls on top of her head. Birdie—skin like paper, pale like flour—appeared even paler than Mayhill remembered, almost translucent, like sausage casing. Mayhill walked closer to Birdie and bent at the waist to meet her eyes like he would a child. "You okay?"

Silence. She looked over his shoulder, out into the pasture, away from the body. Her lip trembled slightly. Shocked into silence.

"You see anything this morning? Do you know this man?" Birdie said nothing, and so he raised his voice an octave. "Birdie Girl...I need you to tell me what happened."

Her brow furrowed deeper in reaction to, Mayhill guessed, the voice that her father Van had said made him sound like a jackass. He straightened up and stroked his belly as if a cat lay upon it. His jeans were tight against his legs that had ballooned with time, and his pants were in no more danger of falling off than they were of asking how the dead man's day was going, but the lack of belt tormented him nonetheless.

He felt Bradley looking at him again, and he turned, only to find Bradley now staring at his arms. "It's blood," Mayhill assured him, which did not seem to assure Bradley at all. "Has Birdie said anything?" Mayhill had never known the quick-witted Birdie to be devoid of words.

Bradley shook his head. "No, sir. Just told me to follow her."

"When'd you get here?"

"Around eight," Bradley said.

"Where's Onie?"

"House."

"See anything?"

"No, sir."

"You find him?"

Bradley shook his head. "Buzzards found him."

Mayhill turned on his heel and paced in front of the body, and rattled off details to nobody in particular. "Knife...rope. Hog trapper prolly...no rifle. Tattoo..." He snorted. "Figgers."

Mayhill yanked at the front of his jeans where his belt buckle normally stood like a monolith, and he breathed in the scene. Something about Birdie's folded arms, the scowl—it reminded him of Van, his best friend, his heartbreak, a man who believed that the law did not apply to him, that the law was a suggestion to be dispensed with when it inconvenienced him. Mayhill realized right then that Birdie wasn't speaking for a reason. Perhaps it wasn't shock at all. Perhaps it was guilt. Dread rose up in his belly. In the untangling of his epiphany, the words dropped from his mouth slowly, carefully, high-pitched. "Birdie...did you...?"

Birdie's gaze met his, her lip quivering.

"Birdie..."

"You think she did it?" Bradley shouted, then lowered his voice and whipped his head to Birdie. "Did you do it?"

"This ain't a courtroom," Mayhill said. "I'm here to help. But don't answer that, Birdie."

Silence.

"Thatta girl." Mayhill winked at her.

Bradley paced away from them, his hands massaging his head.

With that, the unflappable Birdie started to cry, a slow runnel of tears down her face, and she spoke so quietly that Mayhill had to lean in to hear. "I want him gone," she said. "I just want him gone."

"I know you do, Birdie Girl," Mayhill said. He wanted to hug her, but he knew better than to do such a thing. Mayhill tugged his jeans up by the belt loops and held them taut as if there was no waist at all anymore, and looked out at the pasture, the land torn up by pork vermin. He knew he would fix it all for her because that's what her daddy would have wanted, and it's what he would have wanted for his own daughter if he had been lucky enough to have one.

"You gonna call the police?" Bradley asked quietly, and stared straight ahead at the ground.

"Why would I do such a thing?" Mayhill asked.

Bradley shrugged, then gestured his head toward the dead man. "I dunno."

"Private land, private matter," Mayhill said. "And you seem to forget I was the police, young man."

Mayhill lowered his voice to a non-jackass octave and whispered so Bradley couldn't hear. "I'm sorry this happened, Birdie. Had the hogs just come last night…hell, if this asshole just had a Snickers in his pocket, hogs would've eaten him up and problem solved. It's a shame you have to deal with it at all, Birdie Girl, with all you been through." He shook his head at the dead man suspended on the fence. "That's the real tragedy here."

⠐⠄⠂⠄⠂⠄⠐⠄⠂⠄⠐

The only thing Randy Mayhill had ever wanted to be was a sheriff, and he pined for those 842 days like other men pined for a lost love—a Bob Wills-"Faded Love"-wail-into-your-beer kind of pine, a get-drunk-and-wreck-your-truck kind of pine. Even then, that analogy didn't seem heartbreaking enough. He pined for those two and one quarter years like a wiser man might pine for a lost dog because sheriffing, like owning a dog, was all reward. Like a good dog, the law was consistent and loyal. It provided comfort and reliability where the rest of the world hemorrhaged in chaos and rap music. When he lost everything—massaging the law to save his best friend, no less—it was

Van's mother Onie who seemed to understand the depths of what he had endured, even though she was dealing with a loss unfathomable to everyone. When Mayhill lost everything, it was Onie who raised her hands toward the heavens and said, "'Tis better to have loved and lost than never to have loved at all!" And Mayhill, so moved by her recognition of his loss, could only choke out two-word responses for fear he would break down and cry in her bony lap like a fat, tragic baby: "No question!" "You bet!" "Hunnard percent!"

The house Onie had given him then was very small, not much larger than a trailer, but it was definitely not a trailer and, really, it was more than any reasonable man would need. After he left Birdie and Bradley, Mayhill was unable to sit. He paced the house back and forth, but it was so small that he had only five steps each way before he ran into the kitchen or the bathroom depending on the direction.

On a shelf next to the third gun safe was a pair of original 1890s Bean/Cobb detective handcuffs. Mayhill had bought them off of a Mexican antique dealer in Sugarland a decade back. They were so shiny Mayhill could see his reflection in them. Next to those handcuffs was a pair from the WWII Canadian Military, which he almost didn't buy on account of them being Canadian, but when laid out, the interlocking of the cuffs reminded him of a lace pattern his mother stitched at the bottom of hand towels, and they had since become his favorite.

Mayhill's collection took up the entire house, which probably wasn't impressive given how small the house was, but if you considered how small the pieces were, it became impressive all over again. It was this collection and the promises of the police scanner that had kept him going when there seemed to be no reason at all. Today, the waiting had paid off, and Randy Mayhill had work to do! Honest-to-God actual work—not leftovers he pilfered off the police scanner that offered only loose cows and stay-at-home prostitutes.

He had sent Birdie home with the instructions to relax—*relax!*—because she had experienced enough trauma for one lifetime, and he had asked Bradley to come back and repair the fence the next day at eight a.m. sharp. Bradley had asked why—the fence was fine, he said—and Mayhill had said that he had a hunch it wouldn't be. Then Bradley said that is an odd hunch and Mayhill said that Bradley would be better off sticking to fence building than questioning a lawman who had found him standing over a dead body. So, eight a.m. it was.

Back home, Mayhill grabbed the phone receiver off the kitchen wall and dialed.

"Gabby Grayson! Mayhill here."

There was silence on the other end—a moment of calculation—then a voice, small and tentative. "Randy?"

"Hello, Gabby."

"Randy." She said his name like an exhale. "It's been so long. It's so good hear your voice."

Mayhill tipped his head to the phone as if she could see him. "You too, you too. How are the girls?"

"Causin' trouble."

"You know I don't believe that! Those angels?" Gabby laughed, and for a second, Mayhill thought he could smell her perfume, sweet and cheap (gardenias in rubbing alcohol). "Listen, girl, I got a favor to ask. Any missing persons? Anybody?"

"Why you ask?"

"Just helping out a friend."

"You got friends now?"

He made a sound that he hoped imitated laughing, though he didn't find the joke funny in the least. "You my friend, ain'tcha?"

"You know I'd do anything for you," Gabby said.

Mayhill smiled into the phone, the prospects for the day improving by the second.

"But…" she added. "You know I'm not authorized to give names to the public."

"Public? Gabby, you know I ain't public. We worked together a decade."

"We worked together two years. Two years, Randy."

"But we known each other thirty."

"Twenty. High school was twenty years ago."

"Twenty-five," Mayhill said.

"Don't matter," Gabby said. "Could've been a hundred but it ain't right anyhow. Don't do that to me."

"Do what?" Mayhill asked, incredulous. "I'm asking a simple question, and you got a simple answer."

"Yes, it's simple: I cain't! I just cain't! You know that, and we haven't spoken in…well, I don't appreciate you putting me in this position."

"What, the new sheriff gonna get mad at you? I hear he runs a tight ship. He off the ventilator yet?"

"It's not a ventilator!" Gabby said. "It's an oxygen tank, and his mind is sharp as a tack."

"He's eighty-four!"

"He's a veteran!"

"Union or Confederacy?"

"W-W-2! We should be honored that he agreed to serve this community! And in his golden years!" She composed herself. "Just six more months and he'll be the oldest living sheriff in Texas history. Right here in Pine County! Now that is an honor. You don't go and tell me that ain't an honor."

"I'll pray his electricity doesn't go out."

"Randy!" Her voice didn't sound like breath anymore.

"You gonna help me out or not?" Randy asked. "Help out an old friend."

They began to talk over each other, voices louder.

"You haven't talked to me since—"

"He's trying to turn this ship—"

"After everything that happened with Van—"

"You know more than anybody that—"

"High school was a long time ago—"

"But why would you—"

Until Mayhill had had enough and yelled into the receiver, "*Okaaaaaay*, Gabby! You hug those girls' necks for me!" and slammed down the phone.

A sadness stormed Mayhill so violently that he kicked the wall. Pat Sajak, the dachshund, startled. There had been so much potential before interaction with live humans had derailed a perfectly good investigation, and the grouping of him with the common man—the public!—had been too much, as if he had called asking for her bra size and credit card number.

Mayhill hobbled out the back of his house and grabbed a beaten five-gallon feed bucket off his back porch, then filled it halfway from a feed sack of corn he kept just inside the doorway. He walked back to the kitchen and got a stack of strawberry Kool-Aid packets. Personally, he was partial to blue raspberry (blue teeth and whatnot) but the hogs preferred strawberry—everybody knew that—so he mixed it into the corn and churned it with his arm, his right hand as red as Lady Macbeth's.

Mayhill ambled over the hill, navigating landmines of ant beds and bullnettle as the story formed in his head: the dead man must have tried to harm Birdie somehow. A hog trapper—no! a hog trapper rapist!—had come upon Birdie and Onie's tiny house and spotted the innocent Birdie, and then, lulled by teenage beauty—clearly, he had never spoken to her—broke into her house, only to realize too late that Birdie was no ordinary girl as he sprinted across the pasture and into the woods, trying in vain to escape the long reach of her rifle. He turned to shoot in a panic…but alas, a fence! A gunshot!

Fatherly pride swelled up in his chest. Van's little girl taking things into her own hands! Van would have been proud. He hoped—God, how he hoped!—that Van would be proud of him too, because Mayhill owed Van, and guilt makes a man do troublesome things.

The bucket was heavy and bounced against Mayhill's bad knee. He walked past the burn pile and the south tree line, passing a small bunch of hogs sleeping in the woods before he reached the man. The buzzards still circled overhead, and two little bull shrikes still poked away at the dead man's head. Grisly was the word, the blood soaking the man's shirt, the slight stench baking in the heat as the afternoon sun beat down.

Mayhill wanted no traceable record. He would take no pictures, no written notes, but he memorized the scene with his eyes like a good lawman does. The man had a small tattoo of a star on his hand, not like a patriotic star, ostentatious and sharp, destined for flags and Wal-Mart t-shirts, but delicate like a shooting star, a trail blazing behind it. He had a hunting knife, but no bulge of a wallet in his jeans, and for this Mayhill was relieved because then he would not be forced to look at it, to risk his fingerprints upon him.

It was a familiar prayer for Randy Mayhill, said enough times to count on two hands: "Lord, forgive me for what I am about to do."

But never one to surrender entirely, Mayhill always amended it. "But Lord, ye might also consider that sometimes men are left to clean up your messes and maybe thou shalt consider not creating such messes to begin with. Amen."

Justice was not always pretty, and Mayhill had to practice sensitivity like he had to practice most reactions aside from bravado and severity. He knew it didn't matter to anyone but him, but Mayhill removed his hat to pay respects to the dead man, whoever he was, and tried to think real, real hard of the dead man's family and friends to remind himself that no matter the derelict the man had become, he had once been a real person who presumably would rather be alive right now enjoying a chopped beef sandwich, but Mayhill couldn't shake it. For the first time in over a year, he felt what he could only remember now as happiness. Then he set to work at being a hero with a bucket of corn and two dozen packets of strawberry Kool-Aid.

CHAPTER TWO

What went wrong? Mayhill would contemplate the question like a Zen koan for the next few days.

Perhaps the trail of corn had not been thick enough. Perhaps the hogs had not been starved enough. Or was it the Kool-Aid itself? Had the hogs not been sufficiently drawn to it? Had word spread among hog congregations that their favorite treat promised doom, like Halloween apples with razor blades tucked neatly inside?

But really, really, if Mayhill was honest with himself—and every man should be—he knew what had gone wrong: he had left his post. Simple as that. Let's be clear: Mayhill had been dutifully vigilant. He had dozed sparingly and slipped inside only a few times for Dr Pepper and jerky. But it was in these fleeting moments that Mayhill would miss the person who, under the cover of night and trees, removed the body from the barbed wire fence before the hogs even had a chance to go to work.

The night had been dark despite a waning gibbous moon—half full except for a big dent on the side like a smashed orange. Try as he might, his eyes had not been able to adjust in the darkness, and through the binoculars, all he could see was a dim figure where the man hung. Mayhill propped up on the porch, dogs flanking him, and watched for movement. Around midnight, hogs advanced upon the pasture and ducked into a pocket at the end of the tree line, but hours later, Mayhill could still make out the dark, blurry image of the man through the binoculars. Around four a.m., seven deer ran from the thicket. Around 6:30 a.m., when the mockingbirds began to sing, Mayhill left his station and went inside for another Dr Pepper, turned on the scanner for a few minutes (drunk driver, corner store break-in), and then returned to the porch. High, thin clouds had moved in and the rising sun bathed the pasture in an orange glow. He checked his binoculars again and, at first, he thought it was a trick of the changing light, but truly, the man was gone. Just like Birdie had wanted.

But it had not been the hogs.

The signs of hogs are universal, like those of jaundice and lust. There were no rounded tracks pressed like giant coffee beans into the earth. The soil around the man was still intact, not rooted and freshly tilled. The corn remained entirely untouched, save a few pieces pushed into the ground by footprints. Tennis shoes.

Mayhill had been watching the body. But someone had been watching Mayhill.

Staring at the empty fence, he felt almost deaf, confusion plugging his ears like an infection. His brain raced to catch up. The next thing he knew, Mayhill was banging on Birdie and Onie's door and popping his head in front of the side window. "He's gone!" he barked through the windowpane.

Birdie looked up, startled, from the breakfast table. Onie, looking older and frailer than this time last year, sat in front of the television. A car salesman screamed at her from the set.

Mayhill paced the front porch and removed his hat, bumping the long red tube of the hummingbird feeder. He smoothed his right hand over the thinning rivulets that lined his scalp. He wiped the sweat from his hairline, and Birdie stepped onto the front porch. He leapt so quickly toward her that she flinched.

"What did you do with it?" The words sounded more accusatory than he meant. "Where did it go?"

"What?" Gone was the panicked girl from yesterday. She crossed her arms, her father's indignation glossed across her face.

Mayhill lowered his voice and looked around. He clenched his hat so hard that his knuckles turned white, the brim crushed like a flower in his hands. "The body, Birdie. The body."

Birdie tilted her head curiously and tucked a corkscrew of dark hair behind her ear. "I don't know what you're talking about."

CHAPTER

THREE

Bradley Polk had an extraordinary ability to bury his big head in the sand. It was a defense mechanism he had learned early on, and the naiveté had served him well in many regards, primarily in that he was still alive, and if you really think about it, we all have to be a little naive to wake up every morning and think it's worth trimming our neck hairs. His naiveté, however, like the high reproductive potential of the hogs, was a defense mechanism out of control. Despite the staring and the mouth breathing (broken nose, deviated septum) and the opinions of men like Randy Mayhill, Bradley Polk was not dumb. He had simply over-executed his naiveté. It was a misused tool, like a butter knife cutting a tomato.

The night before he saw a body on a fence, Bradley smelled like a rotting sandwich and tried to stay awake as he drove the back way into the woods behind Birdie's and Mayhill's houses. He had slept a total of twelve hours over the past three days, spread out in improbable naps—

one on a bed of sweet feed sacks. His head felt heavy on his thick neck, and his reflection in the rearview mirror was disembodied and unreal; it mocked him like a fun house attraction.

Bradley needed sleep, but like all young men, he needed money more. He wanted to own his own land someday—timberland and cattle-freckled pastures stretched out like a palm slapped on the back of the earth. He would hire men like him, ranch hands and whatnot, like Van had done. Every leftover bit of money went to this dream. As it was now, there was not a whole lot of leftover money. None, actually. He was nineteen years old and still living with his mama, but his mama was thirty-eight and about to get kicked out of her house for not paying rent. She had kicked him out a few days earlier, said not to come back or she'd call the cops. While he didn't care so much about his mother figure, her house was the only place he had to take a shower, and she had made it clear he could not return without cash in hand. Carol Brady she was not.

He was beginning to smell so bad he had to keep the windows rolled down, and the few people he had interacted with, he talked to them at a leper's distance. Buzzards eyed him while he worked. Four buzzards meant *you're gonna get laid*, someone had told him, and Bradley had thought that anyone who would sleep with him in his current condition was not a girl to be slept with in the first place.

The hogs had taken down a large line of fence at Rudy Lyon's, and though Bradley couldn't imagine how he'd have the fortitude to build the fence and then go to his night work after that, he couldn't say no when Rudy, red-faced and drunk, had waved Bradley down on the main highway. Bradley's night job hadn't paid him anything yet, so he had worked all day on the fence—all cutting and digging and tying— and then he drug his overheated, under-slept body to his truck, and headed to his other job where he would work all night until morning when he would wake up and go to Birdie's because it was Wednesday. He always went to Birdie's on Wednesday and Saturday.

Staying awake was easier on the back roads than on the sleepy snakes of blacktop highways. The late summer storms had washed out the dirt roads, and every few feet Bradley would hit a pothole, pop out of his seat, hover a good six inches in the air, crash back down, and then wince at the scraping sound coming from the underbelly of the truck. Even when driving slowly, thoughtfully, a concussion was not out of the question, the beer between your legs would certainly spill, your spit cup sloshing. Jerry Miller's cur dog once popped out the backend of the truck. "Flew like a goddamn angel," he told Bradley, and petted sad Roscoe, the dog's leg in homemade cast of old t-shirt strips and Elmer's glue. Even at the road's worst, when it took a nail-biting, gut-jiggling forty-five minutes to drive only two or three miles, it never occurred to anyone to get out of their trucks and walk, any more than it would occur to a bird to take the bus to Cancun for winter.

Bradley's destination was remote, a series of eight or nine turns in the deepest part of the forest, marked only by memory because he had been forbidden to write it down. Bradley turned down an old, narrow logging road that had mostly grown over with a canopy of low-slung pines. During the recent storm, the oldest trees had lost several branches, which had fallen to the ground in limbs so giant they were almost trees in their own right.

When he had started this job, the instructions he had been given were clear and paranoid: Bradley was to stop his truck just before turning onto the final trailhead, roll down the window, cut the engine, then listen for a good few minutes. Only when he was sure nobody was coming, he could get out, drag the trailhead branches aside, then turn and drive a little bit down the trail. He was then to place the branches neatly back in place, but not too neatly as to be suspicious. Then he could get back in his truck and head to work.

The stench and tiredness had taken Bradley over like a handle of bourbon, and so the night before he saw a dead man hanging on Birdie's fence, he did not follow instructions. He did not stop and listen before he stopped his truck. No, Bradley simply parked his beat-up blue truck at the trail, hopped out with the engine still running, and dragged the big branches out of the way. The branches were heavy, and the old bark dug into his hands in jagged pokes and tore at the fresh bruise on his arm, which made him cuss the uselessness and paranoia of the exercise. Suddenly, Bradley heard a vehicle coming down the trail, heading toward him into the woods, as if it had come from the main highway. At first, he thought it was his imagination, the tricks a mind played on a sleepless man, but then he heard the unmistakable scraping of a vehicle's undercarriage, the thrum of an engine approaching.

"Shit!" Bradley dropped the giant branch, then sprinted back to his truck as fast as he could, his heart pounding in his chest, sure his boss was about to catch him.

He scrambled to his seat and placed both hands on the wheel as if he had just arrived at the trailhead and not skipped any steps at all. Just then, a small, black utility truck rocked around the curve.

It was not his boss.

The logging road was too narrow for two trucks to pass, so the driver hit the brakes and his truck came to an abrupt stop a few feet in front of Bradley's. Bradley froze, not knowing what to do with a stranger here, a stranger who looked him right in the face, could pick him out of a police lineup. Bradley stared straight ahead with his hands gripped tightly on the wheel and scanned the ledgers of his mind for all the possibilities of his next move, but all Bradley could think was: *This man should not be here. This man should not be here. What do I do?*

Bradley had been working in this part of the woods for six months and had only seen hogs and deer. It was safe here, comforting even. Despite the anxiety-clenched instructions to move branches just so and listen for so long, he had never been given specific direction in the unlikely event that he run across a flesh-and-blood human. Because what were the odds out here? Really, what were the odds? One human for every four hundred hogs? No, he had only been given the helpful guideline of, "And if you do see somebuddy…that's when you call in the big dogs." His boss had then curled his hand into a thumbs-up, turned it toward himself, and bounced his thumb against his sternum.

Even now, Bradley couldn't blame the Big Dog. The Big Dog hadn't planned that far because the Big Dog's mind had been on more important, more probable things than a random black Datsun finding its way into the winding log trails of dead, abandoned timberland south of the Trinity. It was safe.

"Hey!" The man leaned out the window, his elbow resting on the frame. "You gonna let me by?"

Bradley finally looked the man in the face. He was tan with dark hair, a face as welcoming as a buzz saw, and Bradley knew immediately he had met him before, but he couldn't remember where. *Think, Bradley!* But Bradley had the kind of young man brain that only registered girls and those who would give him money, so his mind spun aimlessly. Who was he? Was it possible the man was supposed to be there? Should he ask?

"Hey!" the man yelled again. "You stuck or you deaf?"

Bradley didn't lean out the window to respond; instead, he just nodded dumbly through the windshield, and breathed out his mouth. (Make no mistake, Bradley would regret this later.) Almost without thought, he put his truck in reverse and edged slowly into the ditch. The man drove by and eyed him, a permanent scowl. Bradley's heart beat in his ears as he watched the black truck in his rearview mirror. A big wire trap was propped precariously in the back of the man's pickup truck. A rope or two tangled on the side. Two rubber boots stuck upside down where the cab met the bed.

A hog trapper.

Then he disappeared, just a trail of dust snaking around the curve.

Bradley sat in his truck a good while and waited for the adrenaline to burn off. He racked his brain for how he knew the man. A black Datsun. His thoughts circled around Birdie and Van like buzzards— the man had worked for them, hadn't he?—but the thoughts couldn't find anywhere to land.

Bradley then, in the dizzying haze of adrenaline and sleep deprivation, completed the routine. He cut the engine. He dragged the branches out of the way. Then he drove his truck onto the tiny trail and parked again. He dragged the branches back into place to obscure the entrance to trail.

What if the man drove back by? Should he grab his shotgun just in case?

Bradley climbed back into his truck and drove deeper into the trail. The trail was so narrow that the tree branches scraped the sides of his truck and poked in the windows like hands grabbing him. Eventually, he parked again, then walked about a half mile into the forest to the campsite, just as all the light from the day sucked into the trees.

The campsite was sparse. It had a single pop-up tent for the nights when Bradley needed to sleep out there—and nights like these when he had no place to go—and two small camp chairs that slung low to the ground covered in dirt and chalky white bird shit. A beat-up blue ice cooler and an old rusted lantern sat beside the camp chairs. Bradley checked the cooler. One hot beer bobbed half-heartedly near the bottom of the water like a broken buoy. He popped the beer and slumped into the camp chair, exhausted but wired.

Bradley wondered if he had done the right thing, just letting the man go by as if nothing at all was happening out here in the forest. For the rest of his night shift, Bradley sat in a camp chair with a shotgun at his side and stared into the dark. He tried to think about the lyrics to Pearl Jam songs, the land he would one day own, the silhouette of certain girls—anything other than the hog hunter he had let go freely into the woods.

CHAPTER FOUR

Bradley had not shown up at 8 a.m. as promised. And a dead body was missing.

When things go missing in pairs, it is logical to assume that said things are together. Two socks, for example. If two socks go missing simultaneously, no one imagines that one sock found itself in the wrong drawer and the other sock took a puppet show on the road. There was an order to these things, a law, and so it seemed perfectly clear that when Bradley failed to show up, he had proven himself to be a key player. Perhaps Bradley was helping Birdie, perhaps not. But to protect Birdie properly, Mayhill had to find both socks.

The questions pestered him like flies. Who was the dead man? Who had watched Mayhill and stolen the body when the opportunity arose? Had the man done something to Birdie, or Bradley for that matter? And what had he done that was so heinous, so threatening that he found himself shot on a fence? Perhaps the worst question of all, and one he wasn't quite ready to entertain: had something happened to Bradley that he hadn't shown up? There were too many questions.

The real question, of course, was this: what kind of man would attempt to destroy a corpse to save his best friend's family?

To understand why a man would go to such lengths for a girl like Birdie—plain as bread, pleasant as gout—was to understand the loyalty of Randy Mayhill to Van Woods. In the case of Randy Mayhill, the kind of man who would desecrate a corpse, he was the most upstanding man you knew, better than you, really. A man whose moral compass spun in frantic circles because he was the point where all forces of morality converged, and in Mayhill's world, to destroy a dead body for his best friend's daughter—well, it would have been morally corrupt to do anything else.

Mayhill and Van were under contract, it seemed. They were born six months apart and to different parents, but they practically had been brought into this life together. To ignore their mysterious bond was to ignore the laws of nature. It was to be a bird and say, "I think I'll stay righcheer" when the winter wind started howling and the instinct to fly south vibrated every feather.

Mayhill didn't understand it himself. It was a force beyond him, as if long ago, his heart had pledged loyalty to a family who was not all bad, depending on who you asked, but who was not exactly good either. He barely knew himself around them, or what he would do, an almost unconscious force taking him over anytime they were involved. It was an unfortunate affliction, even though Mayhill would never call it "unfortunate," just as a cult member would never call his situation "unfortunate." *The bunker is clean! The dashiki sensible!* Still, the outside world would look upon him, tilt their collective heads, and shake them in pity. What a shame, what a shame, Randy Mayhill.

Back at his house, after leaving Birdie, Mayhill stood in front of the box fan and unbuttoned his pants, releasing his belly like a floodwall. At full capacity, the fan rattled so violently that it threatened to spring loose from the bolts, but it cooled him down and dried his clothes, which were soaked with sweat, his button-down shirt translucent like onion skin. Boo and Atticus stared at him tilt-headed and concerned through the screen door, and Pat Sajak, who suddenly appeared way too fat from pork and belly rubs, sniffed at his boots.

He picked up the county phone book—half as thick as a legal pad and flimsy enough to roll into a tube for fly killing—and thumbed to the Ps. No POLKs, no POLK Bradley. Then Mayhill remembered that Bradley lived with his mama, who had a different last name than him (which tells you something right there!) and he found JOHNSON Lisa and dialed. Mayhill wasn't expecting anyone to answer Bradley's house phone, but he called anyway because that's what you did—low-hanging fruit and whatnot—and it rang and rang into oblivion until the call disconnected and buzzed a fast, angry busy signal that signified nobody wanted to talk to him.

He would have to drive.

If ever anyone were to visit Mayhill, Birdie, or Onie, it would require coordinates and a working ability to navigate by stars. The county dump sat to the south, distant neighbors far to the east, State forest to the west, and the Trinity River to the north. Their closest neighbors were several miles away in every direction, and between them, a dense curtain of pine trees, dirt roads, and logging trails, mostly belonging to Van. One could easily get lost and stumble onto the next property over and not know it, the woods hypnotic and unceasing. There was a main highway that went through town, the kind of highway that was paved with slick black tar, the kind that a cartographer drew exactingly on a map with an inky pen. Then there were the roads that branched from that, county roads paved in cheap gray rock, and then the roads woven into the woods behind Mayhill's and Birdie's houses, which could only be called roads for approximately one-tenth of them. Then they required something else, a different kind of vernacular, a thesaurus, synonyms, variations on the theme of "road": a path, a spoor, a way. As in this "way" to the army ants—their underground den is the size of a basketball court! As in this "way" to Earl Martin's house—*he lived here for eighty years then died when he left the city limits! We think he's a ghost now!* The remoteness of their locale, of course, made the dead man's presence even more bizarre, as if he had dropped out of the sky, freshly shot, and then was retrieved by the spaceship from which he came.

Mayhill would spiral out from Birdie's house, staying on the dirt roads he guessed Bradley might travel, and look for any signs of where the man had come from. Pine trees six stories tall flanked him on both sides, giving way at times to pasture land or a cluster of dead trees. Pat Sajak, the dachshund, sat in the passenger's seat on a folded towel matted with dog hair, a nice protective padding so he wouldn't burn his hide on the hot leather of a truck in the sun. Pat Sajak had become Mayhill's regular companion because he was the first totally useless dog he had owned, and he took him everywhere. Pat Sajak couldn't hunt or guard like the big mutt hunting dogs, Boo and Atticus, but

Mayhill swore to God the dog could smile.

Mayhill came to a fork in the road and made a turn. Who were Bradley's friends? The thought of Bradley made him white-knuckle the wheel. He used to know these things—the vague constellations of people who were connected in discernible ways, that if you needed Shane you went to Dan, and if you needed Lance you went to Nellums. There were hubs around which people orbited like spokes on a wheel. Van had been a hub, and had Van been alive, Mayhill could have found Bradley through him. Bradley had moved from Houston a few years back. Rumor was he had put a boy in a coma, and another rumor was that he had impregnated a gym teacher, but Mayhill couldn't imagine Bradley having the virility for either.

As sheriff, Mayhill had seen Bradley with the cowboys working cattle, slinging a rope like he'd been born with spurs on his feet. Another time, he'd busted up a party where Bradley was the only white guy there, wide-eyed with a red Solo cup in his hand as he edged sideways out the back door amongst a scrum of black kids. Bradley Polk was everywhere and nowhere. Who had he been hanging out with since? Was it possible Bradley was off telling what he'd seen? "Even if he did," Mayhill said out loud, "nobody'd believe him because it's Bradley!" Pat Sajak smiled back. Bradley was nobody to everybody. That was the beauty of Bradley, if there was a beauty to him. Mayhill's grip relaxed on the wheel, and he leaned back and patted Pat Sajak on the head. The air conditioner was so high that Pat Sajak shut his eyes and his short hair managed somehow to blow back dreamily in the stream of air.

Off to the side, Mayhill saw some hogs resting under a cluster of trees, the field around them plowed to soil, and for the first time since the hog plague, he felt an ire toward them. *Y'all had one job to do…*

He looked in the rearview mirror and an old black Datsun truck bounced up behind him, brown dust hovering in a cloud around it. Mayhill thought it was Bradley for a moment: a white guy with a lot of facial real estate. He had never seen the truck before. While it was not unusual for trucks to be seen on the labyrinthine back roads of the woods, he knew most of them because one had to have a purpose to enter the maze to begin with.

The tiny truck whipped around Mayhill, and the driver gunned it as he sped by on a road not meant to be sped upon. The Datsun hit a hole, screeched to a halt, and almost crashed forward. Mayhill slammed his brakes to avoid hitting him, his arm shooting out to protect Pat Sajak, but the dog tumbled into the floorboard with a whimper. The driver, whom Mayhill saw in better detail now, was not Bradley but another kid—practically interchangeable—who was also blond-haired and dirty and looked as if he drove straight there from his parole meeting. The black paint job on the truck was fading, the sides scraped and so beaten that Mayhill was unsure how the truck was still running at all.

"Stay here," Mayhill said to Pat Sajak, and opened the door.

The boy frantically manhandled his stick shift back and forth, and then gunned backward out of the crater. He shot forward, a high-pitched wail as he grated the bottom of the carriage on the rock. Then the boy gassed it again, fishtailing as he sped off, but not before he raised his middle finger for a reason Mayhill couldn't ascertain.

Frank Frank Sam 614. Frank Frank Sam 614.

Mayhill ran back to his truck, his knee stiff underneath him, but by the time he put it in drive, the truck was long gone around the corner. He thought about speeding after him but his truck wasn't that fast, and the boy was clearly heading toward the main highway. There'd be no way to catch him from there.

Pat Sajak hopped back up on his seat. Mayhill held the wheel with his knees and, on instinct, wrote *FFS614* on a notepad splattered in Dr Pepper stains. Then he realized he had no obvious way to look up the delinquent, no way to bring the young man to justice, to talk to his parents, visit his girlfriend at work and suggest, politely, that she was dating a failure of a human being. He had no authority of any kind. He was just a fat man in a truck with his dog and Dr Pepper. He looked over and saw a sounder of wild hogs at work on what appeared to be a carcass. For a second, he was hopeful, until he saw that the carcass had antlers and again felt betrayed by the world.

"Goddammit, Bradley!" he yelled. He slammed his hands on the steering wheel. Then he did a three-point turn to change direction and drop Pat Sajak off at the house before he went to the dump.

CHAPTER FIVE

Randy Mayhill was the only person Birdie knew who would actually kill someone. He had been her father's best friend and all, but even Van had said that Mayhill would never truly be happy until he saw the life drain slowly from another human being. "The heart wants what it wants!" Van had said, and winked at her.

Case in point, Mayhill had been invited by the warden to witness an execution in Huntsville, but wires got crossed and Mayhill couldn't get in, and he had spent the next hour waiting outside, which liked to have given him a heart attack because, as Mayhill said, he "couldn't stand being with all the long-haired protestors who proclaimed the sanctity of life when half of them had punch cards at Planned Parenthood."

Birdie had not known what that meant at the time, but Van had guffawed, a hearty knee-slap of a laugh that made his big teeth fly from his mouth like piano keys. Mayhill was classy at least and did not bully his way through the prison door as he often did in situations of lesser import. Still, Van had said that Mayhill sulked around for a week afterward, as if he had been stood up for prom—which had also happened, but they were never to talk about Goddamn Gabby Grayson.

So to understand Van, you had to understand the kind of man he had chosen for his best friend, a man fascinated with literature and execution instruments in equal measure. Randy Mayhill loved his parents, who died shortly after high school, and he loved Onie and Van like family, and by extension he loved Birdie, and she him, though she had never understood why. He loved his town and his dogs. He loved women but had never found one to settle down with, who wanted to be rescued to the infinite degree that Randy Mayhill wanted to save. Other than that, he was as happy as a man could be. Yet, the last time Birdie saw Mayhill and her father together, Mayhill had been anything but happy.

It was a year or so before a dead man hung on her fence, and Birdie, Onie, and Van had been eating supper when they heard a truck pull up. Birdie remembered the evening vividly because it was one of the rare nights that Van had been home for a meal since his trees were devastated by bad luck and Southern Pine Beetle. That night, the three of them ate mustard greens and new potatoes that Onie had grown, and some beef Jimmy Nellums had given them. Onie and Van had nursed their Miller Lights, and Birdie relaxed for the first time in weeks because her father was finally at the table with them again.

Van looked out the window and saw the dirty white truck rolling up, SHERIFF printed in yellow and black on the side.

"Randy!" Birdie cheered. "I haven't seen him—"

"Dammit!" Van slammed his hands on the table and got up. "Randy."

"What's wrong?" Birdie asked. "Why's Dad upset?"

Onie shrugged and raised her eyebrows, her old lips puckered over the beer bottle.

"Stay in here." Van shoved his heel in the boot like he was mad at it and shot out the door.

"Stay in here?" Birdie asked. "It's Randy!"

"Stay in here." Van spit into the crabgrass that had taken over the flowerbeds, then stormed toward Randy's truck.

Birdie couldn't hear what they were saying but they went at it immediately. Van and Mayhill had always talked in animated ways because they were animated men, their stories flying like bullets, but today they were angry. Even at a distance, Birdie could tell it. They were both tall, all blue jeans and boots. Mayhill took off his hat and swung it wildly and gestured off into the woods.

Their voices rose. Mayhill yelled something indecipherable, arms waving in the air, then pointing at Van, jabbing his finger at him while backing away defensively, as if his finger were a knife. Van swiped at Mayhill's hand. Mayhill ripped his fist back. Then Van threw a punch, and Mayhill ducked. Van threw another punch right into Mayhill's nose. Mayhill swung back and landed a blow to Van's jaw. Van shook it off, yelling at Mayhill, and then, bizarrely, flashed his teeth. A growling dog. A maniacal smile.

"Stop it!" Birdie yelled.

Van front-kicked Mayhill in the knee, and Mayhill went down hard. An agonizing yell from Mayhill, and he scrambled to his feet, only to go weak in his injured leg again and grab at his knee. Mayhill stumbled quickly to his truck and then sped away in a plume of dust, the cats scattering like mice.

Van fumed past Birdie on the porch, his breath heavy. His face was red, his jaw already starting to swell, a tiny split in his lip leaking blood.

His nostrils flared like a bull's.

"Private land, private matter," he said, but Birdie, pale with confusion, wasn't sure who he was talking to.

⠄⠂⠄⠂⠄⠂⠄⠂⠄⠂

A few weeks later, Van would have the fakest of all funerals: a printed program with his name in calligraphy, a gaggle of choir ladies who thought he was now in hell for killing himself, a preacher who didn't know what to say about someone like Van, so full of God and the Devil both. The entire town turned out as towns are wont to do. Onie and Birdie sat in the front row of the church and quivered like divining rods, knowing they were brushing up against something bigger than themselves. Mayhill remained at the back of the church with a brown elastic bandage wrapped around the knee, outside of his jeans. He looked sad and pathetic, and Birdie stood stiff like a utility pole when he tried to hug her because, for the first time in her life, she did not want to hug Randy Mayhill. He was a man who had tried to hurt her father, who could have stopped Van from doing this awful thing, and for that, she could no longer trust him. As he dared hug her then, it seemed that Randy Mayhill was the kind of person who could do horrible things and forget he had done them entirely.

Afterward, Birdie saw Bradley sitting in his truck, just staring away at nothing, naiveté at work, and she wondered if he had ever even made it in the church or if he had convinced himself he was just there for the grape juice.

Onie received Van's ashes in his boot box, and never one for sentimentality, she emptied them as soon as they got home from the funeral. She didn't even go in the house first, just popped onto the front porch, opened the top, and a gray cloud puffed into the air, just as when she had emptied the dust pan earlier that morning. Then Van settled for all of eternity into the crabgrass.

CHAPTER SIX

"Trash is the great equalizer," Van had always said. Even somebodies were nobodies at the dump! You paid for a permit, though it was more like a membership fee, like at the country club. Mayhill didn't know anybody who was a member of a country club, but everyone was a member of the dump. Mayhill had burned his own trash since embarking on a career in hermitry, and trash burning was the only time he or any of the local men could be found in shorts. His own shorts were a ratty royal blue number made out of t-shirt material and holes, a relic from high school football. The task of burning trash left him sweaty, puckered, and red, and if it weren't for the teeth and the coat of ash on his skin, one might swear he was a newborn baby who stood six foot five in jeans he had clearly outgrown.

Virgil Fuller tended the dump and was missing three fingers on account of Desert Storm and friendly fire, and Van had said that

Virgil tried to recreate the hell of war so completely that he decided to tend the dump and marry Patsy Fuller. The fire was the obvious reason for its comparison to hell, but the less nuanced reason was Patsy Fuller herself, who Van and Mayhill agreed was a less attractive, more aggressive version of Saddam Hussein.

A year before, at Van's funeral, Mayhill would overhear Patsy Fuller say that suicide was an offense that sent you straight to hell. "Straight to hell!" she said, her finger pointing the wrong way to the sky, and her underarms flapping like bat wings. She had said it with the same certainty that I-45 sends you straight to Houston, and Mayhill, who worshiped the law and *Lonesome Dove* in that order, for the first time considered hell as a real locale, an inhabitable destination like Puerto Rico or Salt Lake City. But all he could do was imagine Van at the dump, shoveling burnt egg cartons and junk mail into the embers, his white legs singed under tattered shorts, and Mayhill took comfort in knowing that, if hell was real, Van wouldn't have minded the manual labor so much, though he would have minded eternity in shorts. Perhaps, Mayhill thought, that was the hell everyone was talking about.

. · ˙ · . · ˙ · . · ˙

The dump on Thursday was not busy because of the recent rains—no lines of idling trucks, no chivalrous men scrambling to help spinsters unload. Most everyone was content with tending to their own trash, raking up their own pits of hell, but Mayhill reasoned that if Bradley had helped Birdie dispose of a dead man, he would be so unimaginative as to show up at the dump with a body-shaped sack. It's exactly the kind of thing Bradley would do.

Mayhill rolled down his window. Virgil Fuller walked toward him and waved his remaining two fingers (pointer and middle), a perpetual peace sign, and Mayhill had to admit the gesture comforted him. It was a good omen. Since he had last seen him, Virgil Fuller had grown a thick, graying beard, which made him look much older than his mid-thirties. A piece of ash stuck gently to it, as a snowflake might—a Santa Claus in Hell—and he removed it delicately like it was a glittering snowflake instead of the remnants of feed sacks and foil lasagna trays.

"Sheriff!" Virgil cheered.

And Mayhill cheered back, "Virgil!" so happily that it surprised Mayhill as much as Virgil. Mayhill leaned out the truck window and shook Virgil's twin fingers, and it was all laughs, back slaps and where-ya-beens!—just a real nice reunion—until the smell of goodwill rose up like a pheromone and attracted the attention of Patsy Fuller, cueing her to come around the burning pit of trash in a miniature bulldozer to put a stop to all of it.

"Randy Mayhill! Raised from the dead!" Patsy Fuller yelled.

Randy nodded. "I'm sorry to disappoint you, Patsy. How you been?"

"How I been? You don't give a you-know-what how I been. Where *you* been? You disappear off the face of the earth."

"Just taking a hiatus," Mayhill said. "Catching up on my reading."

"Catching up on your reading!" Patsy Fuller had an annoying habit of repeating what people said. "That's what they calling it now? Slinking away with your head between your legs?"

"I've missed our little chit-chats, Patsy."

"Oh please." She rolled her eyes. "Where you been taking your trash?"

"Burnin' it."

"Burnin' it." She eyed him suspiciously. "You gained weight too.

Where's your permit?" Patsy climbed out of the bulldozer and grabbed a rake. She was shaped like an apple and covered in ash so thick she appeared to be a coal miner.

"I'm not dropping anything off," Mayhill said. He watched as Virgil Fuller slinked away into a pile of burning diapers.

"Didn't ask if you was dropping anything off. Asked for your permit."

"Why y'all burning so much?" he asked. The hum of the giant trash compactor was notably silent.

"Compactor jammed last night. Couldn't even squash a cigarette this morning." She studied him again. "We's about to think you died. We see your truck now and again."

"I appreciate your concern, but nah, I'm alive."

"Well, I'd hide too if I was you. I'd never show my face again. I'd get my you-know-what outta town after what you pulled. But that's just me." She eyed him like a specimen. "How's Onie? I heard she's you-know." Patsy pointed to her ear. "I'd lose my mind too. You still stuck in that old shed on Van's place, right? Virgil heard you shacked up with somebody."

"Just my dogs," Mayhill said. Then he regretted the slip because Patsy Fuller launched into a sob story—a real soap opera—about her dog who had disappeared a few months ago and she had six unused bags of Old Roy and what was she to do with a Dallas Cowboys dog jersey—it's not like she could wear it!—and whatnot. Mayhill didn't want to hear it.

"Hogs ate him, I guess." Patsy shrugged her shoulders but her eyes were uncomfortably wet.

"Hogs not doing anyone any favors." Mayhill wished that Virgil would come back, but he knew that Virgil was smarter than that.

"You ain't gonna believe this," she said. "But about a month ago…
somebuddy dumped a bunch of dead hogs out here in feed sacks. Just
right in the ditch. My money's on Jimmy Cason. Feed sacks! That gonna
cover it up? Like I'm stupid. Virgil may be but I ain't." She pointed the
rake at the empty bed of Mayhill's truck. "Why you here?"

"Wondering if you seen Bradley Polk." The words popped out
without him thinking.

"You wondering if I seen Bradley Polk."

"Yes, ma'am."

"Why you looking here?" Patsy eyed him. "Don't he work out by
you?"

Mayhill nodded. "He was doing some work for me."

"You were the sheriff…at one time. Not anymore, of course."

"Of course."

"So you know all about Bradley Polk…"

"I know what people say."

"Dangit, Virgil! Three gone out! Three!" She jabbed the rake in the
air toward a pile whose embers were fading into dark black. Mayhill
guessed this was pile number three, and he tried for a fleeting moment
to understand the dump numbering system, an almost algebraic order
that he had chewed on for years, an algorithm of wood, metal, rubber,
and oil.

"Lemme get this straight." Patsy turned back to Mayhill. "Bradley
Polk. He doing some work for you, and you don't know where he at."
Patsy took much joy from this revelation, as much as if someone had
related that her child had been arrested or his lymphoma had returned.
She propped the rake against her belly and wiped her forehead, the ash
giving way to a stripe of hot red skin.

"I just need to tell him something," Mayhill said.

"You need to tell him something. And you drove all the way out here?"

Mayhill looked jealously at Virgil in the distance who pawed his rake at a smoldering pile. "Ain't too far," Mayhill said.

"Yet you can't wait around your own place for him? Must be sumpin' real important!"

"Hell, Patsy. Just thought he might have dropped off something he weren't supposed to."

"Like what?"

"If he weren't out here, it don't matter!"

"Don't get sassy with me. Not that I have an obligation to tell you anything. Because like I said, you ain't the sheriff no more. Bradley was here first thing this morning. And normally I don't notice him from Adam, but that boy was keepin' a distance from me. Real suspicious. Real suspicious. Like he didn't want to get near me. Stunk to high heaven. Almost felt sorry for him. I don't know what's getting into me. Tell you what, I almost feel sorry for you too. Been a ree-cluse all these years. Robbed by a delinquent. Your life took a real nosedive, Sheriff."

"Did Bradley drop anything off?"

"A man's trash is a private affair. I didn't take this job to flap my lips about people's goings-ons." She waved her arm in the air, her underarm swinging like chains. "You pay him for the day? 'Cause I wouldn't hold my breath you see him again, 'specially if you pay him for the day."

"He's lived 'round here a long time. I can find him if I need him."

"I can find him if I need 'im...you can't find him now!" Patsy said.

"But I got the pleasure of talking to you, Patsy, so it all works out, don't it?" Mayhill put his truck in gear, and it rocked gently forward but Patsy kept talking. For a split second, he pictured himself slamming the gas pedal, just tearing off like when he was sheriff, rushing to see about a robbery. He imagined Patsy going down in a big thud (involuntary manslaughter, twelve-month minimum), freeing Virgil like an abused dog. Mayhill could be a real hero.

He eyed a big pile of sacks towering next to the compactor. If the compactor jammed last night, the sacks must have been dropped off this morning. Bradley. Old sacks of Sevin Dust, fertilizers, and, curiously, old sacks of blood meal. Why would Bradley have that?

"I'd have never hired him to begin with. That's how you screwed up." Patsy gestured the rake to the small house in the distance. "I wouldn't have let Bradley Polk step foot on my place."

"Is that a toilet on fire?" Mayhill pointed to the fifth circle of trash where Virgil flittered near a black sulkiness of rubber tires. "Are you trying to burn a toilet, Patsy?"

"You can burn anything if you keep puttin' it in the fire," she said. She looked back toward Virgil. "Everything breaks down eventually."

. ′ . ′ . ′ . ′ . ′ . ′ . ′

Much to his chagrin, Randy Mayhill had never investigated a murder. Sure, he'd had plenty of thefts, suspected drug dealers, cattle drive-bys, and some of those cases did require a modicum of detecting talent, deductive reasoning like an honor roll high schooler, but it was a small county, a rural county, and most people knew each other, and even when someone did go off the rails, it took all of thirty seconds to figure out who it was. As a result, Mayhill's investigative skills had not had the opportunity to grow past, "Awww, don't be like that, tell me," and he felt in over his head.

At one point when Mayhill was sheriff, a body had been found in the neighboring county. A forester cruising timber had stumbled across a dead woman in the woods, and Mayhill rushed to the scene, hemorrhaging at the words "possible dismemberment." The body (fully membered, false report) was exactly fifty feet into the other county, so the investigation fell in their jurisdiction, and the other sheriff was quite smug about this, Mayhill thought, and paraded around as if he were Columbo even though the murder had been a domestic dispute during a hunting trip and required no more skill than asking, "Who's that woman married to?" Yet Sheriff Columbo had CRACKED THE CASE!, the newspapers declared. *Let's throw a crawfish boil! Put him on the TV! Have a goddamn parade down County Road 1427!* Mayhill ended up with a pile of paperwork and the charge of getting a statement from a lazy-eyed hunter who said only, "I seen her dead." Sherlock it weren't, but Randy Mayhill was nothing if not hopeful.

CHAPTER SEVEN

B irdie Woods, however, could never be accused of hopefulness. No, hope was not Birdie's immediate feeling when Onie pointed to the circling buzzards the day before. And hope had not come to mind when Bradley disappeared and not returned her fifteen frantic calls. Nor was there a cheerful expectancy bubbling through her gullet that morning when Randy Mayhill accused her of disposing of the body of a man he thought she murdered—all with the top button of his jeans popped open because even denim has its limits.

But, oh, how Birdie wanted hope! She wanted nothing more than to see possibility in the world without having to try. Wouldn't it have been easier to be the kind of person whose legs get amputated and automatically thinks, "I reached my ideal bodyweight in an instant!" Still, there Birdie was, boringly dark and anxious and brooding, which appeared just as artificial as Wal-Mart checkout girls who punctuated their greetings with "blessed!"

It wasn't even optimism Birdie wanted after her father died. That would have been aiming too high. Aiming for the moon indeed, Birdie Girl! Birdie just wanted a hint that this world, with its unrelenting stream of accidents and premeditated tragedies, was worth putting on shoes for in the morning, that any of it was worth fighting for in the least.

Her father and her. Everybody said they were just alike—erratic, testy—but he was funny, they said. Hilarious! What had happened to Birdie? All of the moodiness and none of the likability. Without Van, she wasn't right somehow. She was angry. She was darker.

If anyone had been watching, however, they would have been keenly aware that Birdie was trying to be Van. She wore his shirts (flannel, too big). She had started cleaning her ears with his pocketknife—the Russian roulette of hygiene—just like Van had done and all the other men continued to do. Their nails were perpetually black but their ears forever pristine, threatened into cleanliness by the dulled blade of a pocketknife. Birdie's days had become a rehearsal in all things Van, and above all else, he had emphasized that theirs was a family that took care of its own business. "Private land, private matter," he always said. "We fix our own problems."

Birdie locked the door after Mayhill left that morning—something she had never done before or even seen anyone do in person except for twitchy television families unfortunate enough to live in New York or L.A. She leaned her body close to the door, huddled over the knob, and blocked the view of the bolt while she turned it, as if Van could see her lock it and disapprove while she did. She looked at how dirty the floor was, the mud from her tennis shoes tracked back to her room. She needed to clean but her hands wouldn't stop shaking.

Onie's television watching was especially tenacious that day, which meant the conversation would be especially poor. A once voracious reader and pianist, Onie had gotten depressed after Van died—caught it like a virus—so depressed now that it was as if all of her personality emptied into the crabgrass alongside her son. Some days, there were hints of muted conversation. But most days, she stared ceaselessly at the blinking box as if the Houston Honda commercials transmitted a secret code (they didn't). The people in town talked. They mentioned the Alzheimer's and the dementia, that grief could stun the brain so severely that it shut down. Wasn't Birdie worried? But Birdie didn't want to hear it. Her own memory moved like swamp water around the events of the past year. Still, Birdie watched Onie closely for clues, always challenging her, trying to get a rise. Birdie's words and actions escalated higher and higher to the point of explosion, a plea for some reaction, for the goddamn raising of an eyebrow—anything to prove that the once-feisty Onie still existed behind the soundproof shell of grief—which was why it was downright shocking when Onie said, "Was that Randy?" as soon as Mayhill's truck pulled away.

Onie's voice jolted Birdie. She realized then how long it had been since Onie had asked her a question of any kind, and with the television on since sunrise, the effect was not unlike someone waking from a coma and asking for a glass of juice.

"Randy just left," Birdie said carefully. "He's looking for Bradley." Birdie moved slowly across the room and next to Onie's leather recliner so as not to startle her back into silence.

"That's why Randy was here?" Onie's gaze remained on the television.

"Bradley was supposed to show up. He didn't, though." Birdie felt guilty for the half truth, but she felt guilty for a lot of things and she struggled to get that much out.

"Oh," Onie said. It was a response at least.

Birdie didn't want Onie involved in any of it, but she didn't want the conversation to be over either. She was buzzed with adrenaline and needed to be soothed. She picked up the television remote from the side table and turned down the volume, hoping Onie would find her just as interesting, but she just stared at the screen.

"Randy's looking for him." Birdie looked at her expectantly. "I'm gonna stay here and wait for Bradley in case he comes back."

Onie nodded and blinked at the screen.

"Bradley's never stood anybody up," Birdie said.

blink, blink

"Isn't that concerning?"

Onie didn't say anything to this either, and Birdie's agitation spiraled. She wanted to trigger whatever had awakened Onie in the first place. She wanted to tell her everything that had happened, to tell her about the man who had died on their land in the middle of the night, to say, "Remember when you saw those buzzards yesterday? There was a body on the fence…by the tree line." Instead, Birdie shook the remote at the TV and muted it entirely. She got right by Onie's ear. "We think something terrible might have happened to Bradley!"

It sounded halfway comedic.

Onie's eyes didn't change but she grimaced slightly, a microscopic turning down of the mouth and eyebrows, a whisper of emotion anyone would have missed had they not been staring at her with the desperation with which Birdie was looking at her right then. Onie placed her hand on Birdie's, her granddaughter's angry fist still squeezing the remote. Without moving her eyes, Onie curled her fingers around Birdie's hand and grabbed it so firmly it throbbed.

For a moment, Birdie thought Onie was concerned, holding her tightly the way a child might grab the hand of her mother in the midst of uncertainty. Birdie squeezed back, touched by the display of emotion, no matter how miniscule. Onie slowly lifted Birdie's hand high in the air, and then with her other hand, ripped the remote control from her. Then she turned the volume all the way up and settled deeper into her chair in time for *Matlock*.

Birdie had the urge right then to scream, to hit someone, to run away, because this place wasn't safe anymore. But she knew she didn't have any place to go, so she went to her room because that seemed like something a normal teenage girl would do.

Birdie's space was small, a converted old tack closet with wood from floor to ceiling, but it held her bed (twin), a nightstand (bobby pins, ChapStick, a small pistol), and a bookshelf with a picture of Van and her sitting on the back of a log truck when Birdie was a toddler. She stared at the picture, not so much taking in the memory as using it to replace the image of the dead man in her head.

Birdie recognized him. She remembered him very much alive, standing next to Bradley and her father.

Birdie took *Walden* from the shelf and opened it to reveal a flat, pink piece of paper folded into a square a little bigger than a matchbook. The square had once been a feed store receipt, an old-timey one about half the size of a piece of notebook paper with two large holes punched in the top. Used properly, the paper would have been added to a ledger. The paper was thin like tissue, velvet-soft, and meant to be thrown away after a year.

The fine, black ink had faded faster than Birdie liked, looking more like pencil at this point. The creases in the paper would not hold much longer because Birdie had folded and unfolded it so many times. Recently, she had vowed to unfold it only when necessary, always questioning if it was worth the risk of removing it from the book, like a genie she could access limitedly. She unfolded the right corner, then the left, and the note limped open, delicate and wilted, onto her bed. She was lucky to have any words of Van's left, she knew it, but their fragility at her fingertips rattled her every time she opened it, like something dying slowly in front of her. Soon, the only thing that would be left of him would be memories, that he was funny and that his eardrums were probably covered in dozens of tiny scars.

Onie had never said a word about the note, the pink receipt originally hidden in her Bible right there in the New Testament alongside, curiously, an old thank you note from Mayhill. Onie's Bible was the one book Birdie was guaranteed not to open.

"Sermon on the Mount is all you need," Onie had said of the Bible. "Terrible editing. Don't confuse the finger pointing to the moon for the moon!" Onie would then point her long index finger to the sky as if to accuse it of something, as if the moon had mistaken itself for Jesus.

Still, after she found the note, Birdie could be accused of doing just that. If you pressed her on it, Birdie would be the first to say that she might have gone a little crazy, the way grief and anger make you do. The note had become her father in many ways, and she studied it like Onie and Mayhill had studied literature. There was something about the note that captivated her, one of the last things to touch his hands. The big I like a straight leaning pine, and the curious B of Birdie, with the humps not round at all, but pointy like two flags on a sail.

When she first found the note, it bothered her because it changed everything she thought she knew—that her father had been so out of his mind with panic that he didn't think of the consequences, that he had acted on purpose without honest-to-God forethought. The note proved something else entirely: Van had thought of her when he did it! The panic and the giddiness took her over, not knowing what to do with this reordering of her grief: *I love you, Birdie. I'm sorry.* He had been of sound enough mind to write a note! He was sane enough to say *I'm sorry*, and yet.

Over the months, she came to love the note because it was another piece of her Van collection. She loved it so much she stole it from Onie's Bible and hid it in her own sacred text (*Walden*), the triangle flags of the B waving at her, the last evidence of Van alive and so kind and so loving, a plea for understanding when he knew how angry Birdie would be. And when she held it, she couldn't help but respond, as if they were in conversation again. "I know you were scared," she caught herself saying aloud, stifling the fury that threatened to break her open. "I love you. I love you." She began to learn, as all wise women know, that love and rage are intertwined.

Birdie knew the paper still had traces of her father upon it—skin cells, oil from his skin, the sweat of his panic—and she laid with it on her pillow as if the ink could talk to her, louder than Onie's television and louder than the hogs that scuttled by her window.

⠄⠂⠄⠄⠂⠄⠄⠂⠄⠂⠄⠂⠄

Birdie had a difficult time remembering when Onie had much emotion about anything, even though it had only been a year since she got so depressed that she propped herself in front of the television. When she thought of Onie's last spirited moments, she thought of ticks, oddly enough.

When gorged on blood, a fat tick can well up to the size of a small grape. Birdie had plucked one of these epic ticks off Atticus, Van's hunting dog, and crushed it with her foot, which created a cartoony splat of blood on the sidewalk, and Onie, who had never once cared about appearances, said, "Please don't flick ticks in front of guests." Then she smiled at the reverend as she ushered him into the house.

Reverend Brown sat on the couch, hat in hand, and Onie brought him some tea in cream-colored china even though he hadn't asked for any. Birdie had always disliked Reverend Brown. Van had insisted that Birdie's dislike was due to Reverend Brown's freakish widow's peak. Most widow's peaks were delightful and created a heart for the face to nest in, but Reverend Brown's was severe and dictatorial. It touched almost mid-brow, as if guiding an imaginary aircraft to his nose. Birdie found it alarming, as if his face was ordering her to look past his eyes (the windows to the soul, no less!) to his mouth, which as far as Birdie could tell, could only recite Bible verses on repeat. In fact, Birdie had never heard an original line come from it, which, Birdie told her father, was the real reason she didn't like the reverend.

Birdie sat on the floor, the house cat she was, at the feet of Onie's recliner. The reverend and Onie fiddled with their tea, as though neither of them had enjoyed such an exotic and toothsome a beverage as Lipton Regular from the Piggly Wiggly. It was midday, and the sun lit the room like a brightly-glowing greenhouse as if to suggest— mockingly, erroneously!—that this house was a place of life.

"Van had no prearrangements," Onie said much too loudly, as if issuing a challenge. "None. No prearrangements."

"That's often the case in…these kinds of situations." The reverend's voice was bruised with reassurance, a forced sort of diction Birdie was sure he practiced into a Fisher-Price tape recorder. He drew out his sentences slowly, willing the words to slide down his widow's peak into his mouth. "The cause of death will not…what I'm trying to say is… it will not be a problem in the Methodist Church. I mean, you and I know the Catholics just throw a walleyed fit about that kind of thing. But, Methodists, well, anything goes. In case that was a worry."

"You know, Reverend," Onie said. "In the midst of all of this, I can't say I've worried about the Methodist Church one bit."

The reverend and Onie bobbed their tea bags feverishly in their cups as if they were stabbing something to death at the bottom of them.

"Good," he said.

"Good," Onie said.

Birdie smiled pityingly at the reverend. She had recently become empathetic to men who tried but failed in very public ways. "Good," she said.

"Van was baptized?" the reverend asked.

"Every time it rained," Onie said. *Stab stab.*

It was only then that Birdie found it strange that, despite her incontestable emotional maturity, two adults were having this conversation in front of her. The silence grew thick except for the slurps, and Birdie longed for her own tea to murder.

"Perhaps we should keep it simple, then. Psalm 23. Bucolic and all," he said, emphasizing "colic" too much for Birdie's liking.

"You know he wasn't much of a Bible man, Jerry," Onie said.

His widow's peak dropped like a curtain down his face. "You're saying he didn't believe?"

"He believed." Onie placed her teacup carefully on the saucer. "I think it's just a matter of what."

"I'm not entirely sure I—"

"What about Thoreau?" Birdie asked quickly then.

"He believed in…Thoreau?"

"Thoreau was a favorite," Onie said.

"Thoreau is everybody's favorite," Birdie said.

"Well, all right!" The reverend clapped, happy to grasp at this blessed new straw. "Thoreau does have some lovely eulogy poems... 'Every blade in the field, Every leaf in the forest—'"

"'Lays down its life in its season?'" Onie interrupted. "I hardly think that's appropriate in this instance. *Lays* down. Active verb. Implies choice."

"He's talking about grass and leaves," the reverend said. "Clearly, Thoreau wasn't speaking about suic—"

"Don't tell me what Thoreau was speaking of."

"I would never challenge an English teacher on Thoreau, but my point is—"

"I don't want even the hint of a suggestion that Van would—"

"But that's not even what—"

"We're not using it!" Onie slammed her palm on the coffee table. The only sound remaining was the almost-undetectable trickle of Lipton hitting the floor until Birdie got up to get a towel.

With that, they decided Reverend Brown would say nothing personal at all. He would only read a version of the Twenty-third Psalm that Onie had edited to her liking. Randy Mayhill would limp to the pulpit for a reading from "Civil Disobedience" that made the congregation side-eye each other, elbow their neighbors in the ribs: "I was not born to be forced. I will breathe after my own fashion!"

The organist would play Willie Nelson's "Angel Flying Too Close to the Ground," partly because it had the word angel in it, which Onie thought would placate the good preacher who needed to believe that Van was religious in an outwardly recognizable way, despite Van having said that angels weren't good for anything other than shitting on your head.

Birdie walked the reverend to the door. "I'm sorry, Birdie," he said. He wisely offered a hand instead of a hug. "Your daddy was a real firecracker. I loved that about him. I'm just sorry that…" he paused and considered, "…that it ended for him the way that it did."

"Passive voice," Birdie said. "Good choice."

"Take care of Onie," he said. "Losing a child…"

Birdie wanted to scream, "What about losing a parent? I'm sixteen! He chose to leave me! He left me on purpose!" But all that came out was the compulsory, "Yessir," as she pawed at the blood splat of the dead tick on the porch. She wanted to outline it in chalk. Death everywhere.

"He was in a lot of pain. Desperate men don't think straight." The reverend shook his head sadly. "Your daddy was a good man."

It was a simple thing to say, not necessarily profound. Still, in the nightmare of the past few days, nobody had thought to tell Birdie that her father had been good. They had all simply avoided saying he was bad, tiptoed around the fact that he had done this supposedly awful thing, got caught growing plants in a dying forest. Van's goodness seemed to be the one thing everyone had forgotten about him, and in her anger at her father, she had forgotten it too.

In that moment, the reverend's entire visage began to soften; his widow's peak became holy, as if the finger of God rested perpetually on his forehead, choosing him, shushing his doubt, deeming him number one. For the first time in her life, Birdie wanted to leave her land, run away from Onie and the drama of her family. She wanted to jump in the truck with Reverend Brown and go live in a world of certainty and kindness. *Take me to your world! Teach me the Bible! Show me boring, Reverend Gerald Brown. Point me in the direction of Kind!* But off he drove, leaving her behind with an angry old woman and a tick carcass.

"You were rude to him." Birdie closed the door a little too loudly. "He was trying to be nice."

"He's trying to check off a box." Onie walked the teacups to the kitchen. "To come in here implying that Van—"

"I think you're in denial!"

"And I think you've watched too much Oprah!" Onie lifted her head to the light coming in the kitchen window as if to gain strength from the sun, a pond turtle sunning on a rock. "I'm going to my room to lie down for a while."

Birdie wished for sunset—the sun less severe, an appropriate pall over everything, the chorus of buzzes and screeches, the whistles and croaks proclaiming night, anything to drown out the sound of Onie crying.

CHAPTER EIGHT

A fter he left the dump, Mayhill drove into town and up onto the dirt lawn at Bradley's house. Bradley's house was one of the few in town. Like calling the roads "roads," you'd be hard pressed to call the town a "town." It was a loose constellation of buildings: an Exxon gas station, a corner store, a feed store, three churches, a school, and a sign pointing to the next town. A man from New York who wore a hat not of the cowboy variety came to town once—he was an investment banker researching timber prices—and Mayhill took him to the barbecue trailer that the black Baptist church had set up on the main highway because they had the best barbecue in all of Texas. This fedora-wearing man ate his drumstick with a knife and fork, and the blacks and the whites to this day would talk about the man in the hat who used a fork for his barbecue. "LA DI DA," they would say, and the rest would call-and-response a "LA DI DA," holding their unused but always present forks in the air—an inside joke that crossed racial lines even though real estate would not.

Except Bradley's house. The small cluster of homes belonged mostly to black families, a point which had escaped Bradley's mother when she drove through the town at random and said, "This'll do," reaching for a celebratory Bartles & Jaymes. Bradley's house was a small, white shotgun house not unlike Mayhill's, and Mayhill knew this. However, driving up to his house, Bradley's somehow seemed sadder and poorer. A dilapidated house surrounded by trees and hills was charming, bucolic, a relic of a fading rancher's landscape, something city photographers would gawk at in the name of humble, *Grapes of Wrath* and whatnot. But transport that same dilapidated house— peeling paint and cracked windows—into town, next to a shiny Exxon station and a rusted smoking barbecue pit, and it just meant you don't got no money.

Like most of the neighboring houses, Bradley's house had no proper driveway, just a dying area of the lawn that had been thinned with a short investment in goats and a truck broken down too long. Bradley's truck was not there, but Mayhill drove up onto the lawn anyway.

A thin, black dog lumbered from behind the house, panting hard in the afternoon sun. Mayhill got out and the dog trotted up to him, open-mouthed and dumb-eyed. Mayhill scratched her chin, which was beginning to gray through a once-black snout, and noticing no saliva coming from the dog's panting mouth, Mayhill grabbed the scruff of the dog's neck and pulled up gently, released his grip, and the skin remained standing in a soft hill on her back. In the art of pie making, soft peaks meant meringue that was close to ready, but in dog rearing, it was a sign of dehydration. Skin that didn't snap back.

Mayhill noticed a bend in the window blinds, a face pop up in the pocket.

He knocked on the door and took off his hat, and a woman emerged, sunken and slow, dark-eyed. A body that screamed for a steak but breath rotten with fruit.

"Afternoon. Ms. Johnson? Lisa Johnson?"

"Yes?" Hers was a familiar face, not unlike that of a woman he had once arrested. The face of being caught somehow but she didn't know for what yet.

"Bradley Polk lives here, doesn't he?"

Her eyes scrunched into a tired concern. "What'd he do?"

"Oh, no, ma'am. He didn't do anything. I just need a fence and was hoping to talk to him about it."

Her body settled at this. She palmed the slick roots of her hair and patted it down, as if looking for something in the tangles. She wore a faded red sweatshirt with the arms pushed up, which revealed a deep black bruise on her right forearm that matched Bradley's bruise from yesterday.

"I'm Lisa." She held out her hand, a sideways, flopping-fish kind of gesture that confused Mayhill. *Do I shake it? Do I kiss it?*

He grabbed the tips of her fingers, bounced them slightly, and let go as fast as he could. "Randy Mayhill."

She smiled and opened the door as if settling into an old routine. "Come in and talk to me. You're letting the air out."

The house was humid, and a thin stream of air hissed through the box unit in the front window. He was sure she and Bradley had lived there for years, at least since before his sheriffing days, but their house had the look of a dirty hotel room. Mayhill stood awkwardly in the living room, not wanting to sit on the couch. Their house looked like a temporary setup that could be abandoned as quickly as they had gotten the keys. There was a cheap metal bookshelf that held a Bible (Gideon, free), a Reader's Digest Condensed Version of *Old Man and the Sea* (already short, lazy), and a school picture of Bradley from a few years before (chubby, pale, pre-Van). The picture wasn't framed, just propped against the wall in a slouching paper curl.

There was a hole near the doorframe.

"What happened to your wall?" He traced his finger around the jagged hole, the exact size of a large fist. Lisa fiddled in the kitchen and ignored the question, so he raised his voice. "Know where Bradley is?"

"He works." She stared into the open refrigerator. It had nothing but a few wine bottles and a Styrofoam take-out container.

"Thought he might have stopped in for lunch."

"Oooooh, yes!" Lisa said. "Hot buffet waiting for him!" The kitchen counter was sparse, save a shiny orange bag that read CHIPS on the side and a half-empty bottle of Kool-Aid-colored wine. Mayhill nodded, and she picked up the bottle. "So we can enjoy ourselves, can't we? Drink?" She slid a glass across the kitchen counter, old crumbs gathering at the base, and Mayhill took it.

"That dog of yours is thirsty."

"Me too," she said, and uncorked the bottle.

"You oughtta bring her in. Hogs'll get an old dog like that, even in town."

She studied the wine bottle and sniffed it.

"Gotta beer?" he asked. The last time he had had a drink was the night of Van's funeral. He didn't do well with downers.

"No." She whimpered every word as if it were her last breath, every utterance a song of lamentation. "Bradley stole half of 'em. Other half boiled in the car. Forgot to bring 'em in."

"I can't imagine you'd forget such a thing."

"But this rosé is still good." She sniffed the bottle again.

Mayhill hesitated but held out his glass. "That'll be fine, thank you."

"I sometimes drink right from the bottle. Saves dishes." She put her lips to the bottle mouth as if to blow into it, an awkward smile meant to flirt. "Do you still want it?"

"No, thank you." Mayhill put down the glass.

Mayhill had the sudden thought that she could be a prostitute, and with that thought came a wave of concern: that the house was being watched, that he could end up in the papers again, and he had psychic-like visions of being booked by the new, well-ventilated sheriff.

They sat on the couch, and she put the bottle on the coffee table. Mayhill edged himself to the far end.

She leaned back on the other end and crossed her legs. "What'd Bradley do?"

"I said I need a fence, that's all. He's a good builder."

"Cut the shit, Randy."

"Cut the shit. What happened to your arm?"

"Accident at work." She pulled the sleeves of her sweatshirt down, a flash of pink suddenly in her cheeks.

"Why aren't you at work now?" he asked.

"Why aren't *you* at work now?"

"I quit." It was technically true. She searched his face. "I was about to get fired," he said.

"I'm about to get fired too," she said. "Time clock don't work right is the truth about it. I'm 'on leave.'" She made lazy quotes with her free hand.

"Paid leave?"

"Oh, for sure! A paid vacation! I'm looking for something else, though. I'm lookin'..." She trailed off into thought. "Maybe I'll get a real estate license."

Mayhill imagined a drunk Lisa Johnson in a suit made out of sweatshirt material, ushering around prospective real estate clients. *And this trailer has all the amenities for the modern meth dealer: a stove with four burners, a smoke detector, removable paneling...* "So Bradley's paying the bills."

She waved him off. "He hasn't slept here in months."

"He doesn't live here anymore?"

"Said he hasn't slept here." She seemed much drunker all of a sudden, her words vexed and slow. "Oh, but Bradley will shower here! He'll use up all the hot water. Then I have to take a cold bath. A cold bath! Which does no favors for my dry skin, Randy! It's Randy, right? Randy, he eats all my food...steals my beer."

"Sounds like he's gotta girlfriend..." Mayhill thought of Birdie then. "Must be shacking up somewhere."

"Maybe." She shrugged. "I dunno. He don't tell me anything. He showered here last week, and all I was trying to ask about was his job—"

She touched her bruised arm, and something about this exchange was enough to send Bradley's mother into an emotional tailspin, from which she awoke to the pitiful state of her situation. Lisa began to cry, a long, slow wind-up of a wail. "And after all I done for him!" Mayhill stiffened and stood, though the cue didn't stop her. Instead, it seemed to invite her closer until she pulled herself from the couch and moved toward him, her head finding its way to the shelf of Mayhill's gut. She threw her head back—all agony and melodrama—her body still pressed to him so that he could see up her nostrils. "And he don't even care for his mama!"

Mayhill put a stiff arm around her and patted her open-palmed and awkward, a soft spanking to her back. She came up to his chest, and her chin dug into the protrusion of his belly. From this angle, the tears soaked through his white shirt and he could see his chest hairs clearly, worms rising to the surface of the soil after a hard rain. None of this was pretty, he decided, and he gave her a final pat-pat-pat and inched away from her—cautiously, teeth not showing—the way one might step away from a bear.

She was the kind of woman who needed to be touched, and for a moment, Mayhill wished he were the kind of lawman who did such a thing, who felt perfectly at home in a strange woman's embrace. Life is easier the more places you feel at home.

She moved closer again and traced the wet spot on his shirt with her finger. "You could leave him your number. I'll give it to him." She attempted a smile, too spent to flirt. Her fingers pressed harder into him.

"I heard he's working at the Cason's. I'll go by. Gotta see Jimmy about something anyway." Jimmy Cason hadn't talked to Mayhill in over a year, but Lisa knew none of these people, nor that Jimmy Cason would never trust a man like her son to step foot on his land. But "Gotta see so-and-so anyway" was just the thing he would have said when Van was alive, when Mayhill saw people about things and goings on.

She nodded and wiped her nose on her sleeve, leaving a dark comet across her faded red sweatshirt. She cocked her head lazily and stared at him. "You look familiar."

"I used to be sheriff," he said.

She nodded intently, though her eyes were vacant. "I used to be pretty."

Mayhill knew the right thing to say was, "But you are pretty," but he didn't feel like lying, and the difference was that he really did used to be sheriff. He nodded and her words hovered uncomfortably in the air like fumes until he put his hat back on and let himself out.

In the courts of Mayhill's mind, the evidence would be clear. He did not entice the dog in any discernible way. He definitively did not! The black dog—"On her own vo-lition, Your Honor!"—trotted up to the driver's side just as Mayhill opened his truck door to depart, as if she knew something about him, as if she had heard rumors. The moisture in Mayhill's mouth seemed to disappear at once, sucked away by empathy, and he smacked his tongue to the roof of his mouth to generate any sort of liquid while he searched his truck for an empty cup or a hidden well. All he could find were two hot six-packs of Dr Pepper and a roll of paper towels that had gotten wet and dried and were flaking now like papier-mâché. He considered the Dr Pepper for a moment but knew the sugar would surely dehydrate the dog more, and the familiar feeling of utter uselessness attacked him like mosquitos. He looked at the dog and frowned, and the dog, though open-mouthed, seemed to frown too. The dog reminded him of Birdie. "You," the dog said in so many non-words, "have thoroughly disappointed me."

"Shit." Mayhill sighed and patted his knees in two successive taps, an ancient cue the old dehydrated dog understood in her bones, if not in experience (because this was a dog who had never been invited anywhere), upon which the dog scrambled into the truck, ready to make a break from the horrors of insignificance.

"I guess that's how it's gonna be," Mayhill said, and stretched his puffed arm along the back of the seat, then looked over his shoulder to back out of the driveway. The dog sat in the passenger's seat (Dog, yet again, his co-pilot! Ha!) while Mayhill made a concerted effort not to peel out, and he found that for the second time in two days he was smiling like someone who had something to be happy about.

CHAPTER NINE

R andy Mayhill had always imagined himself as front page
news—heroic deeds, not unlike Batman's, plastered across
the front of the eight-page *East Texas Telegraph*, the same
publication that Van had said was the only monthly newspaper to be
published weekly, the same publication Onie required her high school
English classes edit each week for homework.

Van and Onie were right, of course, as they always were. The
newspaper had problems of the hillbilly variety: a regular confusion
of "their" and "there," and more maddeningly, a confusion of "it's"
and "its" and "its." Its', of course, being the jackalope of the English
language. A legendary animal plausible enough to exist—a hybrid of
real—but in the end, not a real thing at all, except to say something
about the person who defended its existence so fully. But it was among
these pages that Randy Mayhill wanted to be celebrated.

"I don't know why you care so much," Van would say, circling a split infinitive out of habit. "They'd spell your name wrong anyway."

A little over a year before he found a body on Birdie's fence, Sheriff Randy Mayhill scrubbed the *Telegraph* for any mention of his name just as his secretary, Gabby Grayson, ushered a shifty-eyed hog hunter into his office. The man smelled like mud and had a Houston Oilers cap pulled tightly over his head, scraggly hair puffing out like duck feathers. A gold cross drooped from his neck.

Mayhill sat in a large office chair with fast-moving wheels, and off-put by the man's apparent nervousness, he attempted humor as he always did when out of sorts: "That cross of yours…it looks like it was built to scale."

But the hog hunter was in no mood for jokes. "I seen some plants. Hunnards of them. Illegal ones." He leaned toward Mayhill and whispered. "Weed."

Mayhill stared at him, blank-faced, not sure he understood.

"Marijuana, Sheriff."

"Marijuana?" Mayhill asked.

"Marijuana."

"And you sure about that?" Mayhill swiveled the chair back and forth, feet dancing beneath the desk. A headline formed in his head. "You serious?"

"I am," the man said. "I wouldn't joke about such a thing. Found it when I's out settin' a trap."

"Anybody tending it?" Mayhill asked.

"No, thank God. And I mean that sincerely." He touched his cross, then looked up and offered thanks to the stained ceiling tiles. "Didn't see no nobody. Nobody seen me. All pine…dead mostly…then the land totally changed. Hunnards of bright green bushes. Green like poison ivy. But I thought that ain't no poison ivy. And then I realized what it 'twas. And I thought, no, you ain't seen that. But I made myself look twice. No way, you ain't seen that. Then three times. And I thought, you seeing that! You really seeing that! I seen it, Sheriff, I did."

Mayhill scribbled "major marijuana farm" on a pad, then added an exclamation point. "How big a plot, ya think?"

"Football field?" The hunter measured the air with mud-splattered hands. "Maybe more."

"Maybe two football fields?" Mayhill asked.

"Could be three?"

"Three football fields!" Mayhill slapped both hands on the desk. The headline should be simple, tasteful in one-hundred-point font: *BUSTED!*

"But then I hot-footed it outta there," the hunter said. "Because I know what them cartels do to a man like me. I seen that *48 Hours* episode last year."

"'Bout those hikers got killed?" Mayhill asked. "I saw that too. State forest near Brownsville?"

"That's it, Brownsville. Couple of hikers stumble across their operation. Shot dead right there…just for seein' it, Sheriff!" the man said. "Them cartels are paranoid. They'll shoot you dead just for being in the wrong place, wrong time."

"Mexican cartels…in our woods!" Mayhill drummed the desk and looked at his new friend, this muddy angel of good news. "You were trapping? Where were you exactly?"

"South of the Trinity. Property bumped up against the state land."

South…of…Trinity, Mayhill wrote on the pad. Then his blue pen trailed off the page, his words slowed as his brain mapped it out. Mayhill swiveled his chair to look at the map behind him.

"That's right," the man said. "Off County Road 1427, I think."

The air in the room changed then, joy evaporated into the ether, headlines disappearing. Mayhill put down his pen and covered his mouth with his hands.

No, no, the plants could not be there. No, no, they could not be having this conversation.

"Do you have experience with illegal drugs?" Mayhill asked. He gripped his feet to the floor and tried not to fall out of his chair. "Is the smoking of marijuana a pastime of yours?"

"Of course not!" The man's face grew troubled. "A family man. A Godly man." He looked up at the ceiling tiles again.

"But you know the plant well enough to identify it in a thicket with, I dunno," Mayhill smirked, "a million other green plants."

"There were so many of them," the man stammered. "Like I said… three football fields."

"Or maybe just one." Mayhill shrugged.

The man looked around the room—for what, Mayhill did not know.

"And who have you told about these alleged 'plants'?" Mayhill asked, air-quoting with his fingers.

"Nobody. Came straight here." The hog hunter seemed proud of himself, overly eager, a quality Mayhill despised—the need for pats on the back and gold stars.

Mayhill ran his hands over his chest and touched his gold star, then eyed the man. "Well, I'm not saying you're lying."

"No, no, Sheriff." The man got up quickly, walked behind Mayhill's desk, and pointed to the map. He dragged his dirty finger across the line, then took a hard turn, and pulled it down the wall. "I parked right here. Then I saw the river. I know my maps."

"You a cartographer?" Mayhill asked. "Work for the highway department?"

"Drove an ambulance in San Antonio for five—no, it was six years—"

"Well, was it five or six?"

"Before that, was a navigator in the Army. Two tours in—"

"And we thank you for your service!" Mayhill said, standing so quickly that the chair shot from behind him and crashed into the wall.

The man stared at him, confused.

Mayhill looked up at the ceiling tiles, hoping to see whatever the hog hunter could see with that cross. But all he could think to say was, "Show me again where you crossed the river."

. . . .

Mayhill loaded two plastic tankers into an old fishing boat in the dark. He scored the weed killer from a small job off of a neighboring county (stolen farm supplies). It was nasty stuff—old and industrial— the kind of poison that housewives had once happily misted on tomato plants but had been outlawed since the seventies (tremors, private part cancers). Even though he hadn't opened the containers yet, just inhaling the residue on the outside of the bottle burned his nose hairs.

It was hours after Mayhill's and Van's brawl in the front yard, with Birdie and Onie looking on, and the confrontation had gone just about how he predicted—Mayhill the only reasonable person ever present in any situation, and Van, defiant and stubborn, punching him right in the face and permanently injuring Mayhill's kneecap in the name of

HIS! PERSONAL! FREEDOM!

Van's words bore through him as he unhitched the boat. "Private land, private matter. It's a plant. No different than a tree. You can get high off pine sap, if you think about it, Randy!" Van had swung and Mayhill ducked. "Did you know you can get high off pine sap? And nobody's outlawing pine trees and whatnot. I'm not cooking meth, Randy. Do you see an exploding trailer? *Do you?* Look at my teeth! I have all of my teeth!" *SMILE*

Randy understood then. Van's teeth were magnificent.

Mayhill wore waders and snake boots because the Trinity quivered in leeches and water moccasins, but these weighed down his bottom half like concrete shoes. He thought about Van and how he had clearly lost his mind, that he had caught desperation like a cold. Mostly, he thought about Birdie and Onie, how they orbited Van like planets circling the sun. What would happen if the sun went to jail for twenty years? Randy Mayhill wasn't obstructing justice. No! He was preventing heartbreak! And if you wanna get sappy about it, preventing heartbreak is exactly what the law is for.

RANDY MAYHILL PREVENTS HEARTBREAK

The moon was silvery, and the frogs were loud.

About a half mile from where the hunter said he crossed onto Van's land, Mayhill stopped the boat and listened. He half expected to hear music blaring through the trees, a perpetual party to which he had not been invited, all hula girls and drug pipes and whatnot. Instead, he heard the silence of the woods and the river, the *slush-slush* of the boat moving through water. He used his paddle to move slowly forward, his breath the loudest sound in his ears.

Mayhill held a tiny flashlight, barely thicker than a pen, near his head and scanned the bank for pipes. The light slithered over loblolly roots and Budweiser cans. If Van were growing near the river, he was surely irrigating from it; it had been too dry otherwise. He paddled forward, moonlight-quiet, then stopped and shone the light again. He could hear something, the low whir of an engine. He saw the flicker of eyes and a jerk of movement: an alligator nestled on the edge. It was a young one, about three feet long, a lace of dark and yellow scales, its throat a whitish gray. It was maybe two years old, just the age that Mayhill wasn't sure if it was on its own yet. Was the mother around? He shone the flashlight around the boat, farther up the bank.

Then he saw them. Two tiny pipes sticking into the river, certainly not conspicuous, spray-painted dark brown to blend into the bank. Smart, Mayhill thought, but the paint had begun to chip off into the water. Just enough so that the flashlight caught a few inches of the shiny white pipe even in the dim moonlight. He flashed back to the gator, eyes flared red in the light. Then, Mayhill moved the light deeper into the thicket, and sure enough, saw a small irrigation pump the size of a mini-fridge, humming like an idling car.

Lord, forgive me for what I am about to do.

With an old hose, he connected the pipes to the tanks and sat impatiently in the boat—an eye on the gator, still scanning the water for its mother, scanning the bank for Van or hula girls or whomever. Mayhill imagined the poison going deep into the land, chugging into the plants. In the morning, and certainly by the next nightfall, they would be dead. Perhaps not dead, but damaged and sickly. A message

Van couldn't ignore. The party shut down, the dancing girls sent home.

Mayhill unhooked the second tank of poison and tilted it backward to avoid spilling the dregs. Then he pulled the dirty white cap out of his shirt pocket and tried to screw it back on the tank, but his fingers were clumsy in the thick work gloves. He bobbled the tank and poison chugged off the side of the boat and into the water. "Shit." Mayhill took off his gloves and worked the lid back on the tanker with his palm. He wiped the poison onto his jeans and could feel his legs sting where it soaked through.

RANDY MAYHILL SINGLE-HANDEDLY SHUTS DOWN DRUG RING

One month later, the day Van died, Jimmy Cason, the game warden, would sit on the corner of Mayhill's desk.

"A bunch of dead fish washed up in the Trinity," he said. "Gator too."

Something about the way Cason said it unnerved him.

"I went to take a look because that's my job, and I do my job." Jimmy Cason got up from Mayhill's desk and paced the room. "What do you think I found when I went down to the Trinity and started poking around for a bunch of dead carp and a belly-up gator?"

Mayhill's hand trembled under the desk. Was it possible? The spilled poison? He leaned back in his chair and looked up, the ceiling tiles still conspicuously silent.

"We know about Van," the game warden said. "If what I heard is true, you were alerted to the situation about a month ago."

No words came to Mayhill.

"A month ago, Randy." Cason slammed his hand on the desk.

He didn't understand how the game warden knew about the hog hunter. Had he contacted Jimmy too? Mayhill rubbed his hand over his mouth and searched for any excuse, any reasonable cover-up, but none came.

"If this is true…" Jimmy Cason said. "And I'm not saying it is. If this is true, it puts me in a precarious situation. I can't imagine what you must have thought when you found out what Van was doing. I can't imagine what you were thinking…not taking care of it right there."

That was me taking care of it right there.

The game warden went on. "I mean, Van's my friend too. I mean, I'm loyal. He's looking at a twenty-year minimum sentence as much as he got going. Twenty years."

Jimmy Cason, you know nothing of loyalty.

"You know how something like this is gonna go. It's your word against his if this hunter wants to press it." Cason stopped pacing and leaned against the desk. "There will be charges. Won't be pretty. Embarrassing for you, embarrassing for the office. Newspapers. TV crews. Whole nine yards."

"The newspaper…" These were the only words Randy would say.

"If what I heard is true, you could be looking at jail time. You! Not just Van. If we did a full investigation…if we asked Gabby if she knew anything…if she could attest to the man being here…"

Randy waved a hand in the air to cut him off. "Stop." He rubbed his palms flat against the desk, the cool wood grain. His head dropped low toward the desk to where he could almost smell the wood.

"Officially, Randy, because of your unique relationship with Van's family…" The game warden continued, his voice much too gentle for

Mayhill's taste. "We have to bypass the Sheriff's office. It's an official investigation now. We will be working with DPS. I just thought you should know."

Later that morning, a narcotics team would raid the land and find Van dead from a self-inflicted gunshot wound (Smith & Wesson .357). He faced a twenty-year sentence for gardening a plant that makes people eat too many Doritos.

SHERIFF RANDALL MAYHILL CAUGHT IN COUNTY COVER-UP!!! ITS' SHAMEFUL! SAYS LOCAL RESIDENCE

Van had been wrong. They spelled Randy's name correctly.

CHAPTER TEN

B ut that was the past. Today was for redemption! Ye shall be born anew! Verily, verily.

Mayhill left Bradley's mother, dropped his new dog off at his house, and watched her drink a half-gallon of water in twenty seconds flat. For a moment, Mayhill felt jealous of the dog because she had a need that was met so fully. She was delivered from hell to heaven by simply sauntering into the sun at the right time. Oh, to be delivered! Oh, to have a half bucket of tepid hose water set in front of one's dry snout! The dog flopped down next to Pat Sajak on the porch, with Boo and Atticus on the other side, and Mayhill realized then her name was Vanna because dog names are revealed; they are not chosen.

Mayhill then drove to Birdie's and Onie's house and knocked on their door, and was pleasantly surprised when Birdie opened it unarmed. Their house was an old barn that Van's father had converted. Inside the door was a large open room with a piano against one wall and a television on the other. A large couch divided the space down the middle like Communist Berlin. Onie had chosen the side of the oppressive television regime.

She turned her head toward him. "Randy!"

He walked over and side-hugged her in the chair. "I'm sweaty," he said, but Onie leaned in anyway.

Birdie had taken a seat at the dining table at the other end of the room, making a Herculean effort not to look at him, lest she turn to stone. He had sat there with Van and Onie and her on a thousand occasions, the table much too large for the space so that they had to shimmy along the wall to sit. Now, he carefully chose one of the dining chairs as far away from Birdie as possible as he stretched out his knee. He took off his hat and placed it on the table.

"Who is he?" he asked. "You know that man, Birdie, and you're not telling me."

She stared out the window, gripping her coffee cup like a lifeline. He could see in her face she was holding something close.

"Where were you last night?" he asked.

"You tell me." Birdie held up her hands to make binoculars around her eyes.

She was right. He knew they had been home.

"Talked to Bradley's mama. She hasn't seen him in a few days," Mayhill said. "Had a big bruise on her arm, just like Bradley. Said he doesn't sleep there at night anymore."

Birdie's face slowly registered concern. "Where's he sleep, then?"

"Thought you might know." Mayhill watched her closely. "He have a girlfriend?"

"No, he doesn't have a girlfriend! I mean, we don't really talk like that."

"He's here all the time," Mayhill said. "Aren't y'all friends? Y'all the same age about."

"And you're friends with all the fifty-year-olds? And all the Mexicans in town are friends with each other?"

"I'm forty-five," he said. And Mayhill wanted to point out that the few Mexicans in town were all friends with each other because they couldn't afford not to be in that town. And if there had been albinos or Icelanders, they'd best be friends with each other too. It was important to stick together in a place like that—except women, because he noticed that women in this town inexplicably couldn't be friends with other women for too long.

"Who's he hang out with?" Mayhill asked. "Where do you see him?"

"I don't know. I'm not in school, remember?" Birdie had never actually told him she dropped out of school, but her truck had still been parked outside their house when school started.

A revelation hit Mayhill, and he leaned in close across the table. "Birdie, is Bradley here now? Are you hiding him here?"

"You figured it out!" Birdie slung her arms to the sky. "He's been here all along! He's under the stairs with Anne Frank!"

"You argue like your daddy. You're like a rabid dog. Your mouth is foaming."

"And you're talking like a jackass."

"Your daddy said that before." Mayhill snickered.

"You're enjoying this, aren't you?" She finally looked him in the eye. "You're honest-to-God enjoying this."

Mayhill didn't argue. Onie glared at them and turned up the television. The screen showed a *Matlock* rerun, a classic in which Ben marches a horse into the courtroom.

"The man's a trapper. I need to know if you hired him," Mayhill said. "Because maybe this has all been just a terrible accident. Maybe just a bizarre hunting accident. One fella shoots the other and you had nothing at all to do with it."

"Name one place that's ever happened before ever."

"It's happened," he said.

Birdie nervously tapped on her cup.

"Could Bradley have hired him?" Mayhill asked. "Onie?"

"Onie loves the hogs. I'm surprised she's not leaving food out for them." She paused. "Did *you* hire him? Did you hire a trapper?"

"You know I'd never outsource such a thing," Mayhill said. "But for the sake of argument, let's say Bradley—"

"Stop it!" Her eyes threatened to cry but she somehow willed any wetness back in her head. "He didn't do anything."

"Then where—"

She looked at him with a kind of desperation that made his heart stop. She was terrified. Mayhill finally got it. She really didn't know where he was, but the thought of him not being okay was too much to entertain right now. Bradley was fine because he had to be fine, because Birdie couldn't live in a world with more tragedy. There was no other option. Mayhill just didn't know what else she needed Bradley for.

"Did you tell Onie about…?"

She shook her head again.

"That's probably best," he said, then leaned in and whispered, "How is she these days? I mean, how is she in the…?" He pointed to his ear.

"Quiet mostly." The bags under Birdie's eyes hung heavy like a laundry line. "She went to the store the other day for milk and came back with a bunch of junk food. She doesn't even let me drink Coke."

"Well, you shouldn't drink that anyway."

"Please do share your dieting tips, Randy."

Onie laughed from the couch—a distinctive cackle that made Mayhill and Birdie look wide-eyed and guilty at each other. Had Onie been listening, or was it the courtroom horse? Birdie softened for a moment, curls bouncing out of her ponytail, the hint of a smile on her mouth. For that second, Birdie was seven years old again and he was Uncle Randy sneaking her sips of Dr Pepper when Onie wasn't looking.

"Why do Bradley and his mama have bruises on their arms?" Birdie asked.

"Coincidence."

Birdie nodded in the way of someone trying to convince herself of a lie. "Maybe," she said, and took a sip of her coffee. It was the first time she had not disagreed with him.

Mayhill got up and grabbed his hat. "Know anybody who drives a black Datsun?"

"How should I know?"

He was about to say, "He looked your age," but he stopped himself because a man learns, a man corrects his course. And miracle of miracles, she was starting to thaw.

"Just stay in the house for now," Mayhill said. He feigned an authority over Birdie he didn't quite believe himself, like the pointless bobby pin trying to tame her hair. "Don't be stupid. Don't go into the woods or anything. Not until we know what's going on." He opened the door to leave and stepped over a congregation of shoes just inside the doorway. "I'm guessin' you already do though."

"Jesus," Birdie said. "People think what they gonna think." She stretched her arm out on the table and rested her head upon it, then traced the outline of the wood grain with her fingers. "A dead body shows up on your land and people automatically think it's yours," she sighed. "That's the problem with neighbors."

CHAPTER ELEVEN

eople think what they gonna think. It was true.

It was also true that Birdie knew something, but as is often the case with memories, she didn't know what she knew. She wasn't withholding information from Mayhill. She just didn't want to experience the wrath of Mayhill's finger jabbing at her in the air, demanding she make meaning out of something that, as far as she knew, had no meaning at all. She had met the dead man with her father, and their meeting had held little significance at the time except to signal that Van was fraternizing with a different sort of man. She didn't even know his name.

Bradley had met him too.

"That man…" Bradley had said quietly as they walked away from the body Wednesday morning, his hands shoved in his pockets. "You and me. We—" But Bradley stopped himself and walked quickly ahead. He might have been crying.

Watching Mayhill drive off now, she desperately wanted to ask Bradley about it again, a conversation to make the memory crystallize, in which she could just pick up the phone, the way she imagined other girls calling their boyfriends. *That man who what? You and me what?*

Birdie had called Bradley's house incessantly all morning, but she called again now. A woman picked up, groggy and irritated. "Who keeps calling!" she yelled.

"Oh! I wasn't expecting…is Bradley there?"

"Nope!"

"Has he been home today?"

"Hell nope!"

"Could you have him—"

"You call again, I'm callin' the sheriff."

Dial tone.

She angrily pecked Bradley's number into the keypad again because she was Van's daughter after all, and an order to stop was always an invitation to keep going. She wrapped the slack of the long cord around her wrist, cutting off the circulation to her hand, and watched her fingers throb white and red. She pressed the receiver to her ear, but the call rang and rang until it disconnected. Birdie slammed down the phone and then poured herself another cup of a coffee, guzzling it down like a Columbian drug lord. She paced the house, heart racing, breath like a funeral pyre, then stepped outside and craned her neck to see if Bradley were anywhere in sight until the mosquitos and heat drove her back inside.

Birdie thought of Bradley's bruises, his mother's bruises, Bradley not sleeping at his house anymore. She was tired of waiting around. She wrapped up in one of Van's flannel work shirts (red and white plaid), tucked the pink note in her pocket like a lucky charm, and racked her brain for any inkling as to what Van would have done in a similar situation, as if the shirt and note would give her insight. But they remained as tight-lipped as Onie, and she knew at that point, if she needed to think, all she could do was drive.

Bradley had shown up every Wednesday and Saturday for the last few years. Van had brought this awkward young man to their ranch, rumors swooping around him like cowbirds, and from then on, he would be there every Wednesday and Saturday until Armageddon. Even after Van died, which was on a Wednesday with a waxing gibbous moon, Bradley showed up three days later on a punishingly humid Saturday to clear brush and to feed the ducks in the tiny pond near the woods.

A week after Van died, Bradley burned the garbage since it was stacked halfway up the barn with the remnants of casseroles and cards. He waved to Birdie and Onie, who sat on the porch numbly, dumbly, taking in the cool fall weather as if they were waiting for Van to come back with the migrating geese. Three months in, Birdie and Onie realized that nobody had been paying Bradley because Van had always done that, and Onie walked out to the pasture in her shirtdress and tennis shoes with a sizable check that Bradley politely declined even though he was the poorest person they knew. In response, Onie returned to the house and emerged with her shotgun and marched back out to the burn pile and said that if Bradley was not an employee, he was a trespasser, and if he did not want to be treated as such, he would take the money and all additional payments moving forward. Bradley, simultaneously touched and threatened by her hostility, agreed.

The memory had always moved Birdie. Bradley was technically the help, but he was also more than the help as the help always is. They were friends in the way of convenience, but he spoke to her with a nervous deference that made her unsure of where they stood. Bradley spent as much time with her father as anybody she could remember, which meant that he knew Van well. Bradley knew his stories and had heard Van speak of the trees and the birds and the moon so much that he would forever look at life through that lens. Bradley could never again look at a tree and simply think "tree." He wouldn't even see pine. Like it or not, for the rest of his days, Bradley would see a loblolly pine in its second year of flowering, twenty feet tall, eight years old and still growing. He would see all of this in a flash of a second, a hundred times over when he walked through the woods. Bradley would never again see a moon. He'd see the anemic smile of a waning crescent or the sleepy sideways eye of the waxing gibbous.

No more birds. Mockingbirds became gossipers, the Patsy Fullers of the avian world. Shrikes became tormentors, guards at Gitmo…

Birdie turned onto the main highway from the tangle of the backwoods and spotted Mr. Boudreaux's truck edged onto the side of the road. In the past year, she visited with her neighbors less and less because a death like her father's invited as much unsolicited commentary as a pregnant belly or a face tattoo, but Mr. Boudreaux's rusted old farm truck drew her in. The backend brimmed with watermelon, and on the bumper of his truck rested a cardboard sign the size of a watermelon that read, unironically, WATERMELON. She wondered how many people actually stopped on this highway, how many cars sped by to begin with.

Clet Boudreaux was a Louisiana transplant—half deaf, half senile, skin like a saddle—and Van had conservatively estimated him to be a hundred and fourteen years old. *But a real virile hunnard plus.* Despite his age, Mr. Boudreaux sat out on the main highway all summer, every one-hundred-degree day until the last watermelon went home with somebody. Van would buy half of them just to get Mr. Boudreaux out of the heat faster. "He's gonna die out there if I don't," Van would say, a sweat mustache sprouting on his lip. They would try to help him load Van's truck, but always the professional, Mr. Boudreaux waved them off, insisting that it was his job as the sole proprietor of his establishment, and this proved to be an exercise in patience, not unlike watching an elderly ant haul twenty acorns up a tree.

Mr. Boudreaux waved his crushed cowboy hat as Birdie pulled into the ditch behind him.

"Hey, angel! How's Onie?" he shouted, all gums, his Cajun and Texan accents a brawl in his mouth.

"Not as good as you." She hugged him. "Surprised the hogs didn't get all your melon."

"Put out some antifreeze…sweeter than sugar." He winked at her.

"Squirrels will eat it though."

But he didn't respond. He just rapped his knuckles on a watermelon the size of two babies. "Sweet this year."

She knocked on it too, and it answered with a nice hollow thud. "You see Bradley Polk come by here?"

From his truck, Mr. Boudreaux could see one of the three roads that fed into their stretch of woods, the way Bradley drove in from town. He was practically her doorman.

"Most days," he said. "Bradley Polk in and out most days."

"Most days?"

"He still work for you, don't he?"

"Just Wednesdays and Saturdays," Birdie said.

He shook his head, disagreeing. "I seen him every day this week."

"You sure about that?" Birdie shaded her eyes with her hand and watched his face. "Bradley Polk's going into the woods every day?"

"Every day. Listen, these hard as a rock, but give 'em a few days… it'll be candy." He rapped a cantaloupe. It was the size of a bowling ball and sounded like a door knock. He looked at her curiously. "You married yet?"

"I'm seventeen, Mr. Boudreaux!"

"You late, angel! Bethard married me when she fifteen!" Fireworks of wrinkles exploded across his face. God, she loved Mr. Boudreaux.

"You got all that land to think about," he said. "You a catch with all that land. But you ain't doing nothin' with it!"

Birdie cringed, the guilt of letting her father's land waste away, but she still thought it was his to take care of. Mr. Boudreaux sensed as much, and touched her arm. "But you got time, angel," he said. "Ain't no hurry. Ain't no hurry for nothin'."

She looked in the back of his truck, the sweat creeping down his shirt in a dark eclipse.

"I'll take all of them," Birdie said. "Cantaloupe too."

· · · · · · · ·

Twenty-three watermelons and ten unripe cantaloupe rolled around in the backend of Birdie's truck. She didn't know what it meant that Bradley was coming into the woods every day. Was he working more than she thought, secretly taking care of them as he had done after Van died? Still, as much as the new information added to the puzzle, it was something else Mr. Boudreaux said that held her captive and wouldn't let go.

"You a catch with all that land."

Bradley had said the same thing the month before Van died. They had been sitting on the tailgate of Bradley's truck, sneaking a cigarette.

"With this much land, you can do whatever you want." Bradley looked longingly out into the woods. "You're sitting on a gold mine. Look at Jerry Miller's daughter. Everybody's trying to inherit that ranch...got men in line for her."

"I thought it was her boobs," Birdie said.

Bradley, pink-faced, whipped his head to look at her and then away just as fast. "Boobs don't hurt, I guess." He stared at his feet and, like eons of men before him, scrambled to make it better for the woman in front of him, only to make it worse: "Well, at least you got land."

Birdie exhaled a dumpster fire's worth of smoke and crossed her arms across her chest just as her dad's silver truck pulled up. Van and two men got out and walked to the shed. One man she immediately recognized as Dale Mackey, a sun-dried wisp of a man who worked with her father for the past few years, and the other, a dark-haired man, otherwise unremarkable except for the surliness he radiated from yards away. The men returned with bags of fertilizer, which they loaded into Van's truck, though none of them waved.

"Where you going?" Birdie called.

"Cruisin' timber!" Van shouted.

It was an odd response, she remembered now, since fertilizer was not required for such a thing, and the trees had largely been destroyed at that point. Still, always eager, Bradley jumped off the tailgate to help, and Van quickly waved him off—"Stay here. Don't need you today. Stay here."—at which point Bradley slinked back to the truck and watched the men closely.

"Who's that other guy with them?" Bradley nervously lit a new cigarette. "He doesn't work on the crew." In retrospect, she should have seen Bradley's alarm as the first clue. A man he didn't recognize, even though Bradley knew all of the men who worked with Van, and the fact that Van didn't want Bradley.

"I mean, do you know that other guy with them?" Bradley asked again.

"I don't know! Gah!" Birdie snapped, still reeling from the realization that the land she stood to inherit one day was as attractive to men as breasts toppling out of a child-sized tank top. She hardly thought of herself as a catch, and despite hundreds of acres of timberland, no male had shown her the slightest bit of attention. Bradley was the only boy who spoke to her with any regularity, and even that was strained—the look of a man treading lightly, the way her father handled rat poison with gloves and a dainty pinch at the top of the bag.

And so in the way that teenagers register everyone over thirty as an amorphous blob of middle age, the importance of a man neither of them recognized would not land. A little over a year later, the dark-haired man would be dead on her fence. But at that moment, he would enter and leave Birdie's brain as quickly as Mr. Boudreaux made a sale on a triple-digit day, only to re-emerge a year later as she drove away from a watermelon stand, melons slamming back and forth like a rock tumbler in the back of her daddy's old truck.

CHAPTER

TWELVE

During his time as a hermit, Mayhill drove to Houston once a month for groceries, ammunition, and bulk Dr Pepper, though don't ask him the last time he'd fired a gun or press him on his Dr Pepper habit. (He could quit anytime and whatnot.) It was a two-hour drive to Houston and worth it because, to this date and to his astonishment, he had never met anyone named Jimmy within the Houston city limits. Not a gas station clerk, not a grocery store bagger, not a homeless man—*HOMELESS JIMMY, NOT GONNA LIE, NEED $$$ 4 BEER*—nobody. The lack of Jimmies had come to be an important draw of Houston, like the Oilers and NASA, if you were into those sorts of pastimes. It was something to put on the travel brochure, because in this phase of his life, Randy Mayhill had not had much luck with men named Jimmy.

At the funeral, Jimmy Cason, the game warden, had called Mayhill a drug dealer. However, his mouth had been so full of chew that

Mayhill couldn't understand him until the sounds decoded themselves in Mayhill's brain on the long ride home after. The tribunal of Jimmies had stood there like a football team, wide-bellied and grim, and Mayhill, once their non-Jimmy adopted brother, had been sentenced to mockery, and unclever mockery at that, which Van would have agreed was the worst punishment of all.

Still, as much as he tried to convince himself that he didn't care about seeing anybody in town, Mayhill missed the people—and he thought of them every time he sped past the smoking Mt. Zion Baptist barbecue pit that signaled the city limit.

Mabel, for example. Two years ago. May of '94. Rumor had it she made a business out of lacing marijuana cigars with embalming fluid. He visited her house on possession with intent to sell, and Mabel—on the porch swing in a t-shirt down to her calves, breasts down to her thighs—had said he needed to loosen up, get laid, and then she lit up a blunt with a Tweety Bird lighter.

"You're a grandmother, Mabel," Mayhill had said as he unclipped the handcuffs off his belt.

"Great-grandma now!" Mabel shimmied her shoulders, all joy. Mayhill gave her his arm, and he lifted her off the swing. "Grandbaby knocked up." Mabel frowned at the handcuffs. "Come on now. I worked with your mama."

"All right, Mabel, but don't make me run again. You know I get mad if I have to run." Mayhill put the handcuffs away and held his hand firmly on her back. "Which grandbaby?"

"You know Jolene."

"Remind me," he said, maneuvering around the potholes and broken beer bottles in her yard. He walked her to the Sheriff's truck.

"Short red hair. Freckles," Mabel said. She moved her swollen legs slowly forward. "Y'all met last year. Solicitation."

"Ah yes, nice girl." He opened the back door, and Mabel grabbed the handles on the frame and pulled herself in with a groan.

"You right, she nice," Mabel said. "We proud of that one, Sheriff. She purdy, she smart. The whole package. Know what I'm sayin'?"

Mayhill hadn't known what she was saying because Jolene had a severe underbite and had dropped out of junior high.

He had heard that Mabel died but he didn't know what from and couldn't bring himself to call anyone to ask.

Also in town: Rudy Lyons. Drunk before breakfast but polite all day. He was a mindful alcoholic, a tasteful one. He never punched anybody, and he limited his drunk driving to the back roads. He recycled his beer cans obsessively. He had a face like a boiled lobster, red and shiny, and a perpetual smile. He had the correct kind of handshake (two seconds, firm without something to prove), and he was ambitious! Rudy Lyons had a dream! A dream to open a bowling alley/bait-and-tackle shop, which when pressed, Mayhill couldn't say was a bad idea at all. "I'd buy that," Mayhill would say.

Rudy Lyons would sigh dreamily. "I know you would, Sheriff. Everybody would. Be goddamn crazy not to."

· · · · · · · · ·

Mayhill hadn't set foot in the feed store in over a year, yet somehow the doors were still open and they always would be. Should end times come as the Church of Christ said, the feed store would remain floating on an island of hot lava, doors open with an endless river of burnt coffee in Styrofoam cups so small they seemed to be made for the hands of infants.

The feed store had your oats, your sweet feed, your pellets, your salt licks, your wormers (cat, dog, horse, *and* pig). In terms of supply, it would not disappoint, and one might even get more than he bargained for. For example, the miraculous crust of dust and dirt on every inch of every surface, even though the supply was largely new. Or opinions on why a man should marry or not marry a girl and how to let said girl down without retaliation in the event that the feed store men ruled against her. The feed store was an unofficial courthouse where one was tried and convicted, where marriages were made and broken, where all traffic was directed.

When Van was alive, Mayhill, Van, and the three Jimmies met twice a day: before breakfast around four or four thirty in the morning, and at the end of day, just before supper, to discuss the day's business before retreating back to the house, to get in bed before eight, and do it all over again. It was consistency, and every man knows that consistency is bliss.

Today, the door to the feed store was propped open. A yellow fly strip dangled just inside like a welcome banner, and even though the sun shone brightly above, Mayhill found himself feeling guarded at the dark doorway as if he were entering a house with a burglar still inside. He wanted to grab the pistol in his boot and put it somewhere more accessible.

Mayhill hadn't expected the smell to draw him in, to transport him the way someone might be transported at a whiff of his childhood home. For a moment, he was every incarnation of his life: a young man with his daddy, then a patrolman, a deputy, and a sheriff again all in the span of the second it took for the smell of sweet feed and burnt coffee to hot-tail it from his nose to his brain. Then, he bristled at the realization that he no longer belonged there. The badge and the smells were not his.

All at once, the tribunal of Jimmies turned to register his presence—Jimmy Nellums, Jimmy Cason, and Jimmy Miller—pointing their heads in the direction of the very large but not-so-much-in-charge Randy Mayhill, a bear of a man, with poor posture, backlit by the sun.

Jimmy Nellums owned the place. He was the richest of the feed store men and had three ex-wives, one of whom who had been wealthy (Arkansas lumber mill) and died in a fishing accident (state champion swimmer, suspicious). The town whispered, but nobody made a stink because the whites around Jimmy Nellums's wife's eyes had shown—a full circle of white around the disc of color, without the tops and bottoms of the irises hidden like they were in normal people's eyes. Everybody knew that this meant she was mean. His wife certainly wasn't pleasant, but had the town had a chance to vote, Patsy Fuller would have been the one decked out in pink camo floating face down in a shallow lake. (Patsy Fuller's eyes were perfectly fine, it should be noted.) Still, Jimmy Nellums had taken his good fortune and chosen to open the feed store, serve the town. He was practically a hero.

Mayhill stood in the doorway, the sun illuminating the dust like beams from heaven. Jimmy Nellums rose slowly and walked toward him. Mayhill felt his body clench as if it were high noon, his breath notably absent.

"Randy Mayhill…" Nellums said with an air of astonishment, as if Christ himself had resurrected before him. "I'll be damned." He held out his hand. The other two Jimmies remained in their chairs, barely a blink between them.

Mayhill shook Nellums's hand and took off his hat. "Jimmy." He nodded to all of them, three Jimmies with one nod.

Nellums, the chief priest among them, returned to his seat in the circle and left Mayhill to face them. If Mayhill had a flaw, it would be his zero tolerance for silence, which was why he and Van had gotten along so well, Van being able to fill up any hole like verbal Fix-a-Flat. The men stared him up and down, a bored, fixed look because Mayhill's was a case they had already tried, the outcome known. He was trash— criminal trash—like Van, they had decided. Mayhill looked around for Barabbas, the thirty pieces of silver. He cleared his throat.

"Gentlemen," he said. "It is amazing to me that you all have aged in my absence, yet I have remained so young and virile."

Silence. He heard Van laughing in his head.

"You've grown though." Jimmy Nellums gestured his chin to Mayhill's belly. "You trick somebody into feeding you?"

Mayhill was not given to nervousness—he wasn't so weak of mind—but at that moment he wished desperately that he smoked or dipped or had a marijuana cigarette laced with embalming fluid, so he was forever grateful when Nellums pointed to the coffee pot in the corner and said, "Coffee's old."

Don't mind if I do.

Mayhill felt the men looking at him as he walked. The grit crunch on the concrete floor beneath his boots echoed through the store. The coffee pot was burned on the bottom, and the black had inched halfway up the bowl in a grainy stain of smoke. The coffee was bitter against the perpetual aftertaste of Dr Pepper in his mouth, his tongue pickled in sugar. The chemical taste that the hot coffee released from the Styrofoam was apparent now.

Nellums had mercifully added a chair to the circle when Mayhill returned with his coffee. Despite the failure of Mayhill's opening joke, it was true: the feed store men had aged dramatically in a year. The lines in their faces deepened, their jowls padded as if saddling up for the long ride of middle age. Mayhill's own face was not pretty, with his nose like a camel where Van had punched him the last time he saw him. It was barely noticeable in the landscape of his face but it was a reminder, like most scars, of a lesson learned too late.

Mayhill sat in the folding chair. It squeaked beneath his weight, and he took his place in the circle.

"Been a long while," Jimmy Nellums said, suspicion smeared across his face. "To what do we owe the pleasure, Sheriff?"

Mayhill snickered at the formality as if on instinct before realizing the intention of "Sheriff." Mockery.

"Just thought I'd stop by." Mayhill sipped his coffee, thankful for something to do with his hands. "How're the hogs treating ya?" he said to the coffee cup.

"They ain't helping me any," Nellums said. The other two Jimmies shook their head in agreement, mourning their many hog-related losses.

"Hogs done a real number at Birdie and Onie's," Mayhill said. "Trying to help them out. Thought this was the place to be."

Mayhill looked around the feed store. The supply had doubled since he was last here: large wire traps outside the door, bait on display, bags of corn. Brown bags with WILD BEAST ATTRACTANT written across the front in non-descript letters. "Appears the hogs have been a real boon to you, Jimmy."

The men looked at each other, a twinkle of bemusement in their eyes that Mayhill felt the overwhelming need to punch. Nellums got up and walked to the dusty checkout counter and lifted a big stack of papers. He returned and gave Mayhill a flier.

"County agent dropped these off."

The flier was glossy, much too fancy for a piece of paper that said

"Hog Trapping Tips" in the same sensitive font reserved for feminine products.

Mayhill read it while the men watched him.

- *Set up multiple traps in multiple locations.*
- *Vary your bait selection among your traps.*
- *Use small enough mesh to catch all hogs, even young ones.*
- *Do not release trapped hogs.*
- *Don't give up! Persistence pays!!!*

It was condescending, like telling a dying person to eat more fruits and vegetables.

"Who's the county agent?" Mayhill asked.

"Some young hotshot." Nellums pulled out his pocketknife and began cleaning his right ear. "Couldn't have been twenty-five. From Dallas. Got a degree in ecology or some shit."

"Y'all using anybody?" Mayhill asked. He looked at the paper.

"When the hogs make me mad enough," Nellums said.

"I'd appreciate a few names if you got 'em."

"Trapper? Hunter?"

"Don't matter," Mayhill said. "Anybody working out by me?"

"You staying at Van's place still?"

"My place," Mayhill said, "but yeah."

"Taking care of Onie and Birdie?"

"I am." Mayhill folded the flier twice into a square that would fit in his pocket.

"I'm sure you are. Man like you cain't stop bein' a hero overnight!" Nellums put away his pocketknife and pulled a pen out of his shirt. He took the flier from Mayhill's hand. "Tell you what..." He scribbled on the back of the square. "There's a fella named Tommy Jones. Been doing some trapping around the county."

"County hire him?" Mayhill asked.

"Independent contractor." He handed Mayhill back the paper. "County won't hire felons."

"Felon? Tommy Jones…I know that name." Mayhill searched his memory for it.

"Didn't Tommy Jones work for Van a spell?" Nellums asked to the group.

"The whole county worked for Van a spell," Cason and Miller said.

Hearing them say Van's name, Mayhill wanted to punch them in their collective guts.

"He's good," Nellums said. "Give him a call. Know he's friends with Dale Mackey out by you. Passed him on the road few days back, headin' out your way." Nellums got up and refilled his coffee. "I'll tell you what, he was carrying a trap almost as big as that truck of his. Teetering like a top! You cain't carry a trap like that in a Datsun. Passed him fast as I could. Damn near blew out the back and into my windshield."

"Tommy Jones drives a black Datsun?" Mayhill perked up. Had the hog hunter set a trap on Birdie's land? "Young fella? Real rough looking?"

"He rough, but he ain't young," Nellums said.

"You'll like him. Right up your alley." Cason winked. It was barely perceptible, but definitively a wink.

"Why you say that?" Mayhill asked.

"Felon," Jimmy Cason muttered, but Mayhill tried to ignore the implication.

"You really ain't never heard of Tommy Jones?" Jimmy Miller asked.

"Should I have?"

"Well," Nellums said, "people talk."

"You the people who talk!"

The Jimmies laughed legitimately now. Hardy-hars all around! The joke had ruled in Mayhill's favor, and he relaxed a bit, though he hated all of them more than he remembered.

"What'd he do exactly?" Mayhill interrupted the laughs. "Why's Tommy Jones a felon?"

Miller shrugged.

"Beat the shit out of his wife," Cason said. "Maybe his kid. Sumpin' like that, but—"

"But they never proved it!" Nellums waved his hand to emphasize the point. His coffee splashed onto the concrete floor. "They never proved it. Tommy Jones's the best hog trapper I ever seen. I hired him at my sister's place, and I tell you what, give him a few weeks and—"

"Lemme get this straight…" Mayhill's voice rose more than he could honestly control. "You hired a convicted felon who beats his wife, and you put him to work on your sister's place?"

"They never proved it!" Nellums and Miller bellowed.

"You've got nieces!" Mayhill said.

"They never proved it!" Cason said, and then pointed at Mayhill. "What's more, *Sheriff*, I'm not sure you of all people are in any position to come around here bestowing upon us your moral authority." The statement was aggressive, but there was something in Jimmy's eyes—a wariness, a steeliness—that made Mayhill realize much too late that he had been lumped into the category of mentally unstable. His best friend had gone nuts with desperation and killed himself, and Mayhill had gone nuts in his own way. And everybody knows that lunacy, like desperation, is contagious. As a result, the Jimmies thought that

Mayhill was just as likely to come in petting an imaginary rabbit as it was for him to shoot up everyone with a sawed-off shotgun.

Mayhill closed his eyes at the revelation of this shifting social dynamic. Then, he swung his fist as hard as he could, and he knocked Jimmy Nellums out cold. Then Jimmy Miller leapt from the folding chair and Mayhill landed a roundhouse to his ribs. Then an elbow to the face of the attacking Jimmy Cason. He pulled the pistol from his boot and stood over the men, daring them to mock him or say Van's name without a pope-like respect again. Three Jimmies! Writhing on the dusty concrete floor, regretting their underestimations of the intemperate and unexpectedly flexible Randy Mayhill.

However, when Mayhill opened his eyes, the three Jimmies sat in their folding chairs and stared at him steadily. They were perfectly still and silent, an air of superiority wafting around them like tailpipe fumes. They were not writhing.

Jimmy Nellums stood abruptly and held out his hand. "Good luck with your hogs." He looked down at Mayhill. "I know Onie and Birdie have appreciated the enormous amount of help you've given them over the years."

The men smirked and looked into their tiny, cold coffees. Mayhill stood too and understood that the judge was ordering him to vacate. The folding chair perked up from the relief, and Mayhill adjusted his belt where the buckle had stabbed mercilessly into the overhang of his gut.

"It was just real good to see you, Jimmy. Jimmy. Jimmy." He nodded in each Jimmy's direction. "Give all your ex-wives my regards." Mayhill walked toward the sun that beckoned him outside, the smells of the feed store now absent in his nose.

"I'll tell Tommy you looking for him!" Nellums called after him.

"That'll be fine!" Mayhill did not look back. He waved his hat and walked back out into the sun, the infant-sized coffee cup crushed in his hand.

Shortly before he died, Van had bought all of the blood meal from the feed store and had told Jimmy Nellums he would have to even up later. In Nellums's official statement to the police, Van had said that his trees were looking good and that they were selling some of the young ones to a German company out of New York for pulpwood. No longer did a forester have to wait for mature trees every thirty years. It was all getting better! No more borrowing! Pay day! Or at least Van had hollered as much as he ran out of the feed store.

Nellums wrote out *20 BLD ML $75* in chicken scratch, then licked his thumb to peel away the pink page on the receipt pad. He shook his head, perturbed by Van's hubris, and placed the pink paper on the counter in the stack of unpaid receipts—receipts reserved for farmers who were a little behind here and there, for men whose animals had been injured at an inopportune time. Still, Van was rubbing him the wrong way.

Hours later, after a meeting with the cross-wielding hog hunter, Mayhill had run in looking for Van. "Haven't seen him…" a Greek chorus of useless Jimmies bounced through the halls. Mayhill's throat had seized and he could barely breathe, overtaken by a predictable outcome presenting itself. He had turned to leave, hurried and panicked, when Nellums grabbed his shoulder. "When you find Van, give him this." He slapped the thin, pink blood meal receipt in Mayhill's hand. "Van's been borrowing too long. I know it's just blood meal, but last month it was a bunch of lime. Then, a roll of barbed wire. Hell, it adds up. I don't know what he's doin' buying all that anyway. Ain't nothin' gonna help his trees."

Mayhill said nothing as Nellums continued to talk. He stared straight ahead and nervously folded the pink paper into a tiny square the size of a matchbook and slipped it in his shirt pocket. "I ain't gettin' anymore blood meal in, you know that! Government regulating the hell out of it. But do I sell it to him anyway? Of course I do. Because I'm a Christian. Van's had a tough go of it. Timber ruined, lost his money and all, but a man's gotta have a limit." The other two Jimmies nodded behind him. "Take care of it, Sheriff."

When the speech was over, Mayhill walked quickly to the truck. He tried hard to pretend that everything was in control, but he knew that it wasn't. He clenched his hand to his shirt pocket, the blood meal receipt burning a hole right through him.

CHAPTER THIRTEEN

Bradley, however, had always liked the feed store okay. He liked the Jimmies who all knew him and shook his hand, but mostly he appreciated the consistency of it. The same men up there every morning and again in the afternoon, drinking the same burnt coffee, sitting in a circle of chairs as if they were playing an imaginary game of Texas Hold'em or confessing their transgressions in AA. The feed store men could trace their roots back five generations at least, and they talked of their ancestors as if they had a daily close personal connection with them, as if they remembered sitting at their knees, learning how to wax a mustache properly. Jimmy Cason's great-great-great-grandfather had fought at Appomattox and had his hand amputated using only whisky and a saw. Bradley didn't even know his dad.

Bradley had moved to this speck of a town from Houston a few years back, and to live here without suspicion, a man needed at least two generations under his belt. The feed store men talked to Bradley how they talked to the black kids: polite and overly friendly, as if to prove to themselves that they were the kind of people who would talk to strange white boys and black kids. They would describe Bradley as a "class act," which was only reserved for people who had been deemed trashy but so far had hidden their low society affliction enough for their tastes.

Six months before Bradley saw a dead body hanging on Birdie's fence, a large bruise had formed on his arm. It had been a familiar scene at Bradley's house that morning. His mother was drunk. Rent was due. He only had two hundred dollars to contribute, which he counted out in cash on the coffee table. His mother, dipping her head like an oil rig as each bill hit the stack, exploded into panic. She reared back and hit him as hard as she could with her rebar forearm.

"Two hundred dollars?" she yelled like an accusation—arms and legs detonating, hair swinging. "Three hundred is rent! Three hundred!" Bradley lifted his arm to deflect and cowered away, even though she was much smaller than him. The boney-ness of her arm struck him like a tire iron, and a deep ache ripped up his elbow. The whites of her eyes flashed like headlights.

Bradley scrambled away from her, but she picked up her purse and threw it at him—lipsticks and matchbooks flying like shrapnel. Then she picked up a pillow. Then a picture frame. She picked up an ashtray that hit the wall by the door. It left a hole the size of a baseball, the drywall jagged and open like a shark's mouth. It hit the floor in a shatter. Bradley jetted out the door, joining the old dog on the lawn, and heard a loud crash behind him, and as he drove to the feed store, he mentally surveyed everything in their living room and wondered what possibly could have been left to throw.

Bradley loaded feed into the back of his truck for an afternoon job. Fumes of dust and oats puffed around him, and his arm throbbed as he shoved the final bags into the bed. The very little rent money he had been missing, of course, went to gas for driving to the jobs he did have. Birdie's house was thirty minutes from town, for example. Jerry Miller's was twenty-five. A back and forth trip to the ranch, then the feed store and back again. He tried not to think about the math.

Bradley slammed the tailgate and turned to see Dale Mackey emerge from the feed store behind him. He had known Dale when he worked for Van; they had cruised timber together with a steady rotation of other men with spotty résumés. Rumor had it that Dale had been involved with Van's operation—the Jimmies said he'd been his partner—and though Bradley had never really thought much about Dale, he knew that Van had trusted him, so he automatically had too.

Dale was the opposite of Van: a pale man with sunken cheeks and stringy hair, thin and jerky-dry. His eyes were dark orbs, but darted like a squirrel's, which mirrored his speech and twitchiness. Every time Bradley saw Dale, he had the urge to give him a sandwich.

Dale nodded at Bradley in recognition and walked over and shook his hand, and Bradley was shocked at how impossibly soft Dale's hands seemed. Could a man use lotion?

"Where you working now?" Dale spit and scratched the ground with his dirty tennis shoe, then cocked his head to one side. He looked at Bradley through dark sunglasses.

"Here and there," Bradley said. "Feeding cattle for the Millers today. They out of town."

"Where they go?"

"Florida, I think," Bradley said. "Disney World?"

"They pay you okay?"

"Yessir."

"Aw, don't lie," Dale said. "You know they ain't paying shit."

Dale laughed big, and Bradley forced a nervous laugh too, sheepish all of a sudden and not sure what to say since he appreciated the work. He stared in the back of Dale's truck: dog food, fertilizer, boots, and a Sam's Club-sized box of candy that Dale always carried around—a quirk Bradley suddenly recalled from before.

"What're your plans, Bradley Polk?" Dale asked.

Nobody had used his full name in recent memory, and it felt good to hear, like he was somebody whose last name mattered. "My plans?" Bradley asked. "Go to the Millers. After that, I dunno." He thought of his mother, the ashtray like a grenade. He couldn't go home tonight. He needed a girlfriend pronto. He could borrow her lotion and have soft hands like Dale's.

"No, son," Dale said. (Nobody had ever called Bradley "son" either.) "Your plans. Plans. You gonna be here forever? You gonna be forty years old building fences? Working for a bunch of sidewalk cattlemen who think they better than you? Sure, they put you to work, but you just try and date Miller's daughter. You see what happens then."

Bradley thought of Jimmy Miller's daughter. She had a body like a porn star but a face painted in orange make-up that dripped in stripes down her white neck. She looked like a tiger.

This is not a problem, Bradley thought, but he understood Dale's sentiment. "Yessir?" Bradley said, trying to fathom any appropriate response.

And then it happened.

Dale pointed at Bradley as if he were picking him out of a large crowd, instead of pointing at a lone young man in a dusty parking lot to whom he had been talking for five minutes. Dale's tone became serious. "I could use you," he said.

Those were his words. *I could use you.*

Bradley remembered them exactly. They danced in his head at night as he struggled to stay awake on his shift, a memory planted to help him make sense of it all later when he slept in the woods at night and kept watch over a garden surrounded by barbed wire.

Initially, Dale and Bradley planted dozens of baby plants. They had met at his trailer that first morning and loaded about twenty large cardboard boxes into the back of Bradley's truck. Each box was filled with twelve small green plants peeking out of Styrofoam cups.

"Grew them myself from seed!" Dale said with the bright-eyed spunk of a third grader. This endeared him to Bradley because, one, Bradley Polk always liked enthusiastic people—*see also:* Van—and, two, it made the entire operation seem about as sinister as a science fair. They got in Bradley's truck and navigated the winding trails near Dale's trailer until they arrived at a remote part of the forest. From there, Dale instructed Bradley how to enter and leave the plot he had found. Roll down the window, cut the engine, then listen for a good few minutes and whatnot. They walked the rest of the way, each carrying one of the cardboard boxes, as if they were moving into their first apartment.

"I didn't know all this land was yours," Bradley said.

Dale had said nothing. He just trudged along and finished off his breakfast of a Moon Pie.

The plot was in the middle of a clearing where dozens of trees had turned brassy and died, so the light was good, but being in the middle of the woods, the plot was also well obscured. The March sun shone down in bright columns like a lighthouse, and though he had worked the woods plenty with Van, Bradley couldn't remember being under the cover of trees when it was this sunny. He and Dale spent the day clearing debris from the forest floor and picking ticks off their ankles. They dug holes and dusted them with fertilizers, then planted the small plants in clusters about six feet apart that Bradley measured off in steps. They protected them with tomato cages and covered them in flimsy mesh blankets, like babies put down for the night. The arrangement was oddly domestic. Their conversations, simple and easy, about the town (judgmental), sports (Oilers), women (difficult), politics (terrible). The risk of the operation was the one thing they never spoke of, Van the obvious cautionary tale, and Bradley had begun to think of Van's name as a spell, as if saying it would incant his bad luck, put a bullet in his brain. But even then, even with Van's last breath circulating through the trees, Bradley didn't think about getting caught.

Dale instructed Bradley to divide a few sacks of blood meal amongst the five-gallon buckets. A fine cloud of plum-colored dust mushroomed into the air after each pour, and the smell of metal wafted between them. Dale waved a gloved hand in front of his face. "Dogs… hogs. They're predators. Squirrels…deer…" Dale said. "Rabbits too… they're all prey. Prey smells the blood. They stay away."

"What about the predators?" Bradley could hear the hogs screeching across the river like a neighborhood riot. Buckets hung heavily from each of Bradley's hand, and he teetered back and forth like a scale.

"Fence'll do fine." Dale walked along the north edge of the garden and pointed to the where Bradley should spread the blood. "Can't hardly get blood meal no more."

"Why not?" Bradley asked.

"Mad cow disease. Regulations. Blood gets in the feed, in your garden. Your brains turn to shit. Bunch of Brits died few years back."

"Oh," Bradley said. He looked around for something to tie around his nose. "Where'd you get blood meal, then?"

But again, Dale didn't answer. He just kept walking the fence line and worked on a Twizzler, but when they got done for the day, Dale tossed him an old shotgun from the back of his truck.

"For the predators," he said.

⁘ ⁛ ⁘ ⁛ ⁘

Dale had a manual, thin and floppy like a phone book, which he carried around with the reverence of a girl's phone number. It was usually rolled up into a tight tube and tucked in the back pocket of his jeans. The cover and the spine had been bound with silver duct tape to keep the tissue-thin pages from tearing off into the wind and, Bradley guessed, to keep the book title safe from passing eyes.

Bradley would visit the site briefly every day to check the fences and fertilizer. Dale largely stayed away, save weekly or so inspections, and Bradley was struck by the trust Dale placed in him. In no time at all, the plants had grown to the size of a toddler, just to his thigh, and were just as demanding, despite being weeds. Dale would compare the caveman-like drawings of the silver instruction manual to the full, lacy plants in front of him. Then he would declare their needs of the week. They would need lime, for example.

"Pine makes acidic soil," Dale said, and tapped the manual with his gloved hand. "We need lime to neutralize it." Then he would hand Bradley five ten-dollar bills. "Get yourself some gas, and hit the feed store up before tomorrow. Lime. And don't—"

"I know," Bradley would say. "Don't say it's for you."

Bradley could have worked at the lumber mill. Dale had worked there for a bit, even though his father died there. "When Daddy got killed," Dale said. "I had to quit school and help Mama." It was one day near the beginning, and Dale leaned against a tree while Bradley pruned. "Nobody thinks I'm smart, but I am. I had to take care of Mama, though. You know what I'm sayin'? She was grievin.'"

"I'm sorry," Bradley said, and he was sorry, sorrier than he felt comfortable feeling. Dale's father had gotten his head cut off at the mill, which sounds like a freak accident to office workers whose primary workplace hazard is changing the water cooler, but it was not an unusual occurrence at the sawmill. Bradley knew of another man who lost his head. It was an *Alice in Wonderland* kind of world. Don't ask Bradley to count how many lost their arms or fingers. A man might as well hand over his pinkie when he signed his employment papers.

What they were doing now came with a different kind of risk, though in the cocoon of the woods, it hardly seemed a gamble. Bradley was thankful to be a gardener. He was thankful Dale had chosen him, and if he were honest with himself, he wanted to impress him. He never missed a day and was always early to work. He was meticulous with the plants, every bug that flew near the mint green buds a personal affront to Bradley and his devotion. Dale referred to it as their operation.

The rains came, and the growing was effortless. No irrigation needed. Just the right amount of sun in a grove of dead pine trees. More and more plants popped up out of nowhere, like their entire venture was blessed—*BLESSED!* Meant to be! They would harvest early October. Dale could pay off a nagging debt. Bradley could afford an acre and a trailer. They would need another man probably. The promise of money grew.

"I know I said ten thousand dollars…" Dale would say, eyes big as the moon, flashing the long *ta-da!* fingers of a magician. "But what would you think of twenty?"

And Bradley, who hadn't eaten all day and wondered if he could sleep at his mother's house that night, was dumbstruck by the idea of twenty thousand dollars. "Yessir," he would say. "I could do all right with that."

The afternoon that Bradley saw a dead man hanging on Birdie's fence, he headed to the garden for another round of pruning before the harvest next month. He tried to concentrate on the colors of the sunset so he wouldn't have to think about the dead man. In Houston, perfect sunsets were a rarity, saved for special days when the sun and humidity mysteriously reflected just so off the smog. Sunsets in the country, however, were a daily religious experience. The tip-tops of the pine trees turned into black steeples, and the sky flooded with an orange hue the color of a sliced-open cantaloupe, shocking but friendly. The clouds were long, deep, and purple like the bruise on his arm. Still, as breathtaking as the sky was, Bradley couldn't shake the image of the man on the fence. He fought to concentrate on the narrow road in front of him and swerved to avoid some hogs congregating in the road.

"You stuck or you deaf?"

Had those been the man's last words to another human being? Would the man still be alive if Bradley had simply refused to move his truck? Would the man be pulling up to McDonald's for a McRib right now if Bradley had yelled like a lunatic to get the hell out of there?

When he got to the trailhead to the garden, Bradley kept going to see if he might figure out exactly where the man had gone. He drove down the dirt road about five more minutes before he saw it: a small Datsun, faded black and crusted with pale mud, backed into the ditch. The black seemed somehow menacing against the brown of the tree trunks, even during a sundown as holy as this one. Bradley stopped his truck and white-knuckled the steering wheel. This was all really happening. It hadn't been a dream.

But something of note: the trap in the back of the Datsun was gone. The hunter had set the trap somewhere in the woods.

Bradley had the urge to get out and inspect the truck, to follow the trail the man might have walked, the path the trap no doubt carved into the forest floor, but he couldn't move. He sat there frozen for a few moments until a dark thought overcame him. If someone saw him there with the truck, they might think he was responsible for whatever fate had befallen the man. But who would see him? Who would have been in the woods in the first place?

The dead man had, for one.

Bradley put the truck in reverse and backed down the logging trail as quickly as he could before he hit the dirt road. He held his breath the entire time.

This isn't your fault. It has nothing to do with you.

Bradley arrived at the campsite, and Jason sat under a lantern hanging from the low branch of a loblolly. Dale had recently hired Jason to join them since the plants and the work had exploded beyond Dale's expectations. Jason was about Bradley's age, but all talk and much too eager.

Bradley knew the work was not as glamorous as Jason imagined and that he had expected a *Godfather* kind of existence, a *Smokey and the Bandit* kind of existence. Theirs would be a dark world of intrigue— all danger, grit, glitz, money, girls. James Bond. Biggie Smalls. Bradley knew this because Jason had expressed his disappointment in so many words: "We're just gardening like some old fucking ladies."

Hiring him had been a mistake. First, he didn't own a truck, and so Bradley and Dale had to shuttle him to and from work (forty miles round trip, three gallons of gas). Though Bradley had never been inside Jason's actual house, he had driven him there plenty of times and knew the part of the county the way one knows hell, mostly a figment of one's mind. It was a dismal place—a small community with cheap land that a developer had used to draw in poor people from all over the state. People would sell their belongings to start life over with "a little piece of land in the country," only to find that there were no water wells, no sewage, or roads that could withstand a soaking rain. It was a community of stranded people, a desert island in the woods. Though he was regularly aware of the poverty in his own life, he was thankful he didn't live there at least. He thought about the community of stranded people every time he drove Jason home, then went to his mother's own tiny house in town and flushed a toilet and drove down the roads fancy-free when it rained. LA DI DA.

Secondly, Jason was unhinged. The kind of volatile young man you didn't want around for a delicate operation. The kind of young man Bradley's mother would have been had she been a young man. But Dale had felt sorry for him, Bradley guessed, and in his Robin Hood mentality wanted to share with Jason. Had Dale felt sorry for him too?

The light lit Jason's head from above and fell perfectly on the long barrel of a shotgun propped against his chair. The lower half of Jason's face disappeared into the dark. The bridge of his nose and his nostrils glowed almost white, slick with oil. Jason's reddish-blond hair was singed a pumpkin orange, all scraggly and stuck to his forehead, as if he had cut his hair himself with a steak knife.

Jason looked dirty. Disgust welled up in Bradley when he saw him—a full-on repulsion—mainly because Bradley knew he had no room to talk or even think such things about another man's hygiene. Bradley hadn't changed his shirt in two days. It was ripped and yellowed at the armpits with SUBLIME written on the front in a fancy font he had seen on tattoos. It had been one of his favorite shirts, though he hated it now with its saturating stench, its desperation. Bradley had mosquito bites on his neck and on his arms that had swollen into small, puffy mounds. The right sole of his tennis shoe had come unglued and the toe flapped like the mouth of a puppet when he walked, an airborne Jordan with one arm raised and legs splayed, flopping up and down against the pine needles.

Bradley grabbed a beer from the cooler. He would get drunk and wash the dead man from his mind, wring him out like a sponge.

"Where's Dale?" Bradley pulled nervously at the pop-top and cut his finger on the metal.

"Dunno," Jason said, spinning a pocketknife between his fingers.

"He been here at all?" Bradley asked. He sucked the blood running from his finger, and then took a deep swallow of the beer.

"Gone most of the day. Checked some plants earlier. Cleaned up some," Jason said. "Be glad you missed him."

Something about the way he said it twisted in Bradley's gut. "Why?" he asked. "Dale in a mood?"

"Tweaked as shit."

"About what?"

"How the fuck should I know?"

"Then what? After he left?" Bradley asked. "He leave? He go home?"

"Jesus, you my girlfriend?" Jason snapped. "Why you asking so many questions?"

Bradley said nothing and drank half of the beer in a few gulps, but it did nothing for him. Dread bloomed in his brain like overnight mushrooms. The dead man, the truck, Dale on edge. Bradley stared into the forest, which appeared much blacker than normal, the crickets like tiny screams in his ears.

"He wants you here at eight tomorrow," Jason said. He pointed his knife at a pile of sacks and wire. "Need to haul all that to the dump and be back here at eight."

Bradley was supposed to meet Mayhill at eight. Dale had never needed him that early. "Why can't you do it?" Bradley asked.

"I got another job," he said. And in the next breath: "You seen that truck?"

Bradley closed his eyes as if he had been caught, but he didn't know what for. "No," Bradley said carefully. "What truck?"

"How the hell you even get around?" Jason flicked the knife, and it cartwheeled into the dirt by his Nikes. "You don't pay attention to shit." He pulled a ring of keys out of his pocket and dangled them like a cat toy.

"Where'd you get those?"

"Glove box," Jason said. "Always check the glove box."

"Did Dale see the truck?" Bradley asked.

"Yeah, he saw it."

Bradley stared at his hands, but they didn't seem real somehow. Something was unfolding slowly in front of him, a picture taking form. Bradley knew then that he would not be meeting Mayhill at eight. "Dale say anything?"

"I thought he'd wig, but he didn't say much." Jason flicked the knife into the dirt again. "Said it ain't a problem."

"How's he know it's not a problem?"

"I dunno. He just said it ain't." Jason plucked the knife from the ground and wiped the blade on his jeans. "Truck's been there a day."

"What's that mean?" Bradley asked.

"Means I'm gonna get me a truck, what it means."

⠄⠂⠄⠂⠄⠂⠄⠂⠄

The next morning, Thursday, Bradley did not meet Mayhill. Bradley, always dutiful and obliging, especially to Dale, went to the dump as instructed. He talked to Patsy Fuller from a solid fifteen feet away, more flies on him than the trash, her eyeing him like a criminal for reasons he couldn't ascertain. He didn't mind it though, her suspicion a comforting constant in his life when everything was turned upside down.

Back from the dump, eight a.m., Bradley checked the plants and tightened some ties where the fence wasn't snapped perfectly to attention. He heard the rumble of a truck, and without thinking,

Bradley hid behind a tree. He had never done such a thing before—not in the comfort of the woods—and he was surprised to find himself doing it now. In a few moments, though, Dale appeared. Bradley, embarrassed, quickly walked toward the garden, hoping Dale hadn't seen him hide. He pretended to zip up his jeans, as if he had taken a quick pee in the woods.

But Dale was too focused to notice the theatrics. He nodded to Bradley and walked the perimeter of the garden in small, quick steps. Dale had the controlled irritability of a man trying to remain cool, as if he had drunk too much coffee and climbed right into a straitjacket.

"You drive Jason home?" Bradley asked, taking up behind him.

"He got a ride," Dale said. He stopped and pulled a plant close to him, inspecting the bud, taking a sniff.

"But he doesn't have a truck." *The Datsun.*

Dale kept walking. Bradley couldn't tell his mood. He didn't seem upset. He seemed controlled, focused, but something was off, something changing—Dale was more business than he had ever seen him.

"I heard there was a truck." *There was a body about a mile from here!* This was what he wanted to say, of course, but Bradley couldn't make the words real and connect the situation in any way to their garden. The outside reality was moving too quickly for his insides to catch up—just dread sowed into his brain, waiting for the signal to sprout.

"Hog hunter," Dale said. "Far enough from here." He squatted down to examine the fence, his knees snapping like sticks, and plucked the bottom wire with a long finger. It let out the low drone of a bass guitar. "Start taking all this down."

"The fences? Still got a month to go. What about the hogs?" Bradley asked, not sure he understood. "Dale, is something—?"

"Take the fences down and watch for hogs." Dale popped back up and started walking. "I got some things to do at the house. Be back in a few hours." Then, just like that, Dale hurried away and disappeared back down the logging trail.

Bradley looked at the fence, stunned and unsure, and felt like a tornado had just touched down and dissipated. Dale had blown off the truck, but now they were taking the fences down a month early. Bradley expected to hear Dale's engine rev after a few minutes, but there was only the sound of the birds. In a few minutes, Bradley walked down the trail to where they parked their trucks, and Dale's red Chevy was still parked there beside his.

Dale hadn't left. He was still somewhere in the woods.

CHAPTER
FOURTEEN

Mayhill had the license plate number of a juvenile delinquent and the phone number for a felon hog trapper, but he still didn't know anything about the dead man, and so he could hardly call his venture into town a success. Still, he could guess that Bradley was alive and smelled bad, at least as of this morning. This was the bright side, and a wise man looks on both sides. Van always said, "If you got a shit sandwich, at least you got something to eat. Kids in Ethiopia and whatnot." It made sense.

A few hours after Dale and Bradley talked hurriedly in the woods, Mayhill called Tommy Jones, the felon hog trapper, to no avail. The Feed Store Jimmies had said that he was friends with Dale Mackey and had been working in the area, so he decided to drop in on Dale. For his entire life, Dale Mackey lived far on the east side of the woods from Van, and one hot Dr Pepper later, Mayhill turned his truck right into Dale's small driveway, which led to an open field that was green and golden like an apple.

Dale Mackey was a malnourished man. Not in the food pantry impoverished way. In the too-many-Mountain-Dews-and-barbiturates way—a man whose body rejected all that nourished and grounded but somehow managed to suck it away from others like a deer tick. After Van's trees all went and died, Van became Dale's latest host, an exposed ankle in the woods that Dale clung to. Rumor had it that he had been Van's partner in the failed operation. Still, when drug agents raided the land, there had been no evidence of Dale Mackey being there at all—not a fingerprint, not a carton of Kools, nothing—which did not surprise Mayhill in the least, because the only thing he could see Dale masterminding was anemia.

Dale had lived there all his life and was a few years younger than Van and Mayhill. His parents were now dead, and their old house stood crumpled right at the tree line behind Dale's trailer. His land was probably three acres or so, all overgrown field, sliced down the middle by a large drainage ditch that could be called a small creek, depending on the prowess of the real estate agent and the cataracts of the potential buyer. In the right light, though, the land could be worthy of watercolors, feathers of yellow and green, patches of syrup-brown dirt the color of Coke.

On top of the small hill in front of the dilapidated house sat a yellowed hunting trailer with a brown stripe running through the middle, a paint job modeled after sandwich meat. A side window was missing, a cut blue tarp placed over the flap. The front door was slightly off its hinges, and the trailer was missing a wheel in the front. In its stead was a small cable spool, which was shorter than the rest and caused the trailer to sag slightly to the right. Mayhill imagined Dale walking perpetually at a slant, his beers sliding down TV trays, his

Jell-O molds forever tilted.

A tawny cowdog, happy-eyed with white ears, trotted up to Mayhill. Mayhill leaned down to scratch the dog's head, only to find that his fingers were now tinted a purplish red. Mayhill sniffed his hand, and then he looked down at the dog again and saw that the dog's entire muzzle was red with blood.

A shed stood a few dozen feet behind the house, chickens skittering around it. Dale's red Chevy was parked in front of it, and Dale unloaded something from the back end. Even from a distance, Mayhill could see Dale's bones poking wildly from under his camouflage t-shirt like a bag of sticks. Dale stopped when he saw Mayhill and walked up the driveway to greet him.

"Randy Mayhill." Dale took off his work gloves and tucked them in his front jeans pocket. "It's been a minute."

"Dale." Mayhill stuck out his hand. "You're looking gaunt."

Dale eyed him a moment, then laughed, revealing in his mouth a cemetery of teeth, a mouth so wide and cavernous that Mayhill was sure he could see Dale's toes.

Mayhill laughed too, and though he hated Dale almost as much as the Jimmy trifecta, he was relieved for someone to finally laugh at his joke.

"What brings you by?" Dale reached into his back pocket. "Twizzler?"

"Cuttin' back." Mayhill patted his belly. "How you been, Dale? Been a year, has it?"

"Long time, Sheriff." He stuck a Twizzler in his mouth.

"Where you working now?"

"Shifts at the mill here and there," Dale said. "Keep it simple."

Mayhill nodded. "I'm sure the mortgage on this place is real reasonable."

"What job you got?"

"I deal in antiques."

"Come again?" Dale cupped his hand around his ear.

"Antiques." Mayhill raised his voice. "Old things. Guns mostly."

Dale smiled and worked the Twizzler back and forth in his teeth, a gummy red mess of a mouth, not unlike the bloody mouth of the dog that sat at his feet. "Not good to live in the past, Sheriff."

"Depends on the profit."

All of this was a lie, of course. Mayhill had never sold a gun in his life because he was the only person on this blue planet who could be trusted with a gun. Few people had the discipline, control, and mental fortitude that gun possession required. Plus, he loved the equipment of justice. Even Goddamn Gabby Grayson had pointed out that his zodiac sign was a Libra—the only sign that was not an animal. Instead, Libra was the scales of justice, always dangling precariously in balance.

"I'm needing a hog trapper, Dale," Mayhill said. "Heard you might have a friend who's doing some work out here."

"Where you hear that?"

"I thought it was ridiculous too…you having friends," Mayhill said. But Dale was done with laughing. "Jimmy Nellums said you knew a man named Tommy Jones. Real good trapper. I was hoping you could put me in touch with him. Birdie and Onie need some help."

Dale's face changed then, a dramatic sinking of his already-sunken cheeks, the blood draining from his already-pale face. He swallowed the last of his Twizzler and put the package back in the pocket of his jeans. "Why you coming to me, then, Randy?"

"Jimmy didn't have his number."

Dale nodded slowly, the look of a man who was calculating, who knew when he was being lied to.

"I can't help you out either, I'm afraid. Haven't seen Tommy in a long time." Dale clapped his hands in front of him, then put on his work gloves. "It's been real good seeing you, but I got to get on with my day." He turned to go up the stairs, and next to a jar of sun tea, Mayhill noticed a stack of empty sacks. He thought of the empty sacks he saw at the dump first thing this morning.

Bradley.

Then Randy Mayhill made a guess. He made a guess—explored a hunch—because that's what good lawmen do. And it was this hunch, this moment that all who heard the story later would surmise was what sent Dale down a rabbit hole, that tipped over the domino that sent the whole thing crashing into chaos. That if Mayhill hadn't said what he said next, that this story would have ended with only one dead body. But that's not the way the story goes.

"How long Bradley Polk been working for you?"

Dale turned around quickly. "Why you asking me about Bradley Polk?"

"Jimmy said he saw him with you." *Lie, lie, lie.*

Dale appeared to think for a moment, his hands twitching, his lips redder than Mayhill preferred on a man, or a woman for that matter. "Bradley does things for me here and there."

Mayhill looked at the dirty, cracked window on his house, overgrown grass, the tangles of mesh wire and tomato cages everywhere, even though there were no tomato plants. In fact, Dale had no garden of any kind to account for the number of gardening tools he had propped by the shed. He did, however, have an impressive patch of poison pokeweed growing on the side of the trailer, almost as tall as Mayhill, thick with purple-black berries that weighed the entire plant down in long arches.

"What is Bradley doing for you exactly?"

"And what exactly do you want, Randy?" Dale puffed up, smile-less, his tombstone teeth hidden. "Or are you just out of things to do today, thought you'd play sheriff again?"

"Didn't mean to pry…didn't mean to pry…" Mayhill held up his hands as if to surrender. "Just need some help with my hogs is all. Thought Bradley just might be the man to do it. Since you don't know Tommy Jones's telephone number."

"If I see him, I'll tell him you're looking for him," Dale said. He disappeared up the cinder block stairs into his trailer—Twizzlers in one back pocket and what appeared to be, curiously, a rolled up silver phone book in the other.

It had gone well, Mayhill thought. Dale was as friendly as he had expected, though he seemed off. He seemed physically ill. Mayhill turned to leave, and as he did, he noticed a bunch of hogs out by Dale's shed, huddled around Dale's pickup. They appeared to be at work on something, and Mayhill moved slowly toward them. The hogs, thoroughly unfazed by the presence of a lesser-being like Mayhill, did not stir at his presence, but were nosing furiously around a few sacks, their snouts the odd pinkish color he had seen on Dale's dog. He walked closer. He glanced in the back of Dale's truck. A Sam's Club box of Twizzlers and a pair of broken limb cutters.

His gut dropped and his face twitched. He felt the butterflies of a first kiss, the kick in the groin of falling in love, because there it was, right in the back of the truck for everybody to see. Sacks of blood meal! Bright as day! Mayhill leaned over and stared right at them, unbelieving of his luck, because in 1996, blood meal was hard to come by, and it was just the thing that Van had used when he was so desperate as to think all of his problems could be solved by growing an acre of marijuana.

Mayhill was startled out of his euphoria by the cocking of a gun. He spun around to see a not-so-anemic, fully-iron-supplemented, downright formidable Dale standing next to his trailer. The gun was not pointed at Mayhill, though it was held firmly across his chest soldier-like, but anyone could see that it was a message, visible and blaring, a Surgeon General's warning tacked on the end of their otherwise pleasurable experience.

"You need to leave right now."

PART
TWO

CHAPTER FIFTEEN

Mayhill quickly scooted away from the well-armed Dale, left his property, and returned home just as thunderheads formed in the sky. A storm was coming. It was nearing night, his dogs needed to be fed, and he was tired. He hadn't walked so much since he was sheriff, and he felt sore, achy, and alive, but still he contemplated the downright poetic offerings of the hogs. Really, didn't it have to be the hogs that pointed Mayhill to a clue that blew the entire thing open for him? Watching a bunch of hogs devour a bag of blood meal like Fun Dip would mean nothing to anybody else, but it was 1996: the height of mad cow disease. Outbreak in Britain! Hysteria in America! Oprah goes on the television, says she's not gonna eat hamburgers. Beef prices plummet! Cattle ranchers sue! No more blood in livestock feed. No more blood in fertilizers and whatnot.

Yet right before he died, Van had bought all the remaining bags in Pine County because blood meal was the best thing he knew for keeping rabbits and deer away from his marijuana garden. His suicide note had been written on a receipt for blood meal. Randy Mayhill knew all of this intimately, tucked away in the arsenal of his mind.

Now, let's be clear. Blood meal was not impossible to get. Yes, it was possible that Dale had, say, driven to Houston and picked up a few stray bags, or bought some extras off an old farmer, but that wasn't even the point. The point was: why would Dale even need blood meal? Dale had no livestock, no vegetable garden to protect. Had Dale ever eaten a vegetable? Was he even able to identify a vegetable on the food pyramid under the sugary pointed tip occupied by Little Debbie snack cakes and Moon Pies? There was simply no other reason why Dale would have blood meal.

Mayhill thought of the *48 Hours* episode and the hikers who had been killed by the cartels. Dale was no cartel—he was barely a full man!—but it all made sense that the hog hunter had stumbled upon something he shouldn't have seen.

God, what if it had been Birdie walking in the woods?

Standing on his front porch, Mayhill's excitement nosedived into vexation as he stared out at the trees. The rain fell in thick, hard drops that sounded like his tin roof was being pelted with nickels. He was flanked by his four dogs, Boo and Atticus on the left, Pat Sajak and Vanna on the right, and for a moment, he had the urge to howl into the night. He was euphoric and overwhelmed. Hundreds of acres of land where Dale could be working—it mocked him with its vastness. It would take him a couple of days on foot to find anything. As sheriff, he would have ordered helicopters, walkie talkies, gear! Yet now he was charged with combing the woods as a singular man, and even then he risked hanging face-down on a fence in his own right.

Randy Mayhill, lest we forget, was not a man to be intimidated by much. Mayhill could call the game warden himself with a tip, a suspicion—oh, the irony!—but what about Bradley? Bradley had a pull over this entire ordeal that Mayhill couldn't fathom. How inconceivable that the story hinged upon someone so impotent, so worthless—like NASA realizing that Earth had actually revolved around Pluto all these years!

Goddammit, Bradley! But Birdie would never forgive him if that boy went to jail. And if nothing else has been established in this story already, it is this: Randy Mayhill would do anything for Birdie.

Mayhill grabbed a sixer of Dr Pepper for himself and filled up an old red water cooler he had from high school football practice—the water being for Pat Sajak—and the two jumped in the truck to search for more information, despite the rain coming down in sheets.

He had never done a stakeout or followed someone in any meaningful way, and on his law enforcement bucket list, these two things were near the top. While this lack of experience may seem unusual for a man who had been sheriff, even if only for two years, the logistics of country life were not conducive to stakeouts or following. This wasn't Manhattan or LA. For all of the space that the country offered in which one could lose themselves—*Come to the country! Be a hermit and die without notice!*—there really was no anonymity, no traffic in which to hide, no store fronts into which to duck. How would it be possible to follow a lone truck down a remote dirt road into a hidden marijuana field and the driver, assuming he had full faculties of sight, not see? At best, Mayhill could walk for miles and miles, only to duck behind a loblolly pine, which even at six stories tall, would offer as much coverage as a yard stick for a man as big as him. The predicament was real.

Mayhill sketched out a crude map of Van's land and the surrounding area: the back roads that butted up against the river, Dale's house, some old abandoned houses, and the dump. Mayhill knew a few of the old logging roads by heart, the tiny veins that had largely grown over now, where he had accompanied Van cruising timber. The logging trails were infinite and largely invisible to Mayhill, though the trails had popped out at Van without effort, like a dog following a scent that mere humans couldn't fathom.

Mayhill would be systematic now. For the next few hours, the rain blinked in and out. He forewent sleep and drove the back roads, the endless branching of dirt road after dirt road that ended at abandoned houses, a bigger highway, or a curtain of trees. He backed in and out of old logging trails because they were too overgrown for his truck to get through. The rain came in waves, and Mayhill would stop to get his bearings while Pat Sajak drank some water. His headlights bounced off trees in a way that revealed new openings that the day curiously obscured. Everything looked suspicious, yet nothing did.

At one point, he turned off his headlights and crept by Dale's house again. Dale's truck was parked out by the shed, hogs rooting near it. The lights in his trailer were on, and Dale's silhouette coasted by the window like a ghost. Mayhill drove on.

Mayhill put tiny Xs over all of the land he had covered. He circled spaces he had not yet explored. He would do them tomorrow. Then he returned to the road in which he had run across the Datsun, and drove the opposite way to retrace the path where the truck could have come from, just in case the Datsun had belonged to Tommy Jones, the hog hunter the Jimmies thought was in the area.

Eventually, the rain got so thick that Mayhill drove home. He settled into his chair and turned on the scanner, but he couldn't sleep for all of the sugar and caffeine, and so around 6:15 in the morning, he found himself waiting on the side of the road where he had earlier seen the little black truck.

And just as the sun burned off the rain and cast the sky in a parade of colors, a tiny black Datsun rocked around the corner. It had come from the main road, but it was heading into the woods.

Mayhill gripped the wheel hard with his left hand, his knuckles white, and he held out his other arm to brace Pat Sajak against the seat. Right when the black pickup was about to pass, Mayhill gassed it, jerked the wheel, and spun his truck in the middle of the road. The Datsun swerved nose first into the ditch.

Pat Sajak barked furiously at the window, and Mayhill jumped from the truck. He ran to the driver's seat to find the man—a boy, really—dazed, fear glinting in his eyes.

Mayhill jerked open the Datsun door, grabbed the boy by the shirt, and drug him out of the truck. The boy was dirty and blond—all youth and fury and swinging elbows, and though Mayhill was much bigger, he couldn't hold him long, the boy fighting like a scared cat, twisting and thrashing in his arms.

"Whose truck is this?" Mayhill's knuckles throbbed under the shirt.

"Mine!" the boy yelled.

Mayhill slammed him against the side of the truck. "Whose truck is this?"

"I said it's mine!" The boy kicked and swung at Mayhill. "Let go!"

"Quit lying to me, son." Mayhill pressed all of his weight forward. Mayhill's knee was killing him, and he wouldn't be able to catch the kid if he ran.

"I found it," the boy said through his teeth. He was filthy.

"Where?"

"Ain't telling you nothin'!"

"Where'd you get this truck?"

"Let me go!"

Mayhill slammed into him harder, and the boy gasped, his face red.

"Woods," the boy said. He swung his shoulder away from Mayhill.

"You just take any truck you find? Where's the license plate? What'd you do with the plates?"

The boy tore from Mayhill's hold. Mayhill grabbed him again and threw him against the truck. Mayhill's elbow caught the boy's lip, and it blossomed in blood.

"You stole this truck," Mayhill said.

"I didn't!" The boy knifed his shoulder toward Mayhill again.

"Are you Tommy Jones?" Mayhill was getting tired. His strength would give soon. "Is that your name? Are you Tommy Jones?"

"Let me go!" The boy spit blood at Mayhill.

"Tell me!" Mayhill dug his forearm into the boy's chest.

"You gonna crack my rib!"

"I'll let you go if you talk to me," Mayhill said. "This truck belongs to Tommy Jones, don't it?"

"I don't know!" He jabbed a shoulder at Mayhill. "I found it."

Mayhill eyed the boy hard but couldn't tell if he was lying. Mayhill loosened his grip, and the boy sloughed his shoulders, cracked his neck.

"Why you so dirty?" Mayhill asked.

"Why *you* so dirty?"

Mayhill looked down at the big pond of Dr Pepper on the front of his shirt, the boy's blood fresh upon it. "Do you know Bradley Polk?"

The boy kicked Mayhill as hard as he could in the knee, then pushed by him. Mayhill grabbed after him, but the boy threw a fist to Mayhill's eye and scrambled to the truck. Mayhill reached for the door handle just as the boy slammed it shut.

"That truck ain't going nowhere! You stuck, boy." He hit the window with his palms.

The boy jammed the truck into gear and slammed the gas. The wheels spat a shower of mud behind them, but the truck only shuddered in place.

The boy sent it in reverse and hit the gas. More traction, the truck about to rock free. Mayhill didn't have much time. He ran to the other side of the truck and slung open the passenger door.

"Get out!" the boy yelled.

The boy gassed the truck again, and it lurched forward, then resettled in the mud. The boy leaned over and struck at Mayhill's shoulder with his fist, the other hand on the wheel, then gassed it again.

Mayhill clawed the glove box open and grabbed everything he could from it. Papers, trash, a tire gauge.

The truck spun free and knocked Mayhill to the ground. The car door swung and hit Mayhill in the face as he fell back. Mud splattered over Mayhill. The truck jerked and peeled away in a zigzag.

Mayhill's jeans were ripped. His leg was bleeding but he still clutched the things from the glove box. He sat in the road, legs splayed like a kid sitting in the sand. He was covered in mud, and his heart beat hard in his chest. Pat Sajak barked from the window.

Mayhill tried to catch his breath. He rolled to his side, then pulled up to his knees, a pain shooting through his bad one. He climbed into his truck, one leg still hanging out because he was too tired to bring it all the way in. He looked in the rearview mirror and examined his forehead. He had a good cut, and it was bleeding badly. Mayhill patted the dog's head. "You scared him, Pat," he said. "Good job."

He felt older than he ever had.

The sun was fully up now. He squinted his eyes in the morning light, then right there in the truck, thumbed through the papers. An old receipt for tires. A flattened cigarette carton. Underneath it, curiously, a map, hand-drawn in thick purple marker. Mayhill studied it a few moments before he understood—the river, the highway, the woods shaded in big loopy scribbles—Van's land. *And there's Birdie's house…Dale's house…Mayhill's house.*

Underneath the map, the truck's registration. Thomas Reed Jones.

Was that boy Tommy Jones? Or was that just his truck? Why did he have a map?

When he looked ahead, the Datsun's thick tracks were etched into the road. Oh, glorious mud! Mayhill had never been so thankful for mud! A perfect trail! He waited a few minutes to give the truck some lead time, then Pat Sajak and he inched slowly down the road and took turn after turn deeper into the forest, until he came to a logging trail far in the woods between Van's house and the river, where another set of tracks joined the Datsun's. A few more turns and he came to a small offshoot so narrow that Mayhill's truck wouldn't fit without getting stuck himself or scraping the paint job off entirely. He got out of the truck quietly, gun ready. He already ached from his brawl, and his eyes stung from the mud and blood. His head throbbed. He walked about fifty feet down the trail, following the tire tracks, which ended at a pile of dead branches. He scanned the trees surrounding him, but there was no sign of the boy or the truck, as if they had disappeared behind a curtain in the woods.

CHAPTER

SIXTEEN

"We're moving it tomorrow!" Dale made the declaration first thing that same morning. Thunderstorms had rolled through most of the night but the tree cover had made sleeping in the tent largely tolerable. Still, at some point very late in the night or very early in the morning, Bradley thought he heard a truck and saw the moon-white shine of headlights off in the distance. It had spooked him, and so he ran from his tent through the woods and slept in his truck. In the morning, he woke to Dale banging on his window. "You hear me?" he said. "We're moving it tomorrow!"

Bradley was damp and stiff-necked, his shoes still wet from the early morning run to the truck. Everything about him smelled like mold, and he itched beneath his clothes. A lacy rash like poison ivy had formed on his groin. He got out of the truck and popped his neck. The overnight thunderstorms had produced a light summer fog that made

Dale, twenty feet away, look like a ghost—an impression of himself, an image on a cloudy roll of film. The air was so thick Bradley felt as if he were inhaling syrup, and the muddy forest floor, the bounce of wet pine needles, like walking on a mattress. All of it unreal.

Bradley rushed to catch up with Dale, who trudged ahead to the garden. "Moving tomorrow? What's going on?"

"Where the hell's Jason?" Dale snapped, a slight slur to his speech, eyelids hopping like crickets.

And Bradley, aware now that he must tread lightly, didn't know how to ask anything else. Something definitive had shifted in Dale overnight, the volume turned up, his nervousness contagious and suffocating, a neurotic second-hand smoke. Each breath seemed short, a countdown to an explosion. Dale grabbed a pair of work gloves from his bag and stretched his hands into them, his long fingers vibrating like guitar strings.

Bradley had taken down all of the fencing yesterday, but Dale hadn't returned to help as promised, and so the job had taken all day, slowed even more by the rain. With the plants all exposed and vulnerable, Bradley stayed up all night to make sure no hogs trampled them or deer ate them in the night, but the thunderstorms had sent all the animals into hiding. Bradley, however, had no other place to go.

Now Bradley gathered up the remaining wire, while Dale, who rarely touched the garden directly, trimmed the dead leaves off the plants with a small pair of clippers. At the far end of the garden that butted up against the thicket, Bradley picked up one of the few remaining tangles of fencing metal and held it in front of him like a giant, rusted tumbleweed.

Then Bradley heard a sound. A loud crack deep in the forest—a branch breaking, a skulking animal. He stopped for a moment to listen and heard the definitive slush of footsteps, the crunch of muddy leaves. *You're being paranoid*, he thought. *Dale has you rattled.* Then, a flash of motion, something bobbing in and out of the foliage, probably a deer or a hog, but impossible to tell. He put the metal down and took a few slow steps into the woods. He thought he imagined it, but then he saw the flicker in the distance again. Definite movement. A low-flying buzzard? A trick of the eye in the otherworldly light of sun and haze?

The figure moved through the trees, about a hundred feet off, a flash of white against the dead, brassy trunks. Bradley's stomach dropped. He couldn't move. It was a person, certainly a person, walking far off in the distance. Pale. Small.

"What you looking at?" Dale suddenly appeared behind him, and Bradley flinched. Dale's voice was urgent and tight. "You see something? You see something out there?"

"No..." Bradley shook his head. "Hogs, I think." He turned quickly to get back to work but Dale grabbed his arm.

"Nah, I hear it." Dale craned his neck.

"Think it's gone now," he said too quickly, just as he heard the unmistakable sound of footsteps approaching—one-two, one-two, one-two—*slush-slush* on the wet mattress of the forest floor. "I'm gonna load the rest of this wire—"

"Shhh," Dale hissed at him, and then under his breath, muttered something that Bradley couldn't be sure.

Mayhill?

The idea had occurred to Bradley many times that, in a terrible twist of fate, Mayhill or Birdie might stumble onto what they were doing, their land so close to Dale's. Still, it was unlikely! Birdie never left the house. She didn't go into the woods, much less wander as far as Dale's property. He had told himself this at least. Now seeing a person off in the distance, he had to consider the possibility of her being in physical danger. *We're just gardeners. It was just a hunting accident.*

Dale crouched down low.

Go away, Bradley thought, *whoever you are. Please, go away. Walk away from here.* He stared at the ground in front of his feet, Dale's arm still firmly on him. Bradley prayed for a sounder of hogs to charge through the woods, to distract from whatever awfulness was about to unfold. "Hogs," Bradley said, purposefully loud. "They were moving through here yesterday. There's a rooting spot right through that thicket."

Dale didn't say anything but inched backward toward his tool bag and retrieved a pistol.

Jesus. Bradley held his breath. Dale took a few slow steps into the woods, crouching for the hunt, his gun ready.

"Dale…"

Dale was tracking the figure, blessedly indiscernible now through the trees. He cocked the pistol, then stretched his gun long and followed the sound. He squinted and moved the gun toward the footsteps, slowly winding the barrel through the air, stalking an invisible trail.

"Dale…" Bradley's voice shook. Dale didn't look back, but Bradley realized then that Dale could use the gun on him, could shoot him dead right there, and nobody would ever know. Jason might stumble upon his body later. Jason would bury him where he fell in the forest and probably delight in getting Bradley's share of the beer.

He couldn't ignore what was happening anymore. He should tackle him. He should try to wrestle the gun from his hand. Bradley's entire body tensed, every muscle twitching to fire. He lifted his fist.

Then, *BANG!* The sound of metal clanging, the tinny sound of a gate slamming shut. Dale jumped and swiveled his head, trying to find the noise. A fawn sprinted past them.

Then, suddenly, in the opposite direction—the sound of footsteps behind them. In the garden. Bradley turned quickly toward the noise and back to the woods, not sure which way to look. Dale spun with his pistol outstretched, hand on the trigger.

"Shit!" Jason ducked and jumped back with his arms over his head. His face was red and battered, a cut on his lip.

Jason.

Dale dropped the gun to his side. "What the hell happened to you?"

"Nothing." Jason touched his lip and smeared blood across his mouth. "What I got to do?"

Dale looked back into the forest, but the figure was gone, thankfully. Bradley blinked his eyes at the sun and tried to catch his breath.

"You said you saw hogs?" Dale asked Bradley.

"Yes, yessir."

"You start cutting on the end here. Keep watch on the thicket," Dale said. "Jason and I gonna clean all this up, load up everything in the truck. Then Jason gonna cut too. We moving everything tomorrow."

Dale walked away quickly then, as if nothing at all had happened, but Bradley couldn't move. He trembled slightly and looked down at his shoes. They were completely covered in mud, no Jordan peering through, the wetness soaking through the torn sole. He floated over himself, a full-on panic and disembodiment. He wasn't sure how he had gotten there, how he had gotten to this point. He watched Jason and Dale moving around and chatting about the day as if Dale had not pointed a gun at him, as if Dale had not almost shot a person walking in the woods. He hated them. Bradley then had a vision—psychic almost—of ripping Dale's gun from his hand, shooting them both Western-style, *BANG-BANG.* He imagined Dale and Jason falling to the ground, their faces in shock for discounting him.

Bradley tried to shake the thought. He didn't know who he was anymore. He loaded the rest of the fencing wire into the back of the truck and surveyed the plot for any trash, any remnant of them being there, except for the camp chairs and the lantern. Those would stay until tomorrow. He tried to lie to himself the way Dale had lied to himself so fully.

"Tomorrow? What happened to October?" Jason grabbed a shovel from the pile of gardening tools, then held it close. "It ain't ready yet. The buds aren't emerald green yet. You said emerald!" Jason walked down a row of tall plants up to his eyes. He dropped the shovel and stared worriedly at the plants. He pulled a limb down to eye level, the bushy burst of leaves and flowers looking him right in the face. He grimaced and pushed the plant away in disgust. "Hell, these ain't even avocado."

"Ready enough. It's ready enough," Dale snapped. He was a man trying to convince himself. "Tomorrow."

Bradley put on some gloves and grabbed some branch cutters. He crouched low at the base of the first plant on the row nearest to him. He nudged the leaves out of his face. Jason was right, they weren't ready yet. Bradley was surprised at how proud he was of the plants after all the months of nurturing and pruning. The plants were gorgeous, the closest he'd ever come to ownership of any kind. It pained him, but Bradley opened the handles wide and edged the blades into the stalk of the plant. He squeezed as hard as he could, and the thick stalk cracked and fell over but was still connected by ropy fibers. He twisted the cutters back and forth, and the bush came free completely. He tossed the pale green plant to his left to start a stack, and even though Dale was watching him, he avoided Dale's gaze. He didn't want to look at him. It hurt to see what a man deluding himself looked like.

The flash of white, pale and small. His stomach churned. He knew it was Birdie. Why had she been out there? Why had she gone so far? And then the realization shook him, his own stupidity punching him in the gut. Of course. *Of course.* They were on her land.

CHAPTER SEVENTEEN

J ust as Mayhill slammed a strange boy into the side of an old black Datsun, Birdie cut a slice of Mr. Boudreaux's watermelon for breakfast and handed it to Onie in her recliner. Birdie stared out the window into the driveway and willed Bradley's truck to appear. Across the pasture, Mayhill's truck was gone. For a moment, she considered he had gone missing too, and an ache of concern sprung up like a fever blister, all surprise and annoyance.

Onie's television was off, which was a promising start to the day, but the sound of her slurping and gnawing at the watermelon was eerily reminiscent of hogs at a trough. It was like she was tasting it for the first time, all ruby-mouthed and happy. It was the loudest Onie had been in a year and had the welcomed side effect of making her look alive.

"Do you remember a man who hung out with Dad and Dale Mackey?" Birdie settled on the arm of Onie's recliner and watched her closely. "He started coming around after the trees died."

"Rudy Lyons," Onie said, pink dripping down her chin. "He wrecked the bailer first thing one morning. Still drunk from the night before."

It was a surprisingly detailed response, though wrong entirely.

"No," Birdie said. "This man came up here with Dad and Dale."

"Rudy Lyons is a good one," Onie said. "Could write pretty well, considering. His mama was totally illiterate. Good people though."

"Onie, I'm not asking about Rudy Lyons. I know Rudy Lyons," Birdie said. "I'm asking about a very specific man. I don't know his name, but he had a tattoo."

Onie wiped her hands on her skirt and turned on the television. This irked Birdie and she wondered if she should just drop it, but Onie was talkative, and in one glorious morning of them sharing a watermelon, the house seemed less tinted with loneliness. A back and forth exchange! An honest-to-God conversation, snuggled up on the recliner! She mentally noted to feed Onie watermelon daily. Maybe it was the sugar.

"This man came up here one time with Dad and Dale," Birdie said over the television. "Bradley didn't know him. I had never seen him before."

"Cat on a hot tin roof," Onie said suddenly.

"What?" Birdie asked, not sure she heard right.

"Cat on a hot tin roof."

Birdie searched Onie's face, suddenly sure she was speaking in code. She scoured her memory. *Yes, yes…Cat on a Hot Tin Roof… Tennessee Williams…or was she referencing an actual cat…there was a feral cat named Emerson…*

Then Birdie followed Onie's gaze to the television. *Wheel of Fortune.* Six words. O's bubbling up across the spaces.

"The damn puzzle!" Birdie said. "CAT ON A HOT TIN ROOF."

Onie grimaced but didn't admonish her language, though Birdie desperately wanted her to do just that kind of thing right then, slap her face, say, "Watch your mouth, child!" To say a normal, predictable adult thing right then (though, let's be honest, Onie had never said normal things). All Birdie wanted was a sane adult around, to be taken care of. She wanted her father, not this depressed shell of a woman who tightrope-walked the thin line of sanity. Hope be damned.

Birdie stormed to the front door and shoved her feet in her tennis shoes.

"Why do you look at me like that?" Onie called after her. She didn't look away from the television, just commenced work on the white part of the rind.

"Like what?" Birdie's voice was bratty and caustic.

"Like you've lost something."

The dead man had fallen oddly close to a break in the trees where a dozen inmates had entered to cut down Van's garden on order of the County. A week after Van died, an unmarked white prison bus rolled up the driveway because that was the closest access to the main field that had been their agenda that day. Birdie had been surprised to find that the men were mostly white—the local pen, of course; black men being locked up for much longer in Huntsville on account of Birdie didn't know what—and they were dressed in the neon orange that allowed escaped convicts to stick out like poisonous mushrooms in the woods.

These were trustees, they were told, part of the community work squad—no murderers or rapists—so they were not chained, just heavy work boots in which nobody could run very far anyway. They were jovial even, laughing like a football team getting off the bus, and the realization of happy prisoners had torn her in two. That could have been Dad. Yes, imprisoned but alive. Alive! She could have talked to him. And Bradley, there on a Wednesday (because all of life seemed to happen on Wednesdays and Saturdays), walked briskly from his truck to stand beside her as if he could sense her outrage. He had never stood that close to her.

"Did you know what Dad was doing?" Birdie whispered. Birdie's gaze was fixed on the men, a blister of orange moving in a line across the field.

"He wouldn't let me near it," Bradley said, then put his hand firmly on her back. She looked up at him, not offended so much as surprised at his hand on her, like he was propping her up. And he stayed that way until the final trustee disappeared into the break of the trees.

. . . .

Birdie was thinking all of this as she marched past the burn pile and up the hill toward Mayhill's along the tree line where they had found the body, repeating Mayhill's taunt of "Do not go into the woods" like a mantra, rebellion hot in her blood. She was always her father's daughter.

I've lost everything, Onie. She touched her shirt pocket, pink note folded up inside.

She broke through the tree line into the woods and beheld it with the same awe as if she had burst through a closet into Narnia. The thicket this time of year was lousy with ticks, which was one of the reasons her father had remained clean-shaven—that and women love a chin dimple. She pulled her socks up tightly around her ankles and kept Van's shirt buttoned at the wrists. The trees were overgrown and cast lacy shadows on the ground, and in her head, her father was telling her they needed to be cut, the entire place cleaned up, but it was too much work for only Bradley and she didn't have the energy or desire to call anybody else to do it. *You ain't doing nothin' with that land.* But in her mind, Van was somehow responsible for it.

Standing in the woods right then—if you pressed her on it—she still believed Van was there somehow. In her weakest, most superstitious moments over the past two days, she had entertained the fact that the dead hog hunter was supernaturally connected to Van. A man who worked for him ended up dead on their land and then disappeared! It was the exact kind of thing that ghost stories were made of, that Van would have adored. Ghosts in the woods, rattling chains, and whatnot. Had this sort of thing been an option in the afterlife, like a college elective, Van would have signed up first day. He would have majored in it. Even dead, he couldn't stay quiet.

The thought simultaneously delighted and spooked her. She walked slowly and tried not to make a lot of noise, though the pine needles crunched like paper beneath her shoes. Off to her right, some hogs rooted in a small clearing, and she stopped to watch them. The clearing was a favorite rooting spot, the ground all overturned in patches, tilled-fresh, the dirt exposed that had long been covered by pine needles. The hogs were small animals, really, to cause so much destruction. Two or three feet tall, ears in jagged rooftop triangles atop their heads. All different colors, red, yellow, black, and white. All precious in Jesus's sight. A whole United Nations of hogs. About three dozen of them, noses under the needles, followed an invisible line of grubs. Birdie's gaze settled on the eyes of a larger black boar, which had stopped its rooting and looked right at her, eyes as black as its skin. They were glassy, almost cloudy, but her presence didn't seem to faze it.

Dad?

The boar dropped its head, thoroughly uninterested, and Birdie, now realizing the full extent of her lunacy, sprung forward to shoo them deeper into the thicket. As they dispersed, Birdie noticed a big wire trap on the other side of the clearing. It was about six feet long and rusted a deep brick red, anchored to the ground with chains at each corner and wrapped around the tree to keep the hogs from ripping it away.

Inside: a large paper-brown lump, like a heap of clothes. Her stomach twisted, her face fell cold. She couldn't believe she hadn't thought it before now. She could find Bradley dead. What had Bradley last been wearing? He had a dun-colored jacket, didn't he? But it was summer! She searched her memory for Bradley's clothes and walked closer, the slow crunch of her footsteps pounding in her ears. *No, no, no, no, no, no.* She stopped and squinted. She stepped and *pop!* A branch cracked beneath her feet.

All at once, the trap shook—a big, violent lurch. A fawn. It was barely able to stand upright but flung the trap in panicked *rap-rap-raps* and banged against the top of the cage, its back bloodied and shredded. Birdie rushed forward, her feet weaving through boobytraps of thicket vines and branches, then flattened her body to the side of the cage. The fawn slammed itself against the metal, eyes wild, all fear. She grabbed the top of the gate and yanked as hard as she could, the metal jabbing into her ribs as she lifted, but it was rusted and wouldn't slide up. Another hard yank and the fawn scrambled out. It sprinted into the woods as the gate slammed down in a tinny *clang! clang!* that sent the birds and squirrels scattering like a riot and sound echoing through the woods.

Birdie, breathless, leaned against a tree and stared at the trap. She didn't remember one being there. Who had put it there? Had Bradley put a trap there? Mayhill? Then the thought hit her. The dead man had put it there. But she couldn't fathom why he had put it on her property and in her woods. What exactly had he run across when he did? She wondered if the trap was the last thing the dead man had touched.

Do not go in the woods. God, she was an idiot! All of the juices of Birdie's rebellion dried up right then, and she ran through the thicket and back to the house, the limbs tearing at her jeans like claws.

CHAPTER
EIGHTEEN

"Birdie!" Mayhill yelled.

While Birdie was off in the woods, Mayhill pounded on the door of her house. He would be modest, he told himself on the break-neck drive over, after he ran the Datsun off the road. He would calmly state the facts and commence the investigation, but he would have to rein in his excitement. He had followed the Datsun right to where they were probably working, hadn't he? *CRACKED THE CASE!* Though he couldn't be sure given the dizzying terrain of the backwoods, he guessed the body had been about a mile from where he followed the truck through the trees.

Mayhill caught his reflection in the door window. He was covered in mud, all rough and tumble, Gus McCrae. Beneath a cut oozing yellow and red, his eye was swelling. Mayhill was a little fat, of course, but for the first time in a while, his outsides matched his inside vision of himself.

"Birdie!" He knocked hard again and then let himself in. Pat Sajak trotted behind him, his claws clicking on the concrete floor, and then sniffed around the kitchen, intrigued by an improbable amount of watermelon rinds hanging out of the garbage can.

The recliner swallowed Onie like a mud pit, while a blonde local newscaster stated calmly at fighter jet decibels that, "It's gonna be hot out there today, folks!" Mayhill wondered if Onie was not just depressed but going deaf too.

"Onie," Mayhill hollered over the television, and walked up behind her. "It's Randall! Where's Birdie?"

"Randall." She smiled at him. Then, upon seeing the gash on his forehead, she frowned. She reached her hand toward his face, and he patted it away. "It's going to be hot today!" She gestured to the perky blonde woman on the screen.

"September in Texas? Damn near psychic!" He picked up the television remote and clicked it off. "May I?"

"What happened to your eye?" she asked.

"I fell." Mayhill tried to hide his disappointment of having to talk with Onie. He loved her but didn't understand what was happening to her, and like most things he didn't understand, he wanted to stay at a distance.

Pat Sajak emerged from the kitchen, sniffed at Onie's feet, then jumped onto her lap.

"You don't know where Birdie is?" he asked. "Not safe, you being here by yourself. Birdie needs to be with you."

Onie petted the dog, seemingly happy to have an animal in her lap. She looked longingly at the blank screen.

"I'm serious here." He paused, suddenly unsure how to talk about the situation in her emotionally-fragile state. "It's just better with Birdie here. I need to make sure Birdie's looking after you if I'm not."

"What's Birdie going to do? Have you seen her shoot?"

"Fair enough, fair enough," he said. "Has anybody been around here? You talk with anybody strange lately?"

"Other than you?"

"Ha ha. I need you to cooperate, Onie," Mayhill said, though he found the joke to be an encouraging sign of her mental state. "You talk with any strangers, I mean. Anybody knocked on the door you don't know? Any trappers…hog hunters…wanting work here?"

"No, I don't think so," Onie said. "Not recently."

"The county send anybody out?" Mayhill asked. "I know they've hired a few trappers, trying to put a dent in the problem."

Silence. She looked intently at Pat Sajak, as if waiting on the dog to answer Mayhill's question. "Some wars are unwinnable," she sighed. "Pyrrhic victory at best." She sounded somewhat like her old self.

"Oh, Pyrrhic, for sure!" Mayhill was impatient. "Listen. Tommy Jones. You know who that is? Fella's a hog trapper. Been in the area evidently…worked with Van. You used to feed all those men on Van's crew, remember that? I thought you'd know him. Jimmy said he's been on the news. You watch the news, right? Before *Wheel of Fortune*?"

"Why was he on the news?" Onie asked. The dog repositioned and dug his head into the crease of her elbow.

"Oh, hell, I dunno. Something about his wife. They couldn't prove it. I don't watch the news, but you do!" He pointed to the dark screen. "Remember? It's gonna be hot out there today!"

She patted Pat Sajak, entirely disinterested in their talk. It annoyed Mayhill, her lack of focus, her lack of presence, as if she were hovering six feet above the conversation. Here he'd spent his entire life fighting to make everything better for everyone, and Onie—she wasn't even trying. All her fire gone. He desperately wished for Birdie to come in.

"Tommy Jones, Onie." He leaned down closer to her, as if trying to entice a snake out of a basket. "Worked with Van. I need you to think. Just focus."

In that moment, looking at her cool, distant eyes, he did worry about her sanity. Perhaps she wasn't just depressed. Perhaps she was losing her mind. What an odd expression—losing her mind—as if Onie's mind had flown away like a baby bird, and she, the mother bird, tried desperately to catch it. Or was her mind losing her, trying like mad to hold onto her spirit? Perhaps her spirit was too big and fiery to need something as useless as thinking anymore.

"Whose dog is this?" Onie asked suddenly. Pat Sajak's long brown body was now curled up like a snail in the fold of her thighs.

Mayhill's heart sank. Had she not remembered him come in? Had she not remembered petting him for the last five minutes?

"That's my dog, Onie," he said carefully. His voice was firmly at a jackass octave, trying not to condescend. "Good boy, that one."

"No," she said. "That's not your dog."

It sounded accusatory, her fire temporarily returned. All at once, Mayhill was back in her high school English class, Onie demanding that he explain the symbolism of the Gatsby green light. *Impossible goals, Mrs. Woods! It symbolizes impossible goals!*

"Onie," he chuckled nervously. "That is my dog. His name is Pat Sajak. Just like on the screen. I know we all hold Mr. Sajak in high regard around here."

"No, he is not."

"He is!" Mayhill said. "He is my dog."

"That's not your dog."

But Mayhill saw what was happening. She was stuck in a loop.

Something turned in his stomach. And though he never backed down from a fight—his wounded eye proof, split like a tomato too long on the vine—this war was unwinnable. He'd just be fighting hogs. Pyrrhic victories and whatnot.

"All right, Onie."

Mayhill clicked his mouth at Pat Sajak, who then looked up at Onie. She shrugged, and the dog extracted himself from the nirvana of her lap. "When Birdie comes around, I need to talk to her. It's real important. Could you have her call me?" Though he wasn't sure now she would remember.

"Not your dog," she said again, and then a few more times.

Mayhill clenched Pat to his chest and walked quickly to the door. He stood on the front porch with his slandered dog and tried to piece together what had happened. The entire conversation had rattled him, thrown him off his game. He had planned to be modest.

For a second, the worst thought settled on him, like shrikes on barbed wire. He had gratitude—no, relief—that Van was dead. At least he didn't have to see what was happening to Onie.

CHAPTER

NINETEEN

Back at Mayhill's house, the phone rang. It had been months since his phone had rung, and he jumped to his feet as if the sound were an intruder to be dealt with.

"Tommy Jones," a tiny female voice said from the other end.

"Who is this?"

"Tommy *Joooones*." The voice was a frantic whisper. Goddamn Gabby Grayson. "You want a guy who's missing? There's a guy who's missing."

"I keep hearing about—"

"He missed parole," Gabby said. "Parole officer got a warrant out for him now."

"When was he supposed to report?"

"Two days ago," she said.

"And they already got a warrant?"

"Because it's Tommy Jones."

"For missing one meeting?" Mayhill asked.

"It's like O.J. missing one meeting."

"I know you aren't comparing The Juice—"

"You have been living under a rock."

Mayhill pictured Gabby on the other end, winding the cord and cocking her head at the curiosity that was him. He put the phone in the crook of his neck and popped another Dr Pepper to help him think.

"Look," Gabby said. "I can't catch you up right now. For goodness sake, turn on the television. Read a newspaper! Ask these 'friends' of yours. But I just wanted—"

"Did he have a tattoo?" Mayhill asked quickly, the Dr Pepper kicking in.

"Tommy Jones? I dunno…" Gabby said. "The news only shows his face. He does not have a tattoo on his face."

"Can you check? This is real important. And don't worry, it's public record. I know that's real important to you."

"Don't be nasty, Randy. Why do you need to know if Tommy Jones has a tattoo?"

"Please, Gabby."

"Lord! Have! Mercy!" She stabbed the computer keys. "And the only reason I'm telling you anything is—"

"Public record. Yes, yes. I'm the public. I understand comp—"

"Star. Right hand." Gabby stopped typing. "Looks like Tommy Jones has a…blue star on his…right hand."

Mayhill was silent.

"Randy?"

"Yes, I'm here," he said.

"Did you hear me? Yes, Tommy Jones has a tattoo. Are you okay?"

Gabby asked. He could feel her looking at him through the phone. "What is this about? You call up—"

"You sure about that? You sure this Tommy Jones person has a star on his hand?"

"Blue star. Right hand. Says so right—"

"White guy? Dark hair?"

"Caucasian male. Dark brown hair. Forty years old," she said. "You're acting odd, Randy. Downright peculiar."

Mayhill paced his tiny kitchen back and forth. He was silent, though he breathed like a bear into the phone. Tommy Jones was the dead man on the fence, but who was the boy driving his truck?

"But I did help, didn't I?" Gabby sounded perky, pleased with herself.

"No, not at all," he said. He tried to swallow the joy that threatened to explode in his chest. "You did not help even one iota."

She laughed quietly on the other end, and Mayhill imagined angels singing, a whole little football team of them storming through the phone line to bring the good tidings of Gabby's giggle to his ears.

"I'm sorry I was gruff yesterday," she said with remorse. "I mean, I know you love veterans. I never should have implied otherwise."

"Thank you." He cleared his throat. "They're what our country is built upon."

"Of course they are," Gabby said. "And don't you have something additional that you need to say to me?"

"And…I'm sorry I didn't talk to you for a year. Then I call back asking for favors."

"And got mad when I didn't do your favors?"

"And got mad when you didn't do my favors," Mayhill sighed.

"What about that? What about getting mad at me?" she said.

"I'm sorry," Mayhill said, his smile as big as watermelon slices. "I'm sorry for all of those things."

CHAPTER TWENTY

"**W**eed?" Birdie whispered. She looked tiny sitting on Mayhill's couch, yet the house seemed much too small all of a sudden with another person in it. Not sure where to stand, he leaned against the second gun safe, and Birdie stared bewilderedly at him, her eyebrows hovering like helicopters above her eyes. "Weed?"

"I'm sure of it!" Mayhill was high off of Dr Pepper and Gabby Grayson's voice, his emotions a powder keg.

"And the guy..." Birdie said.

"The dead guy!"

"The dead guy has something to do with that?"

Mayhill's face wrinkled into revulsion, a full-on contortion that was beyond his control when asked any question with an obvious answer. He looked away toward his dog, who sat beside Birdie on the couch, and took control of his face again, because, logically, Birdie did not deserve such an inconsiderate, albeit totally appropriate reaction. Birdie was not stupid, having the high-priced genes of Van and Onie, yet such a question had just fallen from her mouth without a hint of sarcasm. "Yes…" he said slowly. "I would think the dead guy has something to do with an illegal marijuana operation near here."

"And Bradley's involved," Birdie said.

"Doesn't look good."

Pat Sajak stretched, turned a circle, and then repositioned closer to Birdie. "She's in your spot, ain't she, Pat?"

Which she was, but Birdie only rolled her eyes.

"Dale said Bradley works for him sometimes." Mayhill paced. "But he ain't working on Dale's trailer or anywhere around his place, I can tell you that." A flush of concern came over him as he said the words. Bradley was dim, but looking to Dale for your livelihood was the saddest thing he'd heard of since lacing cigars with embalming fluid. The desperation! He thought of Bradley's mother, the off-brand CHIPS, and shook his head. "Boy doesn't have much."

If Birdie shared Mayhill's newfound humanism, her face didn't show it. She took in all of the information with a stoicism he had only seen in movie mob bosses and Tom Landry, a cool calculation of seeing ten steps in the future. Van had had the same expression, and it made Mayhill nervous.

Birdie walked out onto the porch, and Mayhill and Pat Sajak followed, the heat blasting them like a firewall as they left the air-conditioning. Birdie stood, arms akimbo, and looked out toward the tree line.

"He's doing it near here?" she asked. "Where we saw the man?"

"It's smart, if you think about it." Mayhill looked at the wall of trees off in the distance. "I mean, doing the same thing again. Not like the law will keep checking the same place over and over. Not after a big bust like that." He picked a fleck of dried mud off his arm and was surprised at himself for giving Dale credit for anything. "And he doesn't need irrigation 'cause it's been so wet. Wettest summer in decades. No pipes. Risk is minimal."

"He's on my land, isn't he?" Birdie posed it as more of a statement than a question. Mayhill was unprepared for the vitriol in her voice, and he shook his head, suddenly uneasy.

"It's just a theory, Birdie. I think it's a good one, but nothing has been—"

"But it would make sense, you said. It'd be smart. And the guy—"

"The dead guy could still be a hunting accident. I'm just talking out loud. Brainstorming. Where there's smoke, there's fire kinda thing." He didn't know how much he should tell her. "There's some kid driving like a maniac back there...keep passing him on the—"

"Dale didn't think I'd find out because I don't do anything with all this land...don't do anything except just sit around and watch *Matlock* with Onie! Gah!" She kicked the front porch post.

"Birdie, calm down." Mayhill swooped up Pat Sajak and held him close to his chest. "*Matlock*'s a good show."

She spun away from him as if he had touched her shoulder, which he wisely had not. "And that's why Bradley's helping! Dale hired Bradley as insurance! He knows I'd never call the police on him."

"If you found out."

"If I found out. Gah!" Birdie threw her hands up.

"Birdie..." Mayhill said. "If Bradley's doing what we're thinking, maybe he deserves—"

"Don't say it!"

"Jail?" He put the dog down. "Don't say that a man deserves jail for doing bad?"

"So Dad deserved jail?"

"It was his land. It's different." Mayhill tried to think of all the myriad ways it was different. "Van was good. He just got desperate, made a wrong turn, trusted the wrong people."

"What about Bradley?" she yelled. "He's not good? What's he got?"

"You can't possibly compare your daddy to Bradley Polk!"

Birdie threw herself in Mayhill's rocking chair and rocked so fast he thought she might take flight. "Why would Dale kill a guy and leave him there? It'd just draw more attention."

Birdie had a point. Dale and Tommy Jones were supposedly friends, and the body was a decent distance from where Mayhill guessed they were. Perhaps they had gotten in a fight. Maybe Dale hadn't had time to dispose of the body before Birdie found it.

"I mean," Birdie said. "We wouldn't even be talking about this if we hadn't seen a dead guy. I'm beginning to wonder if we're all..." She looked at Mayhill, and then mouthed, "Going nuts," as if Onie could hear from across the pasture. "Maybe crazy is in the well."

"Big picture, Birdie. Big picture." He leaned against the porch post, his knee still aching from before. "Hunter tracks some hogs through the woods. Comes across a marijuana field. Dale shoots him. Same thing happened on *48 Hours.*"

"Or Dale shoots Bradley." Birdie brought her hands to her face. "That's why he hasn't come back."

Mayhill waved it off. "Dale shoots the trapper...scared to death..." He didn't believe the words himself. He wasn't sure why that boy would have Tommy Jones's truck. "I'm working on it, Birdie. I'll take care of you, you know I will."

"Do you know who the trapper is?" Birdie asked quietly then, but Mayhill could hear it. There was a knowing in her voice.

"You knew him! Why didn't you—"

"I recognized him," she said, "but Dad never introduced me. I don't know his name." Pat Sajak jumped into Birdie's lap, and she paused for a moment to scratch his head. Looking at Pat and Birdie, Mayhill decided then that she needed a dog. A dog could fix this. At least four. Onie had given him Atticus, Van's hunting dog, after Van died. She said it made them too sad to see him waiting for Van every night. Taking Atticus from them had been a mistake, but hell, Mayhill was waiting for Van too.

"His name is Tommy Jones. Jimmies told me he trapped out this way. Evidently, he's a real rough fella…got a record…" *Violent to women*, he almost said, but he stopped.

"Tommy Jones," she said, as if trying to conjure a memory.

He pulled out the map he had found in Tommy Jones's glove box and flicked his hand to unfold it in front of her face, like giving a hound a scent. "You know this map?"

Birdie snatched it from him and studied it. "Why is it covered in mud?" Then a flash of understanding in her eyes. "This is our place. Where did you find this? This is a map of our place!"

"Belonged to Tommy Jones."

"He drew a map of our place? And then he died?" The panic caught in her throat, and Mayhill wanted so badly to fix it right then, but he had no words. "Why was he mapping our place? Why, Randy, why?"

But Mayhill, of course, didn't know. He couldn't fix it, and he had told her too much. Still, he couldn't help but note that Birdie had trusted him enough to ask.

Birdie drove back to her house, and Mayhill laid down for a short nap before Pat Sajak and he would commence their search for Bradley. He turned on the police scanner, which was a mix of fuzz and low beeps—a quiet day, a slow day, a day when Mayhill would have caught up on paperwork, driven lazily down the roads, checked in on the low-hanging criminal element. He fell asleep, as usual, and dreamed of welfare calls, paperwork, drunk drivers.

So it was not so crazy that Mayhill didn't stir when he first heard the sound of a siren—a man like Randy Mayhill regularly dreamed in sirens and alarm bells—but then he heard his dogs bark. He slowly opened his eyes and knew then it wasn't a dream. Lights whirled through his window. Specks of blue and red bounced across into his tiny bedroom like a nightclub. Pat Sajak perched on top of the small gun safe and growled out the window, each bark lurching him forward, his small body casting an overlay of blue and red shadows on the wall across the room. Mayhill scrambled to the window and pulled down the blinds. The sheriff's truck was parked outside his tiny house, lights blazing.

CHAPTER
TWENTY-ONE

ale's trailer made Bradley feel as if he were inside a gullet. The sun behind the tarp window cast a blue glow on the walls, not helping to dissuade from the gullet aesthetic, as if he swam in the innards of a cold-blooded frog, blue arteries and all. After they wiped down and unloaded all the remaining supplies, Dale and Bradley retreated from the heat into the trailer while he made some iced tea. Bradley didn't want to be there. All he could think of was Dale's pistol snaking through the air, tracking the figure through the woods. All these months. *Birdie's land…Birdie's land…Birdie's land.* The words pulsed through him. He had never felt so stupid.

He had been to Dale's place only a couple of times before. First, when they transported the baby plants, and another time when he raided Dale's shed for a shovel after some hogs had died near the grow site. Dale had charged Bradley with the gruesome task of moving them far from the garden because Dale didn't want even buzzards drawing attention to their locale. Bradley hadn't known what to do with them so he drug the smallest of the hogs into feed sacks and unloaded them at the entrance to the dump. He felt bad about this, he did, but where else was someone to dump a bunch of dead hogs in feed sacks?

Bradley sat on the sunken tweed couch while Dale hauled in his gallon jug of sun tea off the front stoop. He watched Dale warily, his mind still back at the garden, how the gun had materialized from Dale's bag. He wondered if Dale kept a pistol under the couch, nesting in the stick-brown cushions.

In the kitchen area, Dale unscrewed the jar and poured the tea into a thermos. An economy-sized bottle of Pepto-Bismol stood like a vase on the kitchen counter. Dale took a swig, then turned back to the thermos and shoveled snowpiles of sugar into it.

Bradley needed to understand what was happening, all the ways he had been duped into doing terrible things, betraying the only good in his life.

Bradley opened his mouth to speak, to ask questions, but then—

"When's the last time you eat?" Dale called from the kitchen.

"Uh...I dunno..." Even Bradley's voice sounded gullible. He shrugged and stared at the photograph of a woman on the wall: flip hairdo, fifties glasses, all sunken cheeks and Indian-high cheekbones. She could have been Dale's wigged twin.

"You been workin' hard." Dale poured a bowl of Hy-Top Toasty-Os and put it on the small side table next to Bradley. Bradley looked at the bowl and back at Dale, confused at first that he was feeding him despite all that was happening. Dale eyed him pityingly. Right then, Bradley tried to refocus on the memory—Dale's gun pointed at Jason, Dale's face fevered but somehow natural, as if he had done such a thing before. But then cereal happened. *Cereal!* The milk now golden like hay. The Toasty-Os tasted name brand. It calmed him. The best thing he'd ever eaten.

Dale hovered at the table and took another drink of the Pepto.

"You doing okay?" Bradley asked.

"Nerves."

"Nerves..." Bradley repeated. He breathed a choppy breath, as deep as he could. "Dale, we about to get caught?"

"You worried about the truck?" Dale sat on the couch beside him. "Second time you said something."

Bradley didn't realize he'd heard him before. "Just seems like things moving fast all of a sudden. Moving it tomorrow. But the plants," he said carefully. "They need another month."

"You told anybody you here?" Dale asked.

"Dale, I would never—"

"Birdie doesn't know you working here?"

"No."

"Randy Mayhill doesn't know you working here?" Dale raised his eyebrows, and Bradley saw it, that new paranoid look that had blossomed overnight like pokeweed, paranoia as thick as Bradley's stench. Dale was testing him.

"No." Bradley shook his head. "Don't know Mayhill too much. Nobody knows about me here. Nobody."

Dale studied his face. "Then we got nothing to worry about, do we?"

Dale leaned forward, reaching for something in his back pocket. Bradley tensed, only to see Dale pull out a package of Twizzlers. He wrestled one out of the cellophane, and sucked on the end, his hands vibrating like an engine.

"I'd say you remind me of me," Dale said. "But I had my mama and daddy. You don't have even that. Men like you and me don't have a whole lot of options. Get decapitated at the wood mill, working for shit until we die. Ranch business dying. No skills. No education. You want a family? You think you gonna support a family on broke fences? You think you gonna support a family being a hand for some trust-fund rancher who treats you like a wetback? Or the Navy? Virgil Fuller lucky he only lost his fingers. Those our only options? Wood mill or military?"

"Work at the prison, I guess," Bradley said, confused. Why was Dale giving him a lecture? "More jobs in the city."

"It's the same anywhere." Dale got up and paced the room, hands shaking at his sides. "You know that. Janitor, cashier at the corner store. It don't matter. The point is…someone else controlling your life."

"I do okay," Bradley said, surprised at the defensiveness in his voice. He watched Dale in his periphery.

"You do *okay*," Dale said. "You a hard worker, I give you that. But you still here because you know." Dale tapped the soft dent of his temple. "You know."

"I know what?"

"You know your life is your own. You know some break is the only way to get your land." Dale paused. "Is that why you still hang around Van's family? You trying to marry his girl? You trying to marry Birdie? Get all that land?"

He hated Dale saying her name. "I'm not trying to marry anybody."

Dale shook his finger in the air, a taunting, knowing thing. "That it, ain't it? Not a bad plan, but I'd be careful if I was you. End up spoiled like Birdie. Sitting on all that land and ain't doing nothing with it. Trees just rotting because Van didn't know what he had. Van and them, they ain't like us."

The bitterness toward Van surprised him. "But you and Van were friends..."

"Van ratted me out the first chance he got. He coulda bought and sold me. I worked for him. *For* him. Someone dictating my life. It ain't like what me and you doing. Y'all don't get it. I'm giving y'all a life. A life."

Bradley realized then that Dale hadn't just expected work; he expected gratitude. He'd worked for other men who'd never even spoken his name, and here Dale was feeding him cereal in the middle of the day, feeding him fried chicken on some nights, talking to him like he was a solider in his army. But Bradley didn't quite know what they were fighting for.

The hunter flashed in Bradley's head again. Dale wasn't just a man trying to get rich; he was a man with something to prove. A dead man near the paranoid, self-righteous Dale. An illegal operation on hijacked land. On one hand, it seemed obvious. On the other, Bradley stared at the cereal Dale placed in front of him. The thoughtfulness, the care. He wasn't sure Dale had it in him. At the end of the day, they were gardeners. They were just gardeners trying to catch a break.

But he had to know.

"Dale...the day before yesterday, when I was at Birdie's—"

"I gotta tell you something." Dale held up his hand to silence him. "Things looking a little different than we thought."

Bradley shook his head, not sure he understood. Dale was going to confess. About Birdie's land, the truck, and...what else was there? What else had Bradley been so stupid about? He realized he was holding his breath.

"Money's not what I said," Dale said.

The money. Of course. Stupid, stupid. Bradley looked down at his hands, trying not to let the rage spill out of him. Of course Dale had taken advantage of him. Twenty thousand dollars had been a joke, a carrot he dangled with nothing behind it.

"How's seventy-five thousand?" Dale winked at him.

And just like that, Bradley Polk disappeared. He wasn't there anymore. He floated from Dale's sad little trailer into a life that belonged to him. He couldn't help it. He saw his land, the sprawling fingers of acreage and pine. Children (three), horses (a long-maned Palomino named Willow), a wife (she would make fajitas, Cheerios, those cakes with the hole in the middle), showers (indoor and outdoor).

Seventy-five thousand dollars. He didn't quite believe it. His life. All of it. Tomorrow. Less than forty-eight hours.

And in the next thought: *Birdie's land, Birdie's land, Birdie's land.* The dead man. Dale swinging that gun. Was that what had happened to the hog hunter? The hunter had set a trap too close to the garden, seen what they were doing. Dale with a chip on his shoulder.

Bradley couldn't speak. He finished his cereal quietly then, his own hand now rattling the spoon against the bowl. On those tree-trunk legs, though wobbly like a newborn calf, he stood up and walked the bowl to the kitchen. Dale's gaze tracked him all the way to the sink, looking at him expectantly with the half-crazed look of a revolutionary. And in that second, with his breath gone and milk dribbling down his chin like a child, Bradley didn't know if Dale was the most terrifying man he'd ever met, or the bravest.

"Thanks," Bradley said, coming back to the moment and the cereal bowl still trembling in his hand. "I mean, you know…in case I never said it."

CHAPTER

TWENTY-TWO

To call him "the new" anything would have been a serious error in descriptor, yet the new sheriff made his way over the rocky driveway and up Mayhill's porch stairs, toting a small oxygen tank behind him. Mayhill was in his boxer shorts but his shirt was still on, though the bottom two buttons were undone, his belly peeking out.

"I knocked first," New Sheriff said. He was very thin and had a slight Cajun accent. A sip of air hissed up his nose, the plastic cannula bobbing in response. "But you's asleep."

"Quick nap," Mayhill said.

"Ain't no quick nap. You was out." The sheriff looked at Mayhill suspiciously, his deep wrinkles like war trenches. "What happened to your face? You look like hell."

"What's this about?" Mayhill asked.

He looked back at the sheriff's truck and saw that someone was in the passenger's seat. He squinted hard to wake up his eyes. A woman. Red sweatshirt. Bradley's mother. Mayhill struggled to breathe. Bradley. Then his thoughts turned to Birdie, and he panicked. Where was Birdie? Was Birdie okay? Where had they found Bradley?

"You look pale, Randy. I know this prolly ain't real comfortable for you. But I'm guessin' you know what this about," New Sheriff said. "Ms. Johnson just here to ID."

"Where was he?" Mayhill said, the breath caught in his throat. "Where did they find him?"

New Sheriff lifted his chin to the black dog sentried on the porch. "Weren't too hard to find."

Mayhill looked around confused, and then rubbed his head with his hands. He closed his eyes, rage and relief duking it out in his brain. "You talking about Vanna?"

"Miss Johnson has reason to believe you kidnapped her dog." The oxygen puffed in his nose. "We'll need you to come down to the station."

·⸱ ·⸱ ·⸱ ·⸱ ·⸱ ·⸱ ·⸱

Goddamn Gabby Grayson.

He hadn't seen her in eighteen months, but upon catching her eyes, he felt that shock of attraction not unlike serving an arrest warrant.

She had aged admirably well compared to their counterparts. A year and a half did not seem like a long time in the grand scheme of the universe, but among the forty-something set, the change seemed almost as dramatic as not seeing a kitten for that long. The feed store men, for example. Brown hair turned half gray in unpredictable patterns—

some salt and pepper, some of the skunk variety. Faces picking up and moving an entire inch south. And the bodies…the bodies! His own body. He was supposed to be dead at thirty from a gunfight, saving women named Clementine and Maybelle. Instead, he was in this gray, sagging vessel he didn't understand.

Gabby, however. Goddamn. She had the same reddish-brown hair that fell in loose rings past her shoulders. Big, happy teeth that proclaimed the world to be trustworthy. A thin waist but big hips he happily rested his hands upon once during a school dance. She wore her self-imposed uniform of a white polo shirt and khaki pants that made her look like a softball coach, no matter the occasion. Gabby Grayson. All business.

Mayhill could see New Sheriff talking with Bradley's mother in his old office, his ancient face bobbing up and down in front of the billboard-sized county map. Mayhill wanted to yell out that Ms. Johnson's son was missing.

What about your son, Ms. Johnson? You gonna get Father Time on that case too?

"We could have worked it out there," Mayhill said too loudly. "He didn't have to make me drive all the way down here."

"He gets out of breath when he talks," Gabby whispered, and leaned over the desk. "I've seen it. That little oximeter goes down to eighty-five. Eighty-*five*, Randy. His oxygen levels should be in the high nineties."

Mayhill wasn't sure what she was talking about and shook his head. "Look, the dog was thirsty…it's a thousand degrees outside… hogs'll get a dog in a second. What about animal cruelty? I'd like to file a complaint. Animal endangerment!"

"Dog's in decent enough shape," Gabby said. "Just a little thirsty is all. I don't like it any more than you, but you do have incredibly high standards. Is it even a teeny-weeny bit possible that Ms. Johnson just wasn't taking care of her dog the way you would take care of your dog?"

"I want a veterinarian!" Mayhill cried. "Call a vet right now to confirm that this dog was just a 'little thirsty.'"

"You know we won't do that."

"The dog was passed out! The dog was dying!"

New Sheriff emerged from the office, a fresh green tank rolling behind him. He stood over Mayhill. "Ms. Johnson is willing to forget the entire thing."

"Oh, how generous of Ms. Johnson!"

"She is willing to sell you the dog for a nominal fee."

"A fee!"

"Yes, a fee, and she will not make a formal complaint."

"Highway robbery!" Mayhill slammed his hand on Gabby's desk. "She abuses a dog, and now she wants me to pay for it?"

"Poor Randy! Still living under the illusion that life is fair!" Gabby had a flair for the dramatic too. She leaned across the desk, and whispered, "Drop the justice, Randy. Sometimes you just have to pay the money."

Mayhill turned back to the sheriff. "How much does she want?"

"Three hundred."

"Dollars? What is this, a royal dog? Did I kidnap the queen's dog?"

Gabby looked at him with an impossible patience.

Mayhill shook his head. He needed to get back to work. "Who do I make the check out to?" he said. He reached into his back pocket.

"She prefers cash," New Sheriff said, the oxygen hissing at him like a cat.

"So what's this all about? The Tommy Jones stuff?" Gabby was getting off work, and Mayhill walked her to her car, three hundred dollars lighter, as the sun was going down.

"I think something bad might have happened to him." Mayhill was exhausted and tired of lying, and the words just popped out. Gabby had a way of doing that to him.

She held a brown leather purse the size of a small cow against her chest. Her eyes narrowed. "Then you need to make a report."

"I'm not going to make a report. I will never make a report."

She sighed, and he could smell orange gum on her breath. "Do you know him? Do you know Tommy Jones?"

"No, I don't know him."

"Then why do you care?"

"I care about my fellow man," he said.

She laughed, and this pleased him very much. Gabby leaned against her old car. "He's a hard one to care about. Beat the you-know-what out of his wife. She's pretty much brain dead," she sighed. "But lots of prayers behind her. Hoping for a miracle. They sold t-shirts."

"What's a t-shirt gonna do? Who sold t-shirts?"

"They...*they*..."

"Who is they?"

"You know...the churches and 4-H and stuff. Civically-minded organizations. *They*. Prayers for Star."

"Her name was Star?"

She grimaced at him, smelling his judgment. "Yes, her name was Star, but it don't matter."

"What kind of name is Star?"

"What kind of name is Randall? I don't know. It's nature! It's natural." She swung her purse around, arms gesticulating wildly. "What kind of name is Rose? What kind of name is Heather?"

"Or Mountain or Polecat."

"Anyway, Staaaaaaar…" She glared at him. "They had fish fries and such. A fundraiser for her medical bills. It was a real tragic story. It *is* a real tragic story. All over the news. Girl had nobody. Just a vegetable in a nursing home in Longview now."

Mayhill had always stumbled over the word "vegetable" in such a context. He wondered how that word had become the euphemism of choice for someone in poor Star's condition. He wondered if Onie would become a vegetable. Then he wondered what would become of him if he were a vegetable. Like Star, he had nobody. At the very least he wouldn't know he had turned into a plant.

"So Tommy Jones murdered her," he said.

"Yes, well, no, she's alive." She made air quotes with her fingers. "They couldn't prove it. A few domestic abuse charges before she got real hurt. That's why the felony, but nobody could prove he hurt her that last time. But people know. We know."

"Then he became a hog trapper?"

"Rumor has it, Tommy Jones was a hitman in Houston!"

"Come on now."

"I'm serious! A hitman! Heard two deputies talking about it. Can you imagine?" Gabby squealed, delighted by the scandal. "I dunno anything about what he's doing now. Guy likes to kill, I guess." She eyed him suspicious-like. "You really hadn't heard about all this? Was a big story for a while about a year ago."

He had stopped reading the *East Texas Telegraph*. And all papers.

He shook his head, feeling like an incompetent child all of a sudden, and pulled his truck keys from his pocket. "It was good seeing you, Gabby."

"Where you going now?"

"Home," he said. "Why?"

"Wanna drive?" Gabby Grayson said. A tiny bubble of orange gum formed on her lips. "'Cause I feel like riding."

Pop.

The moon was a waning crescent, a sliver short of going black entirely, and hung in the sky like a hook. Gabby and Randy exhausted the back roads, and rode mostly in silence, except for a radio station out of Houston that they had both listened to regularly since high school. The radio spewed out sad excuses for country music, which, as far as Mayhill could tell, was just rock and roll sung by Gomer Pyle. The slow, romantic songs made him uncomfortable, not knowing at all what was happening in his world when Gabby Grayson inexplicably wanted to go driving with him, a petty dog thief. He tried not to think about it, the erotic underpinnings of the current situation, though Randy Mayhill was never a man to speak of things erotic or underpinnings of any kind.

Gabby rolled the window down, and her hair blew in the wind like a glorious victory banner until she said she wanted to stop and look at the stars. There was a pasture out by a small pond on the county line. He liked the spot because the trees didn't obscure the sky completely, so he headed that way. Mayhill felt uncomfortable about their destination at first, the entire ordeal seeming too close to the idea of parking, that had he been a different sort of man he might try to make out with her. He had dreamed of such a thing since he was at least thirteen, staring at Gabby's new bra through her impossibly thin white t-shirt at the back of math class, but he had never been a Gatsby, never been a Rhett. He would not know how to make a move if she expected it. Sure, there had been women here and there. A girlfriend in college, wingman nights out with Van, but what was Gabby Grayson thinking wanting to drive with him? This wasn't meant to be romantic, was it? No!

—*Was it?*

—*Release the bull, Randy!*

—*Shut up, Van!*

They were forty-something, not seventeen.

The pasture was covered in hogs, and as he turned off the dirt road into the grass, the field of hogs split down the middle, his pickup inching forward into the crowd. The windows still down, he could hear them shuffle and squeal and move away from them, the headlights from the truck catching their eyes in flickers of red glitter.

When Mayhill saw the hogs thick like this, he thought of Van. Van would have adored the hogs because Van adored disorder and chaos, and chaos calmed Van in the way that a clothes dryer calmed a colicky baby, a harshness that soothed. Van would have loved the way that people railed against them. The epic nature of it all. Man against beast! Captain Ahab versus Moby Dick, Santiago versus the marlin, and whatnot.

Gabby said nothing, head still out the window, delighted by the night, free like a child. He thought he heard her snort at them.

He edged up close to the pond and cut the engine. The hogs were not afraid of them but grazed at a distance now. He got out of the truck and left the low-hum of the radio on. He lowered the tailgate and sat upon it, the truck rocking under his weight. Gabby came around to the back of the truck, leaned back against the tailgate, arms anchored, and hopped backward onto the tailgate. She sat on the end away from him.

They both looked into the field in front of them, their eyes adjusting to the dark and roving landscape of hogs. They moved like a low gray fog around them. Bliss.

"Why'd you leave, Randy?" Gabby asked into the dark.

"Leave where?"

"Oh, I dunno," she said. "Society?"

"I do believe you recall what happened," he said. "You know better than anybody."

"I do," she said. Her voice trailed off as if she were trying her hardest not to keep going. "But it's another thing altogether to become a hermit. You don't wear it well."

He laughed. "I don't wear much well these days."

"You lost your wife, I suppose."

"My wife?" His stomach flipped.

"Van was your wife. You're a widower."

Mayhill wasn't sure what to say to that. Gabby said weird things all the time, like most women he knew. Like Onie.

"Then I was a lousy husband."

"I prayed for you. I prayed for you every day. Still do."

"Prayers for Randy. Where do I buy the shirt?"

"Randy..."

"I appreciate it, I do." But he obviously didn't because Randy Mayhill preferred action at all times. His eyes had adjusted again, and a new layer of stars emerged and doubled the light in the sky. "Been a while since I looked at the stars."

"Why were you a lousy husband?"

He felt uncomfortable with the wording. "Oh, hell. I dunno. It was a weird thing for you to say, so I said something weird back." He pointed to the only constellation he knew. "Orion's belt." Even stars understood the importance of a good belt.

"You weren't lousy to Van. Why would you say such a thing?" Then Gabby gasped almost inaudibly. "Do you think that you somehow...?" Her voice softened, and he could feel her looking at him.

Mayhill didn't say anything.

"Randy?" she asked carefully. "Do you think it's your fault? For Van, I mean?"

He felt a slight clenching of the throat, an attempt to breathe through the shrinking straw of his esophagus. He looked away from her. "You don't know everything."

"I never thought I did, but you talk like a guilty man."

The music from the cab of the truck had stopped, and the low, obnoxious chatter of advertisements cackled from the radio. Her tenderness embarrassed him.

She looked into the black beside him. "I'm gonna tell you something, Randy." She took a deep breath. "I swore I'd go to my grave with this."

Mayhill suddenly felt uneasy, that his sad-sack routine had inspired her to break some personal code. She was the only other person he knew with convictions as strong as his.

"I don't know what you're about to say, but don't say it. I'm guessing you're trying to make me feel better about—"

"They didn't just find Van's operation or whatever," she said. "They didn't stumble across all those plants, whatever they told you, whatever the newspaper said. It wasn't like that."

"Please don't. I got it. It wasn't my fault. I never actually thought it was all my fault," Randy said. It was a lie and a big one. "But a man has regrets...like right now...I regret everything about this conversation."

—*Stop talking, Randy! Let her speak!*

"No, you have more than regret. I can see it. A man doesn't disappear for two years because of embarrassment. You're a hermit, Randy. You have full blown shame, Randy Mayhill. You think you caused Van's death."

"I do not think I caused Van's death."

"You do too think you caused Van's death, and that's too much for one man to shoulder."

"Oh God, Gabby." He felt so embarrassed he considered jumping back in the truck, driving straight into the pond. "I'm fine. Sure, I don't like how it played out in town, the newspapers and such. Sure, a man has regrets. I coulda done more—"

"And it's all clear now." Her face had a look of astonishment, and it was apparent she wasn't listening to Randy anymore. "I've been sitting on this thing, and I didn't know what it meant or why God gave it to me to know."

"Stop." Randy raised his voice. "Don't do this. You can't unsay whatever you're about to say. It's a slippery slope, letting go of your ethics."

She shook her head as to brush off what he said and screwed her courage. "It's important. I know that now. If you have a chance to absolve a man, you do it, Randy. You know that. That was the whole point of Jesus."

He slipped off the tailgate and walked away from the truck, and stared down the hogs. "I don't need absolving," he said. "And I think Jesus would find I make a hostile work environment."

"Somebody called it in, Randy. Somebody reported Van."

He turned and smirked. *Oh, the relief!* "I know that, Gabby. The hog hunter. I know. I met him myself. You were there. Big cross. Smelled like mud."

"No! It was not the hunter!" She shook her head furiously. "Randy, listen! This has nothing to do with you!"

"Then I don't need to know, do I?"

"There was another tip! Anonymous! An anonymous tip!"

"Anonymous?"

"Went above your head," Gabby said. "Called the game warden directly."

"Okay, it wasn't my fault. Thank you for saying so." He tried to sound sincere but knew he was failing. "Thank you, Gabby. That was a kind thing to say. I feel a bona fide sense of relief right now."

"Don't patronize me!"

"I am not!" And he wasn't. He was trying to take it all in but he couldn't wrap his head around why any of this was designed to make him feel better. He felt a sense of relief that it hadn't just been him, but who was to say that his stunt hadn't attracted the attention of yet another person? What did Gabby's revelation prove? Van was an idiot, and Mayhill was one too, albeit to a lesser degree than he previously thought. He paced slowly in front of the tailgate. "I appreciate you… what you're trying to do, but you're a smart woman. Don't matter how it happened. He got caught. At the end of the day, he got caught. You know it doesn't change a thing."

"It does though." Her voice was small again, and she looked down at her hands.

"How? How on earth would that change anything? Van's dead. I lost my job—"

"Because it was Dale," she blurted. "It was Dale who called in the second time. Dale was the anonymous tip."

He waited a moment before responding. He wanted to be sure he heard right. "Dale?" The world seemed to move in slow motion then, his breathing labored, the crickets as loud as car horns.

"Yes." Gabby looked like she was about to cry.

"How do you know?"

"I read the report a few months after it happened, what the game warden wrote. All of it in Van's file. I am so ashamed. It wasn't my place. But it was just so tragic...Van...you. I don't know what I was doing. I just needed something to explain it all." She rubbed her hands through her hair, and then cupped her eyes. "The caller knew the coordinates, Randy. Coordinates."

"That don't mean anything!" Mayhill threw his arms in the air. "Hell, that mud man could have known coordinates."

"Jimmy wrote down his name."

"What?"

"Jimmy wrote his initials once. DM. In the file. Just a little slip, but he did. It was right there in his notes. Jimmy knew who he was talking to. Wasn't just a rumor."

"Dale Mackey..." Mayhill whispered.

She nodded.

Mayhill stared at the pond, the white trail that the sliver of moon cast across the water. "But that's how they found it," Mayhill said. "The poison killed all those fish. That's what Jimmy Cason said happened. I did that, Gabby." He stood in front of her now. "I did the poison. I was trying to poison Van's crops. I was covering it up for Van. I did what they said. I knew and didn't do anything."

"I know! We all know!" Gabby slapped her leg. "Nobody's questioning that you tried to cover it up! But it wasn't the dead fish!

The game warden found the fish after Dale called in. That's when they found the poison. Not because of the poison. Just easier to say that the poison tipped them off. Protects their anonymous tipster. Gets you out of the picture. Convenient."

"After the call…" Mayhill's voice trailed off. He leaned against the tailgate, exhausted. "That's how they knew I knew. I always wondered how the timing worked…" They sat in silence for a moment. "Why didn't you say anything? Why didn't you tell me?"

"If anyone could understand devotion to her job, I'd imagine it's you."

"But to know something and not say it. To not do anything at all. Justice was not served!"

"I believe in the system," Gabby said. "And if the system fails, Dale will stand before God one day."

"Before God? And if there is no God?"

"He'll have to live with it until he dies!"

"Or that asshole's bucked the system twice!"

Gabby sat quietly and did not respond, and so Mayhill had to sit with his angry words, his meanness. She was all grace; with her, he had to be a better man.

"I'm sorry," he said to her for the second time that day.

But Gabby, all decency and goodwill, was already over it. "Why would Dale have called himself in? That's what I never understood," she said. "It makes no sense."

Mayhill shook his head, eyes wide, and rubbed his hand over his mouth, still confounded. "Dale was paranoid. Van probably told him I knew, so he thought it was a matter of time before police were after them. Had to be it. If Dale calls the game warden himself, maybe he could beat police to the punch…I dunno…make sure he wasn't around…pin it all on Van."

"But Van would just say Dale's involved too."

"Well, hell. Dale probably didn't touch anything. Have you felt his hands?"

"And if Van is dead…" Gabby said. "He couldn't rat out Dale. All of it's on Van's land. Just rumor mill then."

"If Van is dead…" The implication hit him like a bullet. "Oh my God." Mayhill couldn't breathe. His chest was caving in.

"I tried calling you," Gabby said. She grabbed his sleeve and pulled him back toward the truck. "You never picked up."

He tried to catch a breath but all he could think was that Dale had killed Van himself.

"I didn't tell you," Gabby said, "because of everything you just told me. I thought it didn't change anything." She looked at him, as if to beg forgiveness. "You left. You left for a long time, and you didn't come back. I didn't know why. Not sure any of us knew why. I mean, yeah, you screwed up. But shame ain't worth that. Shame ain't worth losing your life over. You're too good of a man for that."

It was then that Mayhill finally breathed in deep. He walked back to the truck and sat on the tailgate next to her, not at a distance now. So close he could smell gardenias.

He looked out at the hogs that seemed to be multiplying in front of him. They congregated in bunches a hundred deep, a fast-motion propagation of the species. He felt like he could see the entire world fast forwarding on his VCR, everything unfolding in astonishing beauty and perfection.

He nodded and looked into the night, and he could feel her looking at him. Too good of a man, she had said. The words rung in his ears. The night seemed radiant then. His stomach flipped at the realization that he had been living out the wrong story all along.

That's when it happened. It happened so fast he didn't even register at first that Goddamn Gabby Grayson had taken his large, meat cleaver hand and squeezed it tightly in hers. Her hand was tiny and bird-like, and now it rested with his on his thigh, like he was a man worth caring about, like he was a man who deserved grace. Nobody had touched him in years, and Randy Mayhill's throat caught at the realization that he had found something he had not known was lost.

Then they both turned and looked out at the hogs swarming like locusts around them. He stared at their hands a moment—intertwined, mismatched in size, and couldn't think of a thing to say, his brain notably quiet. He had everything right then. They sat together like this on the tailgate in silence for a long time—this rare and glorious moment of physical contact for Randy Mayhill, this moment of grace squeezed by improbable loss—watching as the hogs rooted happily in the dark.

CHAPTER TWENTY-THREE

"I need to see Van's gun."

After Mayhill left the Glorious Gabby Grayson, he found himself on Birdie's front porch. It was around eleven at night, and his head was so close to the porch light that the moths flittered near his ears, the shine of his bald spot beckoning them like a torch.

"Why was the sheriff at your place?" The worry on Birdie's face was now a permanent fixture, something to work around like the hogs.

"It was nothing. Misunderstanding."

"They had the lights on. Onie was worried." But he could see that she was worried. Onie didn't seem to worry about much these days.

"It was nothing, I promise," Mayhill said. "I need to see Van's gun. I really need you just to trust me on this one."

"You're knocking on our door at eleven at night," Birdie said. "Police at your place this afternoon. Now you're asking for Dad's gun."

"I know it's—"

"And we still don't know where Bradley is." She cinched her arms over her chest, straitjacket tight.

"We'll find him." Mayhill swatted at the moths. "But it's all connected…it's all connected. Can I come in, please? I need to look at his gun."

"And I need to know why!"

"I think something else might have happened to your daddy," Mayhill blurted. "I don't think he killed himself. I think he was shot."

Birdie's face changed right there under the porch light—bafflement and disgust making the slow trek from her brow to her mouth, now perpetually downturned. The look was not quite shock, but more of exhaustion, a bizarre submission to her life's list of horrors. It pained Mayhill to see.

"I can't explain it all right now. But Dale, the weed…" He looked around guiltily and whispered. "This Tommy Jones guy…he might be a hitman. All of it. It's connected."

"Why would a hitman be on our land? With a map." She stepped back inside, pulling the door. "Don't mess with me. It's too—"

"I'm not messing with you!" Mayhill put a foot in the door. "Please!"

"You don't have proof of anything! Hunches don't prove anything."

"You want proof? Then let me see Van's gun."

"Which gun?"

"The gun they said he…used." Mayhill looked at her steadily, the sad reality of the statement wedging itself between them. "Just to put my mind at ease."

He felt like a jackass saying it, that she might care about his mind, much less about it being at ease, what with the laundry list of worries piled on top of her. But like a miracle—the second one that night—

Birdie moved aside, and Mayhill stepped into the dark of the house, leaving the moths on the porch.

The house was quiet; even the television yattered at a reasonable level. The cool, blue light of the screen reflected off the concrete floor and cast the room in a preternatural glow. Onie slept on the brown couch underneath a blanket Mayhill recognized from camping trips, and the remnants of two TV dinners sat on the coffee table. In the kitchen, Birdie slid open a drawer underneath the microwave. She returned with a tiny key the size of a quarter, then motioned for him to follow her into Van's room. Van's bed was made—an old plaid quilt—and Mayhill stopped for a moment to look at the books on the bookshelf by his bed. *The Complete Works of Shakespeare. Walden. The Great Gatsby. The Collected Works of Ralph Waldo Emerson.* They had almost the same collection. He wondered which of these Van had last read.

Birdie opened the door of a largish walk-in closet, and Mayhill stepped inside. A tall gun safe the size of a refrigerator stood on one side, and Van's clothes hung like a thick curtain on the other. He and Birdie squeezed tightly in the middle, the chain from the light brushing his ear. Huddling next to Van's clothes, he was hit with Van's smell. His chest tightened at the unexpected memory.

Birdie handed Mayhill the key, and they shimmied past each other, switching positions. Mayhill sucked in his belly but it embarrassingly grazed her arm anyway. He opened the safe: a Colt Detective Special, a Beretta 1934, and Mayhill's favorite, a Colt Single Action Army Revolver, a pistol that cowboys would have carried in their holsters in the late 1800s. It would be worth over a thousand dollars now, but Van's was special because it had been passed down from Onie's grandfather.

Then a plastic bag, deep in the back corner of the safe.

"This is what they returned?" Mayhill had never known what gun they found beside Van and even he wouldn't dare ask Onie such a thing.

"It's what Onie brought back," Birdie said.

"Christ, she didn't even take it out of the evidence bag." It was a little Smith & Wesson 686 .357. Mayhill crouched slightly and looked through the sight, and then turned it back and forth in his hands. Three-inch barrel in stainless. An L frame. A little beefier to accommodate a seven-shot cylinder. Onie had given it to him when he graduated high school. "He carried it in his truck," Mayhill said. "He wouldn't have used this. He just wouldn't."

"Why are you doing this?" Birdie said. "We know he did it. Everybody said so." But as much as Birdie tried to convince herself, they both knew Van wouldn't kill himself with a gun his mother had given him. Even crazed with fear, Van wouldn't do that.

She stared at the gun in Mayhill's hand, a steely mixture of sadness and rage. "Who, then? Who did it? The agents? The police?" She looked up at him, pleading. She was barely able to say the words, her voice giving out as if she were being choked. Then she nodded, the revelation landing. "Dale," she said.

"I think so."

"They wouldn't have made a mistake like that," she said. "That can't be what happened."

"Not something you'd pay attention to unless you knew Van."

"You'd notice," she said. "Onie'd notice."

"But I didn't know what they found," he said. "I wasn't allowed... Jimmy Cason confronted me...next thing I know Van's dead...I had no access to—"

"Why wasn't someone looking for it?" Birdie's eyes were turning red. "Why didn't anybody suspect anything?"

Mayhill looked at the gun in his hand, baffled.

"Why didn't the police ask around?" Birdie asked. "Why didn't they investigate?"

"Nobody investigates a dead drug dealer." The words sounded harsher than he intended, a buried anger toward Van escaped and run amok.

Birdie whipped her head around, gasping as if her breath had been knocked out. "Dad was not a drug dealer."

"We know he wasn't," he said quickly. "In their eyes, he was though. He was just…disposable then."

"You're saying he didn't matter."

"To them," he said. "Yes, I'm saying he didn't matter to them."

"Why didn't you look into it? Surely you had some contact, you knew something…"

"I was out of it, Birdie. They kicked me out!"

She glared at him. He could tell that the questions in her head were coming too fast and she didn't know what to ask.

"He was desperate," Mayhill said. He eyed the gun in his hand. "Desperate men kill themselves. It made sense."

Birdie slammed her fist into the wall, and Van's clothes rattled on the hangers. Mayhill flinched. "It did not make sense! It did not make sense that he would choose to leave me!"

They stood there in silence, listening to the closet resettle.

"I know, Birdie," he said more gently this time. "But what Van was doing was so crazy to begin with, nobody understood what was going on with him anymore."

"He was not crazy." She might hit him. Birdie was stone-faced now despite the wash of red that settled over her cheeks, her eyes filling. It scraped him raw.

"What he did was crazy," Mayhill said. "Crazy and desperate are interchangeable."

"He had lost all of his money! He was just trying to get it back. On his own land! Just like you said! That's not crazy. That's not crazy."

"He was facing prison. Twenty-year minimum. *Minimum.* You ever visited the prison?" Mayhill asked. "And there for twenty years? You ask any of these men out here. You go up to the feed store and ask any one of them. Faced with prison? They all would have at least thought about doing the same thing. I mean, Van woulda gone to hell on his own terms than heaven on somebody else's. So nobody really questioned...I think *I* might have—"

"But he left a note..." Birdie said, recalculating.

"Well, that's just..." The closet felt impossibly small all of a sudden. He felt hot. "I wouldn't think too much of it." He turned to put the gun back in the safe.

She grabbed his arm, fingers dug deep.

"You know he left a note, Randy. It was in Onie's Bible...where she keeps important things."

"Just one piece of a big puzzle."

"But you gave her the note." She stared straight ahead into the gun safe.

"I found it..." Mayhill said.

"Where did you find it? If you weren't involved...if the game warden or whoever wouldn't let you touch anything." Birdie's fingers dug deeper into his arm. "Tell me where you found it, Randy."

"It was with evidence."

"Where did you find it?" The panic in her voice heightened.

"It was with his things. Gabby was able to—"

"But you didn't even have access to his gun, you said...you didn't have access to his records..."

"Birdie..." The implication was there now.

"You gave Onie the note!" She slammed her fist into the wall again, and a few of Van's shirts dropped to the ground. All at once she materialized the note from her pocket. It unnerved him to see it.

"*You.*" She slapped the pink paper to his chest.

He fumbled to catch it but it floated to the ground at their feet.

"Birdie..." But he didn't know how to finish the sentence. His eyes darted away from hers a split second, and when he looked back, he knew immediately that she understood. Still, he was surprised to find himself defensive. *How could she think that I—?* He wanted to disappear behind Van's shirts.

She stared at the wall.

"Birdie, please look at me," he heard himself saying. He hated the sound of his voice, the pathetic pitch, the inadequacy of words, but it was all he could think to say. If Birdie would just look at him, then he could still control the situation somehow. He could still retain the chance that she might love him like she had when her daddy was alive and they were all happy. If she could just look at him, she might still respect him or see that everything he had done had been with her utmost good in mind.

"We all just love you so much," he said.

She didn't acknowledge him. She was not going to let herself cry, to give him another second of emotion. Her eyes had gone steely and her face was yet again dead to him—not just annoyed and distant in that standoffish teenage way, but dead, all caring and regard for him ripped out by the seams. He wanted to hear Van's voice in his head, to say it was okay what he had done, but Van was notably silent. He looked at Van's clothes, limp and unworn, reminders of how dead he was.

They stood there—the note on the ground between them, Mayhill with Van's revolver in his right hand—and he tightened his grip on the gun, suddenly afraid of Birdie. He wanted to leave, to run out of the closet and out the front door, but he was afraid to move. She could rip it from his hands, shoot him in the gut. Even with her rage and his fear circling each other like dogs, daring each other to make the first move, he couldn't blame her for killing him. It seemed like the right death in a way. She was angry enough, and he was sad enough.

A thunder of final thoughts in his shortish life: Wondering what would happen to her if she killed him. The need to run from the house and dig his own grave to give her an easy cleanup. What would happen to Onie if Birdie killed a man?

"Give me the gun," Birdie said suddenly, her voice cold, emotionless.

"I don't think that's…" Mayhill checked that the safety was on and held it firmly to his side. A surprising thought: he wanted to live. But only to make it okay for her.

"Give it to me." Birdie did not appear angry. She was resolute. He wished she were angry, because calm people were the most deadly, thoroughly convinced of the sanity of their choices. She looked tired, resigned, much older than she should, holding out her hand.

He lifted the gun to give it to her and, in these seconds, considered acutely that these were his last moments. He spent all these years trying to save the world and this is how it would all end. A woman killing him for trying to save her. He wasn't selfless; he wasn't a hero. He might have been the most selfish man he knew.

Birdie grabbed the revolver much too quickly, and Mayhill held his breath. For a moment, she stared at the gun in her hand. Then she pushed past Mayhill, his back ramming into the wall. She placed the gun reverently back in the safe and closed its heavy, black door with the quiet clicking of the latch. Then she left.

Mayhill stood in Van's closet, unsure what to do next. What had just happened? He had just confirmed that his best friend had not killed himself. What should he be feeling? Jubilant? A sense of victory that he had solved the mystery of what had happened to Van? Ashamed that he had never suspected it before? This was justice in action, wasn't it? Goddammit, where was Van? He picked up the note and slipped it in his back pocket. Mayhill wandered out of the closet and stood unmoored in the living room.

Birdie was curled up in Van's big leather chair, eyes on the blue glister of the television. *M*A*S*H* played on the screen. The sepia doctors were in surgery, all masks and laugh tracks in the middle of war. Birdie looked small, the same baby-bird fragility that had inspired Van to name her such a thing. Onie was still asleep on the couch, turned away from the television now, and purring like a lion. Mayhill didn't know how to leave. If he left, he would never see Birdie again, not in any meaningful way. If he kept her in his sight, this family— Onie, Birdie, Van—they would still be his. He opened his mouth, but nothing came out. He walked to the door and let himself out, the latching of the doorknob severing his final connection to Van, but all the way home he whispered aloud to himself, as if Van could hear, as if Birdie were eight years old again and riding happily in the truck beside him, "I'm sorry, I'm sorry, I'm sorry."

CHAPTER
TWENTY-FOUR

After Mayhill left, Birdie pulled herself off the couch. She couldn't stand the sound of Onie's snoring, and even though it was nearing midnight, she got in Van's old truck and left. She needed to drive. Watermelon and cantaloupe rolled in the backend with all the silence of a bowling alley. The hogs swarmed in patches over the pastures, and she could hardly remember what the place looked like before they had taken over. She drove past the dead hermit's abandoned house and remembered the ghost stories Van had told her every time they'd driven by. She'd hide in the floorboard until they passed. And a few miles past that was a large field with a dilapidated house that had belonged to an old black family, the Lewises—a rickety old shotgun house balanced like toothpicks, walls of dried out gray wood. When Van was young in the fifties, he saw a cross burn in the field right in front of it, all eight Lewises huddled together on the porch, horrified in its glow. Every time Van told her that story (many, many times; it clearly haunted him) she looked into the dark expectantly, nervous to see if the cross had reappeared—a memory so ingrained she almost thought it was her own.

She was tired of collecting tragedies, and here was another. She had been duped and someone had killed her father, and yet the first instinct she had was to tell Van—whisper it into his shirts, tell it to his knife as it corkscrewed in her ear—as if he hadn't known.

The note hadn't felt right in her stomach, like chicken eaten a day past optimal, like a berry you eat off the pasture bushes and suddenly you're sure you had misidentified it. Of course the handwriting had not been quite right, but she was sixteen, and what people told her became what was true. That B right there, without any humps, just two angry triangles that looked like flags on a mast, perhaps were not flags at all, but more like fangs.

⠄⠂⠄⠂⠄⠂⠄⠂⠄⠂

"Marlboro Lights, please." Birdie was stricken by her voice as it left her mouth. She sounded like a toddler, a smoking toddler, but a toddler nonetheless.

"How old you?" The man working the cash register at the corner store was not one she recognized. The corner store was the only place in the county that was open past midnight.

"Eighteen!" Birdie said much too defensively. *Gah!* She straightened her back to highlight her breasts, which she was sure had grown lately.

"ID," he said. He took a drag of his cigarette.

She went through the theatrics of digging around in her pockets. "Must've left it." She shrugged.

He shifted from one elbow to the other, settling in for a show. He looked happy about it, some unexpected entertainment on a late night that didn't involve a high shoplifter or a parking lot knife fight.

"I'm serious," she said. "I left my license. I just need these. Well, *I* don't. I smoke a different brand. But these. They're for my grandma."

"Why don't your grandma buy them, then?"

"It's a real sad story." Birdie pulled her pocketknife out of her pocket and carved around in her ear. "She has lost her mind."

"We all have, baby doll."

"Then you know what I'm saying!" She looked at him straight on like Van had taught her. The cashier's eyes were yellow and bulging, old smoke on his clothes, a dirty white polo shirt stained brown with age around the collar. He shook his head in a way that she knew was meant to shame her. He, like the rest of the world, was unmoved by her. She put her pocketknife away.

She wondered why the cigarettes were so important to her all of a sudden, but it was all she could think about. Bad night? You need a cigarette. She learned things from all the television she'd been watching. Also, her father looked eerily similar to the Marlboro Man had the Marlboro Man smiled incessantly. "Look, I just need these," she said to the cashier. "I *need* these."

"And I need a beer," he said. He straightened up then, done with show. "And you need to buy sumpin' and get the hell outta here."

"I'll buy you a beer! You know…for your trouble." She pulled out twenty dollars, smacked it on the counter, then rushed to the cooler at the back of the store—only to register the total absence of alcoholic beverages. She had never tried to buy beer before, but the county, of course, was dry. How had the Baptists managed to ruin absolutely everything? They were worse than the hogs. "No beer." She laughed nervously and walked back to the counter. "I gotta truck full of watermelon though. Best you ever eat. What if I unload a few out front?"

The cashier smirked, real smug-like, Birdie thought, and then he slid the twenty dollars back across the counter to her.

"You aren't going to sell me any cigarettes, are you?" she said.

"No, I ain't."

She nodded slowly and took in another defeat for the day. She flung open the glass door much too hard like some punk movie kid. It was the only power Birdie had, to push open doors.

"I knew your daddy," he called.

"Oh yeah?" Birdie took her turn looking unimpressed, but she felt her father admonish her for dismissing another person. He was always watching, it seemed. So she tried to contort her face into one that conveyed interest. She turned and leaned her back against the dirty glass door and forced a smile.

"I worked for him a spell. You's a little thing." The cashier dropped his hand down toward the ground to show how tall she had been.

"When was that?" Her question was disingenuous. Behind the cashier, an old poster—a cigarette advertisement of a rocket—drew her in. The ad featured a glamorous woman in a bomber jacket behind a cartoon camel launching a rocket. The camel mocked her with his lit cigarette. How long did camels live? Was the camel eighteen? Could the camel have legally bought the cigarettes?

"Awww, I dunno. Don't matter, don't it?" He lit his own cigarette.

She realized then that the man was waiting for her to look at him, that he knew when he was being ignored. But the man, unlike her, was much more used to it. She felt Van's admonishment, the guilt percolate through her.

"Your daddy, he good to us," the cashier said.

"Oh yeah?" Birdie asked. "Who's us?"

"Me. All the men nobody gave jobs to. And we nobody. But your daddy…he didn't think nobody was nobody." He lifted his mouth and blew out a smoke ring. "Ain't nobody nobody, I guess."

Van would have loved the turn of phrase. He would have said it for weeks. She wanted it on his tombstone, but her father didn't have a grave. Only crabgrass.

"Hey," he said as Birdie stepped out the door. She looked back, and the man manifested a pack of cigarettes. He flicked his wrist, and a single cigarette miraculously emerged like a finger pointing at her. Camels. "I know it's not your brand."

She smiled, embarrassed all of a sudden. She took the cigarette and spun it between her fingers like her father had.

"Thank you," she said. She sucked on the end, the flavor soaking into her mouth through the dry, dry paper.

Birdie should have gone straight home—but she had won something, hadn't she?—and weren't small victories like the taste of blood for a certain kind of animal, whetting the appetite? She drove past the corner store and cut the lights as she turned onto Bradley's road, the truck headlights too bold for the midnight darkness of the side street. Immediately, she could see Bradley's tiny house lit up, a jaundiced glow from the front picture window, casting an outline on the blue truck parked to the side of the house. She held her breath. Bradley. She drove closer and rolled to a stop in front of the house. She peered into the dark and saw it was a Dodge, not a Ford; gray, not blue. Her brief hopefulness shamed her. Her stupidity hung on like baby teeth that wouldn't fall out. Of course it couldn't have been his truck. He didn't sleep there.

In the front window, a silhouette of a woman bounced in the distance, sashaying through the light behind the dirty glass, and then a man lumbered into the picture, their outlines connected, and though it was close to midnight, Birdie rapped hard on the door.

"Who the hell!" The silhouette slithered to the door, and a woman peaked her head out. She was long-faced and angry-eyed, about a head taller than Birdie even with her shoulders curled forward like wilting paper. Ridden hard, put up wet, Van would have said. Birdie knew immediately it was Bradley's mother. She could see the hint of him in her features, behind the indignation, behind the exhaust cloud of smoke and wine.

"I'm sorry to bother you," Birdie said. Her voice was frustratingly small again. "I know it's late."

"Well, you are bothering me," Bradley's mother said. "What the hell you want?"

"I'm trying to find Bradley."

"Bradley ain't here." The woman tried to close the door, and Birdie stuck her foot in like Mayhill had taught her.

"You're the one been calling my house all day."

"I can't get a hold of him," Birdie said. "Do you have any idea where he—"

"You need to get the hell off my porch."

"But do you know where he is? I'm worr—"

"Do you know where he is?" The woman mocked her, voice pitched high. "That boy's nineteen."

"But he lives here," Birdie said. "He didn't show up for work, and I was—"

"For work? *That's* who you are." A smile spread across Bradley's mother's face because this was a woman who loved to be wronged. Birdie had showed herself to be a mouse, and the cat was ready to play. "You're his boss! You're his boss and you come to my house at midnight to harass me?"

"I'm not his boss," Birdie said. "He worked for my dad."

"Oh, you're his boss. You're a little mousy thing, ain'tcha? Don't pay him shit, but you can show up at my house, my house, at midnight on a Friday." Her mouth ran like a motor, finger darting back and forth as if following a fly. Birdie saw the bruise then—a landing strip of black and blue branded into her forearm.

Bradley hadn't done that to her.

"You should know where he is!" Birdie snapped. That's what Birdie had come to say, hadn't she? "You're his mother. You're his mother. You should care where he is!"

"Get the hell off my porch." She shoved Birdie in the chest and out of the doorway. She slammed the door, her tirade still blowing like a storm behind the thin window. Bitch this and show-up-again that. Something about the sheriff.

Birdie watched the silhouettes, now like conjoined twins, disappear from the front window, but no other light in the house came on. Standing in Bradley's pitiful yard, she felt sorry for herself, though admittedly much sorrier for Bradley, and she found her empathy encouraging. How awful for the both of them, the neglect of Bradley's mother. The arrogance of Mayhill. The gullibility of her father. The greed of Dale. Onie's stifling depression. Texas summers so suffocatingly hot and sticky. Victims to the weather! Victims to the hogs! It was a pitiful roll call of injustices, and she and Bradley were victims to all of it. It overwhelmed her, and she was tired of taking it.

You need to leave before something happens.

Birdie told herself this, but her legs wouldn't move, her father's rebellion, pulsing like the tiny thread of fluid up her spine. She tried to shake the feeling but couldn't let it go.

She hurried to the back of her truck and felt around in the bed. It was hard as a rock, the size of a bowling ball, and it carried every ounce of rage and transgression she'd ever counted in Bradley's and her young lives. She bobbled it in her hands a moment. A pause.

You should know where your son is.

It all moved in slow motion then: Birdie, with all of her strength, hurling it through the night in a long, triumphant arc, right into the belly of the yellowed house. The deafening shatter. The entire window crashing down like a waterfall.

Then Bradley's mother, red sweatshirt clamped over her bare chest, running into the light, gasped—wondering what had happened and knowing what had happened all at the same time—until the moment she squinted, and all at once realized that something very different had transpired than she first thought. Because surely it was not possible that this thing rolling over the carpet of glass—shards sparkling like glitter—and coming to a slow stop at her feet was a cantaloupe that some mousy little thing had lobbed through the night.

. : . . . .

Speeding away, Birdie felt that anything was possible. She felt indestructible. Something was taking the shape of hope. Something suggested that hope was coming. She lit the cigarette and sped down the highway so fast that the truck seemed to fly underneath her, the wheels precarious and slippery, much faster than she had ever gone. Maybe it was the nicotine rising to her brain, or maybe it was the window rolled down, her hair whipping her face so hard it stung, but all she could feel was invincibility right then. Was it relief? A way of looking at the world that before an hour ago seemed impossible?

Birdie hit the gas harder, the trees whirring by. Maybe she could outrun the facts that she would be forced to put together, more feelings to come to terms with, more emotions to assimilate—all this complicated grief and whatnot. She didn't want to do it! She knew what the right response was: she should be horrified! She should feel enraged that someone had taken her father from her, but all the disgust and anger had escaped into the oddest of weapons—a cantaloupe! HAHAHAHAHAHAHAHAHAHAHAHAHAHA! *Oh, Dad, you should have seen! A melon plunged through that window.* And where all the rage had been, a weird giddiness settled instead. A grin spread across her face, headlights knifing the night.

She sped up and the steering wheel jerked violently beneath her hands. She had never driven this fast, and as long as she sped forward, she could fly into the night with this new feeling, this feeling that something was different, that the grief and anger had moved now, that it wasn't so stuck, that suddenly she was strong and had control over her life. She had evened the score. She had scored a cigarette! Something unexpected was cracking open inside of her. She couldn't be sure what it was until she felt the words rising up in her throat like a single tiny soap bubble floating out of the dishwater, and she wanted to zip around town and scream it into the night air. She wanted to send the dozing cowbirds flying into the dark and spread the news to everyone like a frantic carrier pigeon: *Dad didn't leave me on purpose.* Birdie leaned out the window, hair slashing like whips, and yelled out into the empty highway. "You hear that, everybody? He didn't leave me on purpose!"

PART THREE

CHAPTER
TWENTY-FIVE

"**D**o you think Dale would have shot you?" It was early evening, and Bradley was stewing on a mess of information. The money. It was more money than he could ever imagine. But the next thought: Dale's gun. Dale's gun winding through the air and then pointing right at Jason. What would Bradley have done if Dale shot Jason? Would Dale have shot him too? And the next thought: the money again.

"Dale ain't gonna shoot nobody," Jason said. "Just on edge. I seen him puke three times yesterday." Jason sat on the camp chair with a paper plate full of fried chicken in his lap. Grease smudged his mouth. Bradley stared at his own plate of fried chicken, battered an inch thick. Dale had made it himself for dinner. "To take care of his boys," he had said like a father. He had killed the chickens himself.

But Bradley—simultaneously terrified and elated—couldn't eat. After leaving Dale's, he had worked his body hard the entire day. His arms ached, his hands had blisters, his legs were quivering. His fingers remained in a perpetual curl, trained by the limb cutters. His stomach rumbled for fuel but he just took tiny sips of beer as if it were ginger ale and he had taken to a sick bed. The cicadas' song plugged his ears. Dale had retired to his house for the evening. Stacks of depressingly avocado-colored plants lay in heaps around the woods, but they still had more to go before tomorrow evening. Tomorrow would be brutal.

"He pointed a gun right at you," Bradley said. Dale was a riddle he couldn't figure out, but he desperately wanted him to be good.

"Bad shit's gonna happen," Jason said. "Look around! You ain't working in a daycare! You're in a cartel! You gonna eat that?"

It is not a cartel. We are gardeners.

Bradley handed his plate of chicken to Jason. "You just wanna think you're in a cartel," Bradley said. "This isn't a cartel."

It is not a cartel.

A cartel was a dangerous game run by men named Guillermo in crisp white shirts with machine guns. He had learned as much on television. Bradley, to the extreme contrary, was a fence builder, ranch hand, and part-time gardener, and he reminded himself of that fact at all times when he began, much too late, to doubt his life choices.

It is not a cartel.

But part-time gardeners did not make seventy-five thousand dollars. He wondered if Dale had promised Jason the same. Where had Dale even gotten the extra money? Bradley had been too stunned to ask. Or maybe he didn't want to know.

"Getting a little money is all," Bradley said. "Not a big deal."

"Ain't a little money," Jason said. "What are you going to do with it?"

"Get a shower."

"Oh hell. What you really gonna do?"

"I'm serious," Bradley said. "All I want."

"That's your problem right there." A wad of chicken hung from Jason's mouth and tumbled onto his plate. "You think you better than everybody."

Bradley was silent.

"Well, LA DI DA!" Jason said.

"I'm not better than anybody," Bradley lied.

Jason didn't say anything—just wiped his hands on his jeans and crumbled the two plates into a plastic grocery sack. Bradley couldn't tell if he was really mad, and this made him uncomfortable for some reason, as he suddenly wanted certainty about everyone around him. He was surprised to find that he really, *really* wanted to talk with Jason right then.

"I don't think I'm better than anybody," Bradley said. "I just want normal stuff."

Jason nodded and lit a cigarette. He sank deep into his camp chair, an unlikely therapist, and listened intently. Bradley felt oddly grateful.

"I just wanna be somebody," Bradley said. "Somebody people pay attention to."

"Go on." Jason nodded, his face suddenly inscrutable and thoughtful. Then he took out his pocketknife and began to clean his ears.

Of course the money had ballooned in Bradley's brain since talking with Dale. No longer was just land possible. An impact was possible. The way Van had operated, employing the whole town practically. Bradley explained that he wanted to be the kind of man who came into a little money and did something noble. He wanted to do something the newspapers would write up, the television would talk about, like if he signed an NFL contract and bought his mama a house.

This happened every year on the local news, as if it were a national holiday. A giant of a man about Bradley's age stood over his tiny mother, them both wearing expensive wool baseball caps with the team logo, the jersey much too large on the mother. Them both crying that she deserved it. She had taken him to practices since he was this high and went to every game in the rain and whatnot. Bradley felt a quiver of guilt every time he saw the scenario play out because Bradley only wanted to be a good man—that's all he'd ever wanted! Still, he knew that if the Dallas Cowboys signed him tomorrow, he would under no circumstances buy his mother a house. He probably wouldn't even buy her the oversized jersey.

"I mean," Bradley said to Jason, emotional all of a sudden. "What kind of man wouldn't buy his mother sportswear?"

But Jason wasn't listening anymore. Somewhere in the midst of Bradley's monologue, Jason had grown bored. He had taken the camp lantern, laid it across his lap, and was now carving something in the bottom with his pocketknife. The light flickered like a horror movie motel as he worked. Even though Jason had only half listened, Bradley felt appreciative of him in that moment. He felt an unexpected closeness to him because he had shared something about himself, which is probably why he felt emboldened enough to learn forward in his chair and say: "Jason…that truck…it belonged to someone. I need to know who. I need to know what happened to him, and I think you know."

"Jesus! Why do you care so much about a Datsun?" Jason squinted one eye and scraped at the bottom of the lantern. His lip was still swollen. "I'll find you a goddamn truck."

"I don't need a truck." Bradley chose his words carefully. Was it a mistake to talk to Jason about this? "I think something happened to the owner."

"Why does everybody care about that truck so much? I mean, shit!" Jason spit, red-faced and mad, and Bradley braced himself, not sure why Jason was so agitated. Who else had cared about the truck? Dale didn't seem to care. Bradley watched him closely. Jason gripped the knife handle and pulled it hard against the lantern. He turned the lantern upside down, the light bouncing in an eerie shower on the tent, then he blew the paint flakes away. Jason, satisfied, hung the lantern up again, then pulled another cigarette from his front pocket and lit it.

"Why you think something happened to him?" Jason asked.

"You know what happened..." Bradley was testing him. "I mean, you have his keys, you took his truck."

"I ain't a liar." Jason took a drag off his cigarette. "Okay, maybe I am a liar, but no lie about this. Why you think something happened to him?" Jason cocked his head curiously, and Bradley understood that Jason really didn't know anything. Was it possible that Jason's world was so simple that you see a truck on the side of a road and it's yours, like an unclaimed ball on a playground?

Bradley tried to keep his face steady, to not give anything away. He stared into the dirt, but his brain kept seeing the dead man. Three little shrikes poking away at dark hair. The slumped body, the plaid shirt. He tried to think about the money. *Tomorrow, tomorrow.*

"Hey!" Jason punched him in the arm, and Bradley flinched. Jason's gaze was urgent almost; he was now looking to Bradley to tell him something. He needed assurance. "What are you talking about? Why you think something bad happened? Just because some idiot left a truck in the woods?"

"Nothing," Bradley said, shaking his head. "It's nothing. Guy was an idiot." He tried to change the subject. "Has Dale seemed sick to you lately? I mean, he looks bad…peeing all the time, hands are shaking like he's…"

Jason ignored this and sucked hard on his cigarette as if he were getting the last few drags before class. "Why you think something bad happened?"

Bradley had never seen him think more than a second about anything; he looked worried. Jason's face appeared yellow and aged in the golden light of the lantern, even though he was just eighteen, a year younger than Bradley. He could see just how dirty Jason was now: white oozing pimples popping up around his temples, his nose red and porous, his face still roughed up for a reason Jason wouldn't tell. For a moment, Bradley felt sorry for him, the way you do when you think you're smarter or luckier than somebody else. Looking at Jason, he wanted a shower more desperately than anything he'd ever wanted in his life.

Jason stubbed the cigarette out in the dirt, then grabbed the lantern off the tree branch and handed the flashlight to Bradley. "Come on," he said. "I gotta show you this."

⁘ ⁙ ⁘ ⁙ ⁘

They moved through the thicket like an unfortunate Lewis and Clark.

Bradley scanned his flashlight along the ground for snakes, despite Van having told him that they never came out at night. Jason, forever naive and trusting, seemed unfazed by the possibility of snakes, and he held his lantern high. The light bounced off of the low tree limbs. They could hear hogs off in the distance, a sound in the dark that oddly comforted Bradley because it was a sound he could recognize definitively. Even as they marched, flies pestered Bradley's entire body. He smelled like a corpse.

They were on the edge of the thicket when Jason stopped. "There," he said. He pointed with his cigarette and lifted his lantern higher. Bradley shined his flashlight ahead of him, a single beam of white light quivering in the darkness. Bradley squinted and waited for his eyes to adjust. Then he saw what Jason was pointing at: a large mound of dirt, covered haphazardly with sticks and pine needles.

"What is it?" Bradley asked.

Jason motioned for him to follow. They moved closer, and Bradley became quite aware of what Jason was seeing. His stomach dropped.

"Who did that?" Bradley asked.

"Saw Dale working back here the other morning after you went to the dump," Jason said.

Bradley thought back to that morning, when Dale said he was headed home but still lurked in the woods.

"I mean," Jason said, "it looks like a grave, don't it?"

Bradley said nothing, but it did, it looked just like a grave, a long pile of dirt that someone had tried to obscure. It probably had been well covered by the underbrush but last night's thunderstorms had beaten it all down again. Did Jason even know about the dead man? Had Jason seen him too? From where they were now, the man had been on a fence not too far away. Bradley wondered then if he should tell Jason what he had seen. They could make a plan to escape it all together…head straight up I-45…

"Yesterday," Bradley said, "when I was working at the Woodses—"

"I lied," Jason blurted. He looked away from Bradley into the trees now. "I didn't find the keys in the glove box. Dale gave them to me. Said to ditch the plates, take the truck to my house. You know…just keep the truck off the main road."

Bradley felt sick. He couldn't run away. Dale would know. Bradley tried to imagine a life where he didn't know anything about anyone.

"Let's go back," Jason said. "Spooky shit, right?"

Back at the campsite, Jason grabbed another beer from the cooler and handed Bradley one without asking. The two sat in silence for a long while, chugging their beers as if trying to chase something away. Jason pinched his beer can between his knees and carved again at the bottom of the lantern in between nervous drags off of a fresh cigarette. All of the illusions about their situation were crumbling.

"What are you thinking?" Bradley was desperate again to talk. He wanted his therapist back. He wasn't sure how to get through the next few seconds, much less the next day.

"What are you, my girlfriend? What the fuck you care what I'm thinking?"

"Nothin'," Bradley said. "Just talking." He did sound like Jason's girlfriend.

"Well, Oprah, I was thinking about the money." Jason rehung the lantern, done with his scratching, and got another beer. "A lot of goddamn money."

"Well, what are you gonna do with it?" Bradley asked.

"I'm gonna buy my mama a house."

"Your mama's in jail."

"When she gets out, I mean." Jason chugged the beer. "Five to ten." He snapped his fingers. "Flies by like that."

CHAPTER TWENTY-SIX

Saturday morning. Bradley always worked Wednesdays and Saturdays, but he wasn't here to work.

Hummingbirds flittered near a tube of red syrup that dangled outside of Birdie and Onie's window. One hummingbird rammed its tiny head into the window, a loud glass-rattling thud. It fell a bit, but caught itself, and then rose up again only to hover some more.

Bradley stared at the bird and admired its tenacity—he would never have such resilience—and then he turned his gaze back to Birdie's door, only to find that he couldn't lift his hand to knock.

The grave had been the tipping point. The grave was the final straw that sent Bradley Polk, three days late, back to Birdie and Onie's first thing in the morning, ready to confess, to tell Birdie everything, to beg for her help in extricating himself from this un-extricat-able situation. The riddle of Dale had been solved, and all of it had gotten too much for him to take. His future land, be damned. His future, period, be damned. He looked at his gnarled hands, a mosaic of tiny cuts and dried blood, and he willed his right one to lift and curl into a fist and knock on their door like a strong, competent man would do. His hand politely declined.

Walking over from the garden, he knew exactly what he would say: not in sentences necessarily but in concepts. He would come clean. He just needed the cloud of regret to distill into actual words that Birdie would understand. He was not a bad man, the right words would say. He was a man who had made a mistake, who was trying to follow a dream not unlike the one Van had. His bad choices—without him knowing!—had bumped up against her world, and he was a thousand kinds of sorry for that. He would swear on a stack of *Playboy*s he hadn't known it was her land until recently. Did those words even exist? The right words needed more time to bake.

He turned to leave.

Birdie flung open the door.

She stood there a moment and eyed him steadily as if to be sure it was really him. Then she reared back with both arms and shoved his chest as hard as she could. She pushed him so hard that Bradley—a good head taller than her and body like a linebacker—stumbled backward and grabbed the porch rail so he didn't fall to the ground. Her eyes were wide, the whites around them showing, and her dark brown hair pounced like an animal atop her head.

"Where..." She breathed heavy, seething. "*Where*...have you been?"

He hugged close to the porch railing, unsure what to say, and touched his chest where she had shoved him. He felt himself cower, his shoulders curve. Birdie looked pale, her eyes dark and sleepless, the familiar kind of face he saw when he looked in the mirror, except hers was washed and beautiful.

"I thought something happened to you," she said. She visibly softened, like clothes going limp. Her face had turned from pale to pink.

Bradley's heart clenched. She had feared for his safety! She had worried about him! His own mother didn't even care where he was. As sad as it was, the possibility that anyone might be concerned about him had never entered his brain. (Naiveté works in all ways, doesn't it?) He couldn't breathe and his chest tightened in the confusion of it all—a baking-soda-and-vinegar mix of shame and redemption that threatened to erupt in him. Bradley looked at Birdie as serious as he had ever looked at anyone. He looked her in the eye the way a man— that's right, a *man*!—looked people in the eye. And Bradley Polk was a man! He would be brave. He would own up to his transgressions. He would bow to the consequences and do right by her and Van and Onie. He cleared his voice and with no hint of shame, he said so boldly that the hummingbirds shot like torpedoes away from the porch: "Birdie! Could I please have a shower!"

Bradley had not found the right words.

Nor did he have clean clothes with him. He was thoroughly unprepared for life, as usual. At school without a pencil. He had not thought it through when he asked for such an intrusive thing, and was now standing in the stall of Birdie's shower, washing off weeks of grime, shocked at himself that he could dare ask Birdie to clean his body in her home. Perhaps he was a man after all. The water snaked down his tree-trunk legs and pooled brown at the drain. He marveled at the ribbon of bright pink soap in his hands, perfume-sweet like fake raspberries and flowers. Small rashes had formed under his arms and around his groin from the sweat and filth, and the soap and hot water happily stung at his wounds like antiseptic.

Standing in the hot shower, it was worth all the awkwardness, he decided. For a second, he could almost forget about Dale and Jason and the dead man and this out-of-control thing he found himself tangled up in. He imagined living out the rest of his life in this shower, his castle of a beige plastic stall purchased at Sam's Club. He wouldn't need food. He would subsist instead on bliss and berry-scented suds. He would subsist on Birdie's grace. The marvel of soap foaming under Bradley's armpits. He imagined his ashes spread in this shower, swirling down the drain in a winding gray river. *And there goes Bradley Polk…well, folks, he tried.*

When he got out, he saw that Birdie had left two—count 'em, *two!*—towels, thick as mattresses, as well as a pair of jeans, underwear, a blue plaid shirt, and a fresh pair of tube socks. He dressed and emerged from the bathroom, steam bellowing from behind him like Axl Rose bursting onto stage. The shirt was too tight on him. The buttons threatened to pop, and the pants were a bit short, but he was clean— the miracle of hygiene having descended like a dove and alighted on him and whatnot. He wiggled his toes in the tight hug of the socks.

Onie had moved to the front porch. As she rocked in the high heat of the day, her head bobbed in and out of the kitchen window. The hummingbirds flittered at the ruby feeder above her head.

Birdie sat at the kitchen table with two cups of coffee. She smiled softly when she saw him, but Bradley still didn't have the words. "You can sit if you want." She slid a cup of coffee across the table. "I put your clothes in the wash."

He rubbed the sleeve of his shirt. It was soft and worn. "Are these Van's?" It was the first time he said his name in months.

"Is that weird?" Birdie asked.

"No, no, I don't think so." *In fact, I feel oddly moved.*

"I don't think so either." She took a sip of coffee, her gaze still on him. She was exhausted, her eyes dark like her hair. Still, she looked somehow lighter today, happier, but he couldn't imagine why. It couldn't possibly be him. "You can keep the clothes," she said. "It's silly for us to have them. Onie said so. She's not too sentimental." But Bradley noticed that Birdie wore an almost identical shirt to the one he was now wearing. It swallowed her like a cloak. She tucked a wisp of hair behind her ear, a bizarre mixture of flirtation and steeliness. He wanted to talk about the dead man, the truck, all of it.

"What do you do here all day?" he asked instead. A dumb question.

She gestured her head toward Onie on the porch. "Dad would have wanted me here. You know, to take care of Onie…with her problems now." Birdie pointed to her ear. "I read all day. I mean, I take care of Onie, and I read all day."

"It's good to read," he lied, and they nodded in unison. "Thank you for washing my clothes. I'm sorry you had to touch them."

She laughed lightly, a breathiness to her voice. He had made her laugh! But then the laughter stopped, and a silence took over. He could feel it in his belly, he could feel it coming. The winds changing. The way cattle stirred up long before a storm cloud formed.

"Where's your truck?" Birdie asked.

There it was.

Birdie put down her coffee and crossed her arms across her chest. She didn't even look out the window for his truck.

"I walked."

"You walked? You live in town," Birdie said. "Your truck break down?"

A pause. They studied each other's faces. A stand-off of who was going to say it. Then it all came out in a desperate flood: "I swear to God I didn't know where we were, Birdie. I swear to God. I thought we were on Dale's place, and then I realized too late..." Bradley couldn't help it; his eyes were beginning to tear. The shame was suffocating. These were not the right words either.

"It *is* Dale," Birdie said.

"It wasn't supposed to be like this...I don't know how to explain it but—"

She held up a hand to silence him. They sat quietly for a moment and watched Onie rock back and forth, her head appearing and then disappearing in and out of the window, ticking like a hypnotist's watch.

"Dad did it too," she said quietly. "Desperate men don't think straight."

She looked impossibly sad, like these were words she had rehearsed in her head a thousand times, resigned to this fact about the men in her life, that they had all disappointed her so thoroughly. It was a merciful absolution.

"You know what happened to the man," Birdie said.

Bradley wanted to be back in the shower where the world made sense. There would be showers in prison, he consoled himself. He took a deep breath. "I honest-to-God don't know who he is. I mean...I recognize him. I know we saw him with Van that time. Remember that?"

"Mayhill thinks he's a hitman."

"A hitman?"

"Why would he be here though?" Birdie asked. "Why would a man named Tommy Jones be dead on my land?"

"All I know...there's a truck. I know it belongs to him. And Dale... he's paranoid...and I think he might have..." He still didn't have the words, now flummoxed by a new twist. "A hitman?" Bradley looked out the window. His panic was taking flight. Frantic hummingbirds with nowhere to go.

"He had a truck?" Birdie asked.

"A Datsun. It was parked off that logging trail where Van—"

"A Datsun? Randy asked about—" She stopped, as if searching for a thought buried too deep. She rubbed her face with her hands, the first hint of fear peeking through. "The truck's still there?"

"Jason has it."

"Who the hell is Jason? Who all is out there?" She jabbed her fingers in the direction of the woods. "I mean...Dale, you, this Jason person...this Tommy Jones just lands here. Why was he here? Why was he so close to the house? Was he Dale's friend? Was he trying to hurt—"

"You should call the police," Bradley said. The words popped out. Suddenly, these were the only words that seemed like the right ones. "Call the police."

Silence. The house was so quiet Bradley could hear the grind of Onie's rocking chair on the front porch concrete.

"Who is Jason?" Birdie asked again, all defeat and exhaustion. But she couldn't seem to stop looking at the bruise on Bradley's forearm.

"I know I owe you all of that," he said, "but I'm not going to rat him out too. Just do what you need to do. But don't go in the woods anymore." His voice started to break. "I'm sorry, I'm sorry...just don't go in the woods. Call the police."

"I'm not calling anybody." Birdie tapped Bradley's bruise very lightly with one finger, an odd little tap that wriggled hotly through him. "Don't go back there," she said. "Don't."

He watched her hand now resting on his arm, but he couldn't speak.

"I don't know what kind of money he's promised you. You know I can't near match any of that," Birdie said. "All I've got is land." Her voice was soft and even. "Dale's dangerous though. Mayhill thinks he's a murderer. And you're right there with him. Everybody around him ends up dead."

Bradley nodded, and they didn't talk anymore. He considered not returning to the garden, he did. Of course, it was all he could think about. But what then? Where would he go? Looking over his shoulder his entire life? They sat in silence, both in Van's shirts, the grate of Onie's chair soothing them like little children. They both knew he would be going back into the woods. For that moment, though, with Birdie's fingers resting on his arm and Bradley smelling of Van and raspberry soap, they pretended that he wouldn't. They pretended that there was another option for Bradley Polk, that he didn't know too much already, that he wasn't already in too deep. Delusion was a lonely game, he knew. But for that moment, he wanted no one else but Birdie's company in it.

Birdie got up from the table and leaned against the counter. She looked ten years older, a woman now—somehow transformed with the cool boldness of Onie and the wild-eyed rebellion of Van.

"I'm not calling anybody," she said, and crossed her arms. "But tell me exactly where I shouldn't go. And tell me exactly when I shouldn't be there."

CHAPTER

TWENTY-SEVEN

" **Y**ou smell like a whore."

When Bradley got back to the camp, Jason was alone with a militia of empty beer cans strewn around his chair. His words were slurred, and he slumped to one side, despite it being ten in the morning. Seeing drunk people during the day had always unnerved Bradley, like seeing Halloween pumpkins in November.

Bradley said nothing and breathed in the scent of his clothes for the hundredth time since walking away from Birdie's. The fragrance was starting to fade from his nose, which saddened him, but the shirt was still soft and not stuck to his skin the way his Sublime t-shirt had become a familiar membrane. For the first time in a long time, he felt calm and clear. Unflappable. *A man!* He just had to get through today. The truck to pick up the plants was coming this evening.

"I've been thinking about last night, what you said." Jason lifted his head, an unsteady bobbling motion, a melon impaled on rebar.

"What, are you my girlfriend now?" Bradley said.

"I'm serious, man."

Bradley shuffled through the beer cans. "You gotta clean this up before Dale—"

"I've been thinking about the grave." Jason had caught Bradley's nasty disease, naiveté turned to debilitating overthought. He'd been up all night with it like a fever. "We're in serious shit. Dale might have killed somebody, man."

Bradley looked in the tent for a trash bag. "You ain't working in a daycare."

"But I was thinking this too…been up a while thinking about all this. Maybe Dale didn't kill nobody. I know, I mean, this may sound crazy, but what if he found somebody dead in the woods? What if he just buried somebody?"

"That's the stupidest thing I've ever heard." Bradley turned and looked for Dale over his shoulder. He handed Jason a bag, then started surveying the site for the minutia of their previous few months— wrappers, cigarette butts, chicken bones. They would be gone tomorrow. Tomorrow.

"He finds a body, and he buries it," Jason said. He wadded up the bag and threw it under the chair.

"Why would he just bury a body?"

"Gotta keep the heat off us," Jason said.

Bradley grabbed the garbage bag and slapped it on Jason's chest.

"It was on *48 Hours!*" Jason said. "Mexican cartels! They gonna do a big deal…they want the police off their asses…so what they do? They throw a body on the rival cartel's turf. Police go running toward the dead body, taking the heat off them…rivals all get in trouble. It's win-win."

"Unless you're the dead guy."

Jason kicked at a can on the ground. "Jesus, when's the last time you watched TV? TV's how I know things. Mark my words..." he slurred. "Rival cartel."

"This is not a cartel!"

"Somebody dumps a body here. Dale hides it before nobody can see it." He slapped his leg. "Make sense. Dog shits in your yard, you clean it up. Even if it ain't your dog."

It was crazy, but Bradley couldn't help but think of the dead hogs Dale made him get rid of just because he didn't want them drawing attention. He thought of Dale hovering around the woods, away from the garden, the day after the dead man appeared. Was it possible?

Bradley poured a cup of water out of the cooler and handed it to Jason. "It's gonna be hot today. You gonna get sick."

"Dale can do whatever he wants." Jason took a half-hearted sip of the water. "Shit, you give me fifty thousand dollars, I ain't never gonna say a word about nothin'...I'll forget your name entirely. For seventy-five thousand, I'll forget you and everybody you ever know. I don't know nobody. For a hunnard..." Jason continued to name his price and things he'd forget in impressively accurate twenty-five-thousand-dollar increments, until he passed out with his head tilted back and mouth open. The water cup fell from his hands onto the ground, while Bradley set to work alone cutting the last several dozen plants and counted the minutes until the deal was to be done. Some of the plants were almost six feet tall, their stalks an inch or so thick. Some of them required wood saws if the branch cutters got stuck and couldn't be twisted free. His blisters from yesterday were still raw and threatened to break open. Bradley sweated through Van's tight flannel shirt, but he didn't mind because the smell of raspberries floated around him like a cloud all over again.

⁛⁖⁘⁙⁖⁖⁘⁖

"Why's that truck still around?"

Bradley hadn't heard Dale coming up behind them. Dale stormed over to Jason and stood over him, still passed out drunk in the camp chair an hour later. "Get up," he yelled, and yanked Jason by the shirt. Jason's eyes got wide; he was confused and wobbly. He stumbled forward and ripped away from Dale.

"That truck! Why's it still here?"

"I drove it," Jason said.

"I said to get it away from here."

"I didn't have a ride. I've been keeping it off the main roads."

"Get it away from here! Get Bradley to drive you! I know you ain't that stupid." Dale looked at all the cans, and the whites of his eyes flashed. "Why you hammered in the day, boy?"

"I ain't nothin…" Jason tried to walk off but stumbled a bit.

Dale kicked the pile of cans at Jason, a blue one flying up and hitting him in the leg. "You are lit! Tonight, Jason, *tonight*. Look at all we gotta do. No time for this!" Dale looked sick and ghostly, paler than normal.

Jason grabbed some cutters and ignored Dale entirely.

"You know what? Get outta here!" Dale ripped the cutters from Jason's hands. "You can't be here like this. We can't do crazy. Get that truck away from here! Now!"

Bradley imagined Jason speeding drunk down the highway in a truck with no plates. Nothing to stop to him from telling a patrolman everything.

"When you want me back?" Jason said.

"I don't! I don't want you back! You ain't gonna be here tonight, boy. Just gonna be Bradley helping load. Fewer the better anyway." Jason looked like he'd been punched in the face, but Dale kept talking. "You're gonna get paid, so what you care? Get outta here."

Jason shook his head, as if waking up all of a sudden. He pointed at Dale. "You ain't gonna pay me. You lie. You're a liar."

Don't, Jason.

"I'm paying you, boy," Dale said. "But you need to go right now. Can't have this shit."

"I saw what you did back there, Dale," Jason said.

Don't say it. Please don't. Bradley braced. *Don't taunt him.*

"Leave now," Dale said. He turned and walked toward the plants.

Jason paused—and for a moment, Bradley thought he was going to leave—but then, Jason turned slowly and charged at Dale, knocking him hard to the ground. Dale scrambled from underneath him and hurled himself on top of Jason, then straddled him. He pinned him beneath his legs, fists to his face. Jason tried to fight but couldn't swing his arms.

You're so much stronger than him, Jason. What are you doing? Fight him! Fight!

Dale threw blow after blow, wrecking ball fists on long, thin arms. Jason floundered underneath him, choking. He was starting to go limp, starting to go silent, the drunkenness overtaking him like a drowning man. He wasn't fighting back. But Dale didn't stop.

"Dale!" Bradley leaped and grabbed the back of Dale's shirt with two hands, yanking him off of Jason. Dale stumbled back into the dirt and wiped his face. Bradley knelt over Jason. He was barely moving.

"Jason…" Bradley wriggled Jason's chin back and forth. "Jason!"

Dale mumbled something and tried to sit up, but then collapsed back onto the ground.

Jason popped up like a stunned animal. He shook his head, eyes disoriented and wild. His face was badly bloodied, his already-swollen nose starting to swell even more. A streak of red on his hairline turned his blond hair brassy. He turned and spit a mouthful of blood, then pulled up onto his knees and vomited. Bradley jumped back, suddenly protective of his clothes. Jason scrambled to his feet and pushed past Dale, who grabbed at him again, but Jason ripped free.

"Get out of here!" Dale called.

Then Jason screamed the thing that Bradley had been thinking for the past two days, a full-throated roar perfected only by certain young men. "We didn't sign up for this shit! This ain't what you said! This ain't what you said, Dale!"

In a few minutes, they heard the sound of wheels spinning off into the woods, and Bradley realized then that they were all probably going to prison if they survived the night. But when he looked at Dale, he was just unwrapping a Moon Pie, pale and sweaty, shaking his head, saying to nobody in particular, "Boy gettin' paid. Boy gettin' paid."

CHAPTER TWENTY-EIGHT

T o talk to Gabby was to be born again. To talk to Gabby was to have the Baptist preacher dump Mayhill in a plastic kiddy pool and proclaim his sins forgiven! To talk to Gabby was to understand how all these people got hot and bothered about Jesus and his whole sin-forgiveness racket. A man goes around feeling terrible about something, his whole life drowning in gas station beer and contrition, and with a touch of Jesus's proverbial cloak (or in Gabby's case, a vision-inducing polo shirt), ye are born anew! *Me? Yes, ye!* Weights lifted, chains cast off and whatnot. Randy Mayhill felt light. He felt clear. His pants were comfortably snug, flexible in the knee but supportive in the crotch. He felt downright religious, eyes alight, and saw the possibility in the world for the first time in years. Grace was real! Justice was real! (And just when he was beginning to doubt Its existence!) With a new faith in himself, Randy Mayhill knew the only logical next step.

Dale had to die.

Now, this may seem extreme, because everything about Randy Mayhill seemed extreme, but he had always had the suspicion that Dale had to die, the way he secretly knew that billboard lawyers and dog molesters had to die. It wasn't that their existences had been mistakes from the beginning or that they should never have shot screaming into the world to begin with. It was that a wrong turn had been made along the way, and the road back was impassable, washed out by floods, blocked by fallen trees, an army of hogs waiting to devour.

This was not a matter of revenge. Sure, Dale had killed Van and Tommy Jones (for reasons he could only guess) and he had taken advantage of Birdie's land—and Bradley, for that matter—but, no, it was not revenge. Revenge was for scorned ex-wives and small-town football teams. This was of greater consequence. This was karma. Wasn't it karma? A Hindu principle, if he recalled correctly—a lovely law of cause and effect that Randy Mayhill espoused every moment of his life even if he was not Indian. The Christians had it too. Eye for an eye and whatnot.

Mayhill knew how it would play out. Dale would sell all of the weed to some drug kingpin who leached off the rural folk like everyone else in the country; he would take the money, maybe giving Bradley whatever money he promised, maybe not, and then he would split town and leave his little trailer (and dog too, probably!) abandoned like all the other abandoned houses in the country. Nobody would miss him. Nobody would care. No justice would be done. Flash forward six months later, and Mayhill's and Birdie's lives would not have changed, and Dale—all teeth and neck tendons—would be parasailing in the Mayan Riviera.

Mayhill could call the law, and he considered this option—he considered it seriously, he did. He considered it in earnest for almost five minutes. Had Randy Mayhill not devoted his entire life to the criminal justice system? Had he not graduated from Sam Houston State with a master's—a *master's!*—in criminology and written a thesis entitled *Reform: A Modern Folly?* He had indeed (A+ for research, a troubled look from the professor) but then he thought of New Sheriff. Him rolling up in the squad truck, attached to an oxygen tank like a hobo on the Hindenburg, breathing in Mayhill's victory even if he could not form a singular breath on his own. It made his knee ache.

Mayhill was pretty sure he knew where the garden plot was, but he would have to confront Dale, and how might this go? Dale was paranoid and likely to shoot back—a dead Tommy Jones on a fence, case in point—and Mayhill was honest enough with himself that his size had become a problem. There would be no skulking, no sneaking, no spry surprise attacks at six foot five. Even with crouched posture, Mayhill clocked in at six foot three. There were no linebacker ninjas.

Or he could wait at Dale's trailer. Confront him head on, remind him of his crime—"Hey! This is for Van!" *Kapow!*—shoot him then and there. But Dale was probably quick, much quicker than him. He considered just standing at a distance and ambushing him in the night when he slinked out to his truck, but the idea of a surprise attack also seemed sneaky and cowardly—something Dale would do. Is that what Dale had done to Van? Snuck up on him in the woods? He couldn't imagine Dale doing anything so labor intensive.

An entire CBS mini-series of scenarios played out in his head, assassination attempts from the simplest (sniper drive-by) to the most complex (Rube Goldberg machines, infinite knives) and Mayhill twitched as he thought about it.

He chose a gun from the safe closest to the bed, and he placed a target on a large live oak twice as wide as him. Then realizing his mistake, he removed the target and placed it on a young post oak, skinny and gaunt like Dale, and spent the entire morning at target practice.

He would go tonight. Each time he pulled the trigger, he thought of Van and that his entire life had prepared him for what he was about to do.

CHAPTER TWENTY-NINE

O n Saturday evening around sundown, Mayhill drove up to Birdie and Onie's. Onie was working in her garden, and mosquitos swarmed in a cloud around her. Onie saw him and wiped the dirt off of her hands, then held up a zucchini the size of a child's leg.

"Can you believe it?" She cheered as if they had been in the middle of a conversation, him right beside her the entire time. She waved the zucchini back and forth like a club. He realized this was the first time he had seen her away from the television since Van died. Maybe she was having a good day.

The two of them walked inside, and though nobody was there, the TV blared a new evening episode of *Wheel of Fortune*. Onie plopped the zucchini on the counter and paused to watch the final puzzle as if it were breaking news.

"Let's see it!" A human and slightly-staticky Pat Sajak wound his finger in the air and pitched it to the three blanked-out words on the puzzle board. "Go. Hog. Wild." And in an instant, an elfin-looking woman in a purple dress was twenty thousand dollars richer. The television audience went crazy, and Onie smiled.

"Very appropriate," Mayhill said. "I guess Birdie is out. I was hoping to talk with her."

I was hoping to beg her forgiveness.

"We don't need anything," Onie said. The words sounded harsh despite her smile.

"That's what I hear," Mayhill said. "Where's Birdie?" Her truck was still at the house, the door to her room open.

"She said she'd be back tonight."

"Tonight? But she didn't drive." He looked out the window at her truck and tried to swallow his concern. "Did someone pick her up?"

"I don't think so," Onie said.

Mayhill bristled at the thought of her walking the land alone. He bristled that Onie didn't know exactly where she was. Perhaps she was mistaken. He tried not to think about her out there, though every instinct in him was to find Birdie right then, to protect her from Dale or Bradley or hitmen or whatever else lurked like a disease among the loblollies.

Had all of this taught him nothing? Still the thought nestled in the back of his mind. Surely, she hadn't gone into the woods. She wouldn't be so stupid, not with the possibility of what was out there.

Onie washed her hands in the sink, got two cream-colored teacups from the cabinet, and then heated up the teakettle even though it was a hundred degrees outside. Mayhill walked around the barn and looked at the place, how bare it seemed without Van, without Birdie. A big brown couch much too nice for the space, the piano too nice for the space, a breakfast table in the corner that he placed his hat upon. The house was small but his boots echoed as if he were in a cavernous museum.

"You're a good man, Randall." Onie leaned against the sink and watched him while the water heated. "We're lucky to have you."

Randy turned to look at her. He felt unexpectedly choked up, a lump in his throat. "I don't know if—"

"Shhh…" She scrunched her face and held her finger to her mouth. "Van wouldn't shut up either." Onie looked beautiful in the way that an old tree looked beautiful. Her face reminded him of tree bark, carved in cross-hatch lines. She turned off the stove and poured the water. Onie walked into the living room and handed him a cup.

"Awww, no, thank you, Onie. Hot as hell."

But she pushed the cup into his hand. He took the tea and blew across the top.

Onie plopped down in her recliner. Van's recliner was empty next to hers but he couldn't bring himself to sit. "We weren't always a good family," she said. "I think that's why we latched onto you. You were always good. Always a good man."

"You latched onto me, Onie?" Mayhill's throat caught at the thought of anyone latching onto him. He bobbed the tea bag in the water and looked again out the window, unable to meet her gaze. He didn't know why she was saying these things. "Onie, please stop. Please, really. Stop."

She looked up at him all twinkle-eyed—delighted in his discomfort, it seemed. She always looked at him with impossible love, as if he were a man who didn't have to earn it. It made him tense.

Mayhill kept quiet and walked around the house. He looked at the books on the living room shelf. Emerson, Hurston, O'Connor, a condensed encyclopedia that he, too, had been suckered into buying just because the salesman had made the Odyssean-like effort of finding them in the middle of nowhere. He put his teacup on the shelf and thumbed through the O'Connor. Flannery's face had the same delight and deviousness that Onie's had before Van died.

"A good man is hard to find." Onie nodded to the book in his hand and winked at him. Definitely a good day.

"I miss Van," Mayhill said to change the subject. It was the first time he had ever said it.

Onie didn't respond to this—just drank her tea—and he was glad because he regretted the words coming out of his mouth. He wasn't allowed to grieve in front of her because her loss had been so tremendous that his barely counted. She loved Van more than anyone.

He put Flannery back on the shelf. "Birdie hates me."

"Well, there's only ever one satisfactory conclusion for a hero," Onie said. Another odd thing to say. True, of course, but odd. "Even Jesus didn't try to save people the way you do."

"I heard he saved all of humanity."

"Where'd you hear that?" Onie asked.

"I get all my gossip from Patsy Fuller." He looked out the window at the hummingbirds drinking at the feeder. He needed something from Onie but didn't know what. "Patsy Fuller said Van was in hell."

"Maybe so," Onie said.

He spun on his heel and looked at her. "Onie, you don't really think—"

"The kingdom of God is a hand!" She held out her right hand, thin skin with liver spots like camouflage, and flipped it back and forth. "Heaven looks terrible."

"You're losing your mind, Onie."

"Now that is heaven."

Silence. She stabbed her tea bag at the cup. Maybe she was depressed, but her mind was still good.

"Why'd you say that wasn't my dog?" Mayhill asked. He picked up his hat to leave, but Onie just looked at him blankly. "Yesterday," Mayhill said. "I had my dachshund here. You said he wasn't my dog. Little long-haired thing."

Onie's gaze was on the television again, and she rocked back and forth in the recliner. "Is it your dog?"

"Yes," Mayhill said. He looked her right in the forehead.

"Then why give credence to what an old lady says?"

Randy smirked and turned again to watch the hummingbirds. Two of them moving a mile a minute just to stay in one place.

"Birdie thinks I'm going crazy," she said.

"After Van…you just got so quiet."

"A person gets quiet," Onie said, "and everybody thinks they're nuts."

"But you've never been quiet."

"I've never been nuts either."

Mayhill cocked his head and smirked.

Onie wagged an excited finger at him. "Awwww, Randall." She chuckled with an affection that stole his breath. "I knew you wouldn't buy that one."

CHAPTER THIRTY

Of course Onie had been right about the dog, and this was disconcerting.

It had all begun with the police scanner. In most households, personal police scanners had gone the way of rotary phones and young people making eye contact, but in many households, they were as much a fixture as the television. After Van died, Mayhill sometimes felt as if the scanner was talking directly to him. He had always felt that way even when he was a boy, when he listened to the scanner the way his parents had listened to Hank Williams, for inspiration and meaning.

At one point, though, the scanner had been talking to him. He had been the sheriff, and it had told him all he needed to know about his domain—all of the misery of the past perfect tense. It had alerted him to house fires, domestic disturbances, suspected meth labs, child neglect, and loose cows. Cows on the loose made up half of the work of his patrolmen. A Houston deputy had inquired about the percentage of Mayhill's cow-related work, and the deputy had laughed at the answer, but Mayhill, for once, was not defensive. Until that deputy had helped lift a dead, bloated cow off of a dark highway, cars swerving to miss it, the man had no room to talk. They could keep their crack houses and sex crimes, which Mayhill got to enjoy on top of dead cows too, thank you very much.

After he lost it all, Mayhill spent a good few months moping. He thought of what jobs he might be qualified for, but Sam's Club Security Specialist was as long as the list got. During those months, he silenced the scanner and refused to listen to it—defiantly—the way one might burn his ex-wife's records, the song they first danced to. He couldn't bring himself to turn it on. Then, one night, when he was giving up booze for Dr Peppers and eating frozen pizzas every night, in a haze of what-if insomnia, he reached out like the Creation of Adam, with a single finger, and pressed the flat, beige button. A galaxy of problems crackled through his house again, and his whole world opened up. He was no longer confined to the unsolvable mess of his own problems. He could again tackle the problems of other people, which, for some reason, were so much more solvable and the answers so much more obvious than his own. For the first time since he handed over his gold star like a hangdog schoolboy, he felt like he could breathe again. He felt that there was finally, finally some goddamn possibility!

Lucky for Mayhill, and unlucky for everyone else, that particular night was brutal, one of those nights in which the stars aligned in the shape of a dazzling pile of shit for everyone underneath them. There was a big fire out toward Mitday (possibly arson), and on the other side of the county, there were—count 'em!—three drunk drivers at the county line. A party out of control (strippers, homemade explosives).

Near the dump, somebody had reported a cow loose on the highway, and Mayhill knew then that nobody would be dispatched for a loose cow, not on a night like that.

He put on his jeans, which did not offer the comfort they had months before, and slipped into his truck and drove into the night. He wouldn't find anything. He often didn't on these calls, but they had to be checked.

It was out by the dump, and despite the chaos, it was a glorious night—beautiful, cool—and he rolled down the windows and let the wind blow in, even with the charred remains of people's lives hanging in the air. He passed a bunch of hogs, their eyes glinting in his headlights. He drove a few roads and when he pulled onto the main highway, his headlights fell on a big white mound, like a pile of sand in the night. It was a cow, dead in the ditch, stiff-legged and peaceful, and thankfully off the road. Mayhill was disappointed for the cow's death and his continued uselessness, but the outcome was not unexpected. At least no humans had been hurt.

When he turned to drive back, he saw a pair of eyes flash in the dark. The reflective eyes of an animal. Then, his headlights caught a little dog, a dachshund, emerging from the ditch. He recognized the dog immediately as the dump dog that belonged to Patsy Fuller. Despite living out his days at the dump in piles of scraps, the dog appeared underweight—unlike Patsy Fuller, he noted—his little ribs showing more than Mayhill liked, his deep brown fur slightly gray from the ash. He was not an abused dog. He was taken care of just fine, but he was not a celebrated dog, and a dog was meant to be celebrated, with padding on his bones.

Mayhill knew that the right thing to do was to drive that dog right back to the dump and drop him off at the Fullers' front steps because this dog, treated decently enough, should return to his rightful owner because that was the law. Still, seeing Pat Sajak looking like hell, he began to consider that he didn't need rules to be the hero he knew he could be. He could judge the world by his own compass and what it needed. Mayhill opened the door to his truck and held out a piece of beef jerky. *Lord, forgive me for what I am about to do.*

Back at his house, after talking with Onie, Mayhill stir-fried some pan sausage and mixed it with dry dog food from a high-dollar Houston pet store populated exclusively by homosexuals. He poured the greasy concoction into the china bowl his mother had served Thanksgiving mashed potatoes in. His own mouth watered at the memory. He settled his large body into the leather armchair, bowl in lap, then double-patted his large legs, and an expectant Pat Sajak popped onto his lap and put his head in the bowl, which Mayhill secured with one hand to prevent it from crashing to the floor.

Mayhill chuckled and patted his back while he ate, the sun going down slowly. When the feast was done and night fully-baked and black, Mayhill and Pat Sajak loaded into the truck and the dog snuggled into his old matted towel for a sleepy ride.

The dump looked astonishing at night. Islands of red embers covering an area the size of a football field, an occasional low blue flame feathering out of the ground. The Fullers' house had a single porch light on, an anemic flickering yellow.

He rolled up the window to keep the low, lingering smell of a barbecued world from getting in the truck, and felt the shock of regret at this being anyone's home. Mayhill cut the engine and Virgil was already standing outside, using the excuse of a visitor to light a cigarette. Even in the dark, Mayhill could see Virgil's face was still dirty from the day. Virgil worked harder than anyone he knew, and all he had was Patsy and chronic bronchitis to show for it.

Mayhill got out of the truck and shook Virgil's hand. "I figured you had enough smoke, Virgil."

Virgil laughed and took a drag. "You out late. What can I do for you?"

Mayhill walked around to the passenger's side of the truck and opened the door. Pat Sajak jumped out and sniffed a frantic and invisible trail, zigzagging his way to Virgil.

"My God! Is that—?" Virgil dropped the cigarette and crouched down to meet the dog. He scratched him frantically, and Pat Sajak turned over to reveal his belly. "Patsy!" Virgil turned and yelled into the house. "Patsy! Get out here!"

Mayhill braced. "Evening, Patsy." She wondered out of the house and looked more tired than he'd ever seen her. In the porch light, she appeared wounded and battered, much smaller than her bark.

"Leroy!" she squealed. "Is that you?" She picked the dog up in her arms and his long body squirmed excitedly. "You've gotten fat! You're a fat little piggy!" For a moment, Mayhill could see a shadow of who Patsy had been in her teens. Severe and intense, always, but without the bite—her features had been filed down. Without the years of worry about money. Without the decade of being spit on as a guard at the prison because that was the only job she could find around here. Without the years of worry that her husband would blow up in Afghanistan.

"Where'd you find him?"

He couldn't look at her, but watched the embers burn off to the side.

"Patsy, I'm embarrassed to say I found him a while back on the road out there. Didn't put together he was yours until you said something the other day."

Virgil kept his eyes on Mayhill, a tired smile, an exhale of smoke cloaking him like a magic trick. He knew.

"Found him a while back...put it together," Patsy repeated. She squatted down to scratch Leroy's back. "Guess you ain't too stupid after all!"

Mayhill nodded, oddly moved by what was meant to be Patsy's rare attempt at a compliment.

"Stay for a beer, Sheriff?" Virgil asked. "You a hero around here now. Heroes drink free!"

"Nah," Mayhill said. He shook Virgil's hand again. "Got some place to be. Y'all have a good night."

They petted Pat Sajak like a soldier come home, and Mayhill was glad for it, but he rushed to his truck as a wave of sentimentality threatened to overcome him like stomach flu. As he retreated quickly into the dark, Patsy yelled after him. "He's almost as fat as you!"

"Thank you for noticing, Patsy!" he yelled out the window.

"His Aikman jersey ain't even gonna fit now!"

"Good!" Mayhill yelled as the reflection in his rearview mirror filled with embers like rubies.

CHAPTER
THIRTY-ONE

The second time Birdie saw Tommy Jones:

At the beginning of August 1995, a few weeks before Van died, Birdie worked on supper (greens, bacon) while Van slept in his new leather recliner. Onie was in the garden watering the squash when the phone rang.

Birdie answered and then handed the phone to Van.

"Aight," Van said, deflated. "Be there in a few."

"Where you going?" Birdie asked.

"Gotta pull somebody out. Stuck behind Earl Martin's house."

"Who is it?"

"You don't know him." Van moved slowly out of the chair. His normal, bouncing energy had been replaced with a lethargy that made her ache. He grabbed his keys off the counter.

"Well, who called you?" Birdie asked.

"Dale."

"Dale got stuck?"

"No," he said.

"Who, then?"

"Some trapper."

"Why won't you tell me?"

"You don't know him!" Van said. "Not a secret."

"Can I come?"

"You don't need to come," Van said.

"Why not?"

"He's not a man for you to meet."

"What's that mean?"

"Jesus, Birdie!" Van slammed his hand on the counter. Birdie jolted and looked out the window. He lowered his voice. "Why you care so much? Just somebody stuck in the mud. I'm gonna go pull him out. Dale doesn't have the chains."

She didn't say it, but they both knew why she cared so much. Van had been short and distant lately and regularly fell asleep in the recliner before the Ken dolls of the ten o'clock news came on. She had barely seen him the past few months since his trees all went and died.

"Come with me," Van said.

She ignored him and stirred the simmering pot. She knew her father hated nothing more than to be ignored. It was the greatest transgression against another human. She guessed this was why he gave too much attention to everyone he met, no matter how little they affected his life.

"Come on," Van said, louder this time. "Don't be like that."

She watched the bubbles of the boiling water roll to the surface and pop, and she thought about keeping her silence going. She could ignore him more and punish him infinitely for his recent neglect, but more than that, she wanted to spend time with him again.

"Aight," he said loudly. "I'm leaving now. I'm opening the door. I'm walking out the door."

With that, Birdie quickly turned off the burner and trotted out behind him.

Van's truck had always been impossibly clean, especially for a man who worked in the woods, the leather seats sometimes so slick with Armor All that Birdie would slide a good half foot forward anytime he braked. Now his truck was dirty. The inside was covered with mud and grime and an entirely different set of tools than she was used to seeing. Where there usually was a rope and measuring tape, there were giant branch clippers and a few different sizes of gardening shears. A shotgun lay on the backseat next to a thin phonebook inexplicably covered with silver duct tape.

She moved a dirty pair of gardening clippers from the passenger's seat and squeezed the handles open and closed, which made a piercing squeak over and over and over until Van said, "That's annoying as hell." She opened the glove box to put them away, but the glove box was packed with stacks of paper and his little .357 revolver on top. She squeaked it one more time out of obligatory rebellion, and then begrudgingly placed the clippers on the floorboard.

"How's school?" Van asked.

"How's school?"

"Yeah, how's school!" Van said. "What's wrong with that? What's wrong with asking about school?"

"It's boring."

"School?" Van asked.

"The question!" Birdie said. "Well, and school too."

Van smiled and pointed to an old oak that had been struck by lightning out in the pasture. "Storm got it good." It was split right down the middle, a jagged black scar slicing down the trunk. "How's English? What you reading?"

"Thoreau," Birdie said. "So that's good."

"Onie helping you?"

"Helping me with what? I can read."

"Thoreau's her favorite," Van said.

"Thoreau's everybody's favorite."

"True." He nodded. His face looked tired. Everything about him looked tired. He had lost weight and his cheeks had become sunken and looked more and more like Dale than himself. He had lost all his verve, just like his trees had lost theirs. "You know his mother brought him donuts every Sunday?" Van kept his eyes on the road.

"Whose mother?"

"Thoreau's."

"She did not!" Birdie said. They hit a bump, and she bounced hard off the seat, then grabbed the handle above the passenger window.

"She did!" A hint of animation came back to his face, obviously pleased that he had told her something she didn't know. He drummed on the steering wheel. "That right there is why Onie was the best English teacher."

"Because she crushes your idols?"

"How is that crushing your idols?"

"It's hardly living deliberately if you're sucking down a jelly roll your mommy brought you every week."

"How is it not?" Van looked at her, baffled. A hint defensive too.

"Live your ideals and whatnot, but take the help when it comes along. You gotta grab at your opportunities!"

"A donut is not an opportunity!"

"Who says?" Van shouted.

"I say!"

Van smiled, forever impressed by her feistiness. "Who's teaching English this year?"

"Meyer." She gripped the handle tighter at another bump and cocked her head to prevent a concussion.

"And he's coaching football too?" Van asked.

"He calls him H.D. Thorough," Birdie said.

"And he ain't jokin', is he?"

"He ain't jokin.'"

Van shook his head. Birdie shook hers too. A joint lamentation of all the poor rural kids deprived of Transcendentalism during football season. This exchange seemed to restore the normalcy between them, and they rode in silence on the roller coaster of the back roads until they came across a small black Datsun stuck in the ditch at a sharp turn in the road in a part of the woods Birdie had rarely seen. Dale's truck was parked on the road behind it, and Dale and another man sat on the tailgate. The dark-haired man she had seen before with Bradley. The one Bradley worried was taking his work.

Van hooked the chains to the back of the man's truck. He slid some two-by-fours underneath the tires. Van gassed his truck, while Dale and the other man pushed the little Datsun backward until it emerged from the mud.

It was one of the few times she had seen Dale exert physical effort, and the hog trapper, though obviously a product of the country with his hat and boots, did not acknowledge her presence like most gentlemen did. He did not stick out his hand or take off his hat. He barely made eye contact, an oddity given the over-politeness of country men toward women of any age, especially given that her daddy had just pulled him out of a ditch.

"What's wrong with that man?" Birdie asked when they both got back in the truck.

"I dunno. He's friends with Dale?" he said. "Why I didn't want you to come."

"You shoulda stopped me."

Van raised his eyebrows.

She smiled and looked out the window. She was struck by the brassiness of the dead trees. They were so red against the green ones they appeared to be on fire. Their land had turned to hell.

"That was the man Bradley and I saw you with the other day," Birdie said. "Bradley thought you were mad at him since you didn't let him work."

"You and Bradley got a thing going?"

Birdie looked at him aghast.

"What? You could do worse than him. Hard worker, nice boy… real nice boy."

"Dad, no…we're not…no…" She shook her head and willed the blood to go back into her face. "But you're not gonna fire him, right?"

"Why would I do that?"

"You didn't want Bradley coming along the other day. Just thought maybe—"

"I would never fire him."

"Then what's Dale and that other guy doing that Bradley can't?"

Van didn't answer. They rode in silence until Van, as if he still had a conversation going on in his head, said, "A man like that is too desperate for money." But Birdie didn't know if he was talking about Bradley or the other men.

When they got back to the house, Birdie finished supper while Van tinkered in the shed.

"Where'd y'all go?" Onie asked.

"Helped Dale pull some guy out of the mud." The steam off the greens stung Birdie's face.

Onie shook her head, a shock of concern coming over her. "Black truck?"

"Yes."

"Your daddy trusts too many people," Onie said.

"What's that mean?"

"What I said."

"Who is he?" Birdie asked.

"His name is Tommy Jones, if you must know," Onie said, but Birdie would not remember this.

⠃⠂⠄⠒⠂⠄⠒⠂⠄⠒⠂

The morning that Van would die, around the time that the game warden asked Randy Mayhill for his badge, Birdie rushed to her truck to leave for school. She was late for the twenty-minute drive into town, but she had *Walden* in her bag and a biscuit so hot in her hand that she had to wrap it in a paper towel. The butter had bled through the towel and was dripping in a golden river down her wrist. Van scuttled out behind her, also late, and also with a biscuit in his mouth.

"Van!" Onie shouted at him from the garden.

Birdie remembered the moment vividly now, another memory shaken loose, more details coming into focus. She watched from the truck.

Onie was on her knees, a trowel in her hand, and she clawed at the dirt like it had wronged her. She looked dramatic, as if in a movie. "As God is my witness…" all Scarlett O'Hara and whatnot. "Van!"

"I got men waiting on me!" Van yelled back. He waved the biscuit out his truck window. "Home tonight!"

Onie sat in the dirt and watched her son drive off, a black Datsun waiting at the end of the driveway, following Van to work for the day.

CHAPTER THIRTY-TWO

G abby Grayson had called Mayhill superstitious once. When they had worked together, she had read him the *Houston Post*'s horoscope every morning while they drank their first cup of coffee, and to this day, when he drank coffee, he had the undeniable feeling that something was missing—like drinking it black when you're used to having it with cream. He was missing someone to tell him how his day was going to go.

"Libra. Oooooh…you'll be lucky in love, Sheriff!" Gabby had cheered.

Mayhill would avoid her eyes completely and will the red that snaked his neck like a noose to fade.

"Aquarius," Gabby read on. "Ugh! You'll make sound decisions? Tell that to the divorce lawyer! Ha! Let's trade, Randy!" She put down the newspaper, her lipstick leaving a mark on the cup the color of a crabapple.

Now, Mayhill's superstition was alive and well as he picked out his outfit for his reckoning with Dale. Three days ago, four buzzards had brought him luck. He had known it when he saw them. What was the statute of limitations on buzzard luck? Was he still operating under their goodwill? Had Dale seen the buzzards too? If so, how exactly did that work?

His jeans from three days ago had not been washed—in fact, he'd worn them the entire three days, they were that comfortable—so they would offer looseness and flexibility, but they were also smeared with Kool-Aid and hog's blood, the pink note still tucked in his back pocket. Still, he decided that the litheness of his broken-in jeans would be an asset tonight should he have to run. He was slow enough as it was, and he needed every advantage. He would wear the shirt from last night—now forever marked as a relic of luck—because Gabby Grayson had held his hand. He wrapped his knee tightly in an ACE Bandage.

Another game-time choice: he decided to wear a bulletproof vest. The vest had stood stiffly in his closet like a decapitated torso, and he knew he should return it to the sheriff's office since it was technically county property, but the county never asked for it, so he never felt inclined to return it. He had packed it up with his pictures and maps. The irony was not lost on him: a vest given to protect him though he had never fired a shot or dodged anything but the occasional spit. It had been an entirely useless garment.

The vest was gray and of medium thickness. He took it off the hanger and worked his thick arms into the holes. It didn't fit, the vest meant for a leaner male specimen, so he inhaled and fastened the zipper underneath his gut. The zipper would latch, but it would not zip up more than a few tortured inches, so the front flaps of the vest flopped open like pages of a book, functioning like a visual runway to guide any future bullets safely into his heart. But his back would be safe and so were parts of his sides. It was something.

He opened the gun safe. He needed a lucky one, and this was easy, his own .357, the same one Dale had used on Van, and so it made sense to him. It was poetic. He slid it into the holster on his belt. An energy was in the air, and Mayhill shifted from foot to foot, antsy. The dogs picked up on it too, seemingly unable to get comfortable. Much circling, much circling. Much repositioning as dogs do, only to get up and circle again. It wasn't even a full moon, yet the hairs on the back of his neck stood pole-straight.

He felt the definitive presence of someone else in the house, to the point that he quickly turned on all the lights and checked the rooms. No one was there. *No one is there, Randy!* But he couldn't shake the feeling that the house felt claustrophobically small all of a sudden, as if it were packed with people, packed with a past.

"Birdie?" he said, a quiet voice coming from him. "Bradley?"

He stuck his head outside and looked at the trap (empty). Off the porch, deep in the dark, he saw a few hogs, and so he waved his hat to scatter them away. Then he closed the gate to the trap because he didn't want to bother with it. Lord knew he didn't need the meat. "Hello? Birdie?" He wondered if Birdie was back at the house with Onie yet. He walked to the kitchen and picked up the phone to call Onie, but then put the handset back on the receiver.

He patted his dogs goodbye and took a quick look in the mirror, his eye puffy and black but healing nicely, and stepped out into the night.

Mayhill pulled his truck into the ditch and cut his headlights about a quarter mile from Dale's trailer. He had driven slowly so that his truck made as little noise as possible, no scraping potholes to give him away before he even had his chance. When he got out, he held the door firmly and pressed it closed until he could hear it latch, and even that sent a crack of sound through the woods he was certain would alert Dale to his presence.

He clenched his gun and walked slowly down the road to Dale's until he saw the trailer's dim yellow lights sparkle through the pines. He steadied his breath. Mayhill stayed near the tree line and walked quickly across Dale's excuse of a lawn, and then turned abruptly, gun drawn, and stood with his back against Dale's trailer. Mayhill crouched down as he skulked around the edge, as if Dale might jump from behind the pokeweed.

Dale's dog trotted up to him, and anger welled up in Mayhill again. Skinny dog out at night. The poor dog would get killed sooner or later. Mayhill had prepared for the dog because God is always in the details, and Mayhill was downright holy in this regard. He pulled a few strips of jerky out of his pocket, and the dog gobbled them up and licked Mayhill's hand. "Stay," Mayhill whispered. He scratched him behind his white ears and then side-stepped to the front of the trailer.

Dale's truck was not there.

But this didn't mean anything necessarily. Their operation was near here, he was sure. Perhaps the truck was parked there. Perhaps Bradley had it.

The plan was simple: Mayhill would knock, and then he would shoot. Knock and shoot. Knock-shoot. Knock-shoot. It echoed like a mantra in his head. Mayhill wouldn't touch anything. He'd drive away slowly and calmly into the night, no doubt taking Dale's dog with him. No one would ever know.

He held his gun firmly and walked up the concrete stairs, which Mayhill was thankful didn't squeak like wooden ones. At the door, he turned slightly to the side and stretched out his arms. He inhaled deeply and steadied the gun. Then he knocked loudly on the door with his left hand. Mayhill clenched his jaw.

Lord, please forgive me for what I am about to do.

But nothing happened. Nobody answered. Ten seconds, thirty seconds, forty seconds. Nobody. He leaned his ear close to the door. No shuffling around inside, no footsteps. He looked behind him. Dale's dog watched him from the bottom of the steps.

Mayhill breathed in again and knocked even more loudly again.

Again, nothing. A minute, two minutes. No sound. Then Mayhill turned and looked out at Dale's property and out at the shed behind his house.

"Shit." Mayhill dropped the gun to his side.

It was then that Mayhill heard the low grumble of a truck. He hurried down the stairs and hid in the dark beside Dale's trailer. The dog followed and stood next to him in the dark. Mayhill fed him another piece of meat, anticipating that Dale's truck would turn into the driveway any second. The sound was moving closer, the engine growing louder, but no lights were coming through the trees. He moved to the corner and looked in all directions for the hint of headlights. Surely, the sound was not coming through the thicket. No truck could maneuver back there.

Just then, movement in front of him. Mayhill's eyes struggled to adjust. A black truck, camouflaged entirely, blinking in and out of the trees along the road. Headlights off and going much too slowly, stealthily. Just like Mayhill had moved a short time before.

Mayhill started off toward his truck. The dog trotted behind him.

"Stay," he told Dale's dog. "I'll come back for you." And by the end of the story, Randy Mayhill most certainly would. But the dog looked away as if he didn't believe him.

CHAPTER

THIRTY-THREE

Mayhill again cut off his headlights, this time about a half mile from the trailhead where he had followed the Datsun's tracks through the mud. Really, Mayhill liked this option better, confronting Dale where he had dared to trespass. There was a symmetry to these things, a poetry.

With a black wall of woods to his right and a black wall of woods to his left, he thought of Bradley and what it must have been like to work here in the blackness. Had it been thrilling like this moment, the scorched summer air filling your lungs like water? Or had it been frightening, him forever on edge, like watching a horror movie on repeat?

He stepped through the curtain of the woods. The trees could make you feel claustrophobic, or they could be like a blanket that insulated you from the rest of the world. He understood then how Van might have felt invincible in his woods, where his daddy and granddaddy had worked, that nothing bad could ever happen there, the invisible hand of immortality infusing him with false confidence. Van hadn't been crazy. He had felt too safe.

The forest was inordinately quiet but alive—a sleeping giant pulsing with energy. In the blackness, with the canopy hovering six stories above him, he felt almost as if he were hallucinating. Tree after tree, hypnotic.

—*You're a good man.* Onie's voice bellowed in his head.

—*You treat life like hand-to-hand combat.* Van's voice popped from the thicket.

A chorus of voices in his brain worthy of Macbeth.

"Shut up!" Mayhill whispered.

—*Who's the one going crazy?*

Mayhill stepped quietly through the thicket. He pushed through a lattice of broken branches, edging his belly through, the jagged sticks tearing at his arms and legs. A branch poked him in the back, but through the vest, it felt like a stiff finger.

"What were you thinking, Van?" He had never said the words out loud, though he had thought them a thousand times. He stepped over a large fallen branch. Van had died not too far from here. It was a terrible thought, but instead of spooking him, the idea comforted him somehow. Right then, a bird—an owl maybe—flew overhead and rustled the pine needles. "Goddammit, Van, I'm not falling for your shit."

—*I didn't say anything.*

Mayhill heard movement. Hogs. He approached a small clearing, and the hogs seemed to turn and follow—an organism moving along with him—because animals did that with Mayhill. Still, the blood on his jeans from days before—wouldn't that have repelled them? But the

Kool-Aid! Mayhill had an army, which made him nervous. He worried about drawing extra attention, but perhaps it was genius! The hogs with him, an auditory camouflage. Suddenly apprehensive, he tugged at his vest to close up the gap, the base of the zipper digging hard into his gut.

He kept walking and tried to ignore the feeling, the voices in his head. Perhaps he really was going crazy. Perhaps that's what happened to Van: the kaleidoscope of the woods made him nuts.

Then he heard voices, real ones this time. A few more steps, and he saw the faintest light. A small camping lantern lit the scene in the clearing up ahead. Two chairs. A pop-up tent deflated on the ground, as if it were being packed up. Dale's head. Bradley's head. *Bradley! Alive!* Fifty hogs rooted to the left of him. Mayhill crouched low. He stopped to watch, and he touched his gun.

CHAPTER THIRTY-FOUR

T he deal was to be done at ten p.m. with a guy Dale would only refer to as The Mexican, though his name was Omar and he was white. And Bradley would know such a thing because his neighborhood in Houston had been predominantly Mexican, blooming with *taquerias* and La Michoacanas. Omar was also from Houston but had spent every weekend in Galveston working on his tan, thus Dale's nickname for him.

Omar had come to see the garden a few months before, and Bradley hadn't liked him at first sight (glowing teeth, overly-aggressive walk). He had introduced himself to Dale but not to Bradley, because Bradley, lest we forget, was nobody. Omar was a wannabe gangster not unlike Jason, but unlike Jason, his connections were apparent and went beyond men like Dale. He wore a large gold watch, and the soles of the most recently-released Jordans (1996, Air XI, patent leather) did not flop when he walked, his toes forever dry and shiny. He smelled like cologne.

After the many months of work, all there was to do was to wait in the dark yet again. Bradley had watched plants grow for six months, yet the last day had felt, for reasons obvious to everyone, excruciatingly long. He could hear gunshots in the distance all day. They were hunters, Dale had assured him, though Dale hardly seemed confident either. Bradley had seen Dale throw up twice that afternoon. He had slinked off behind a tree, and Bradley could hear the sickness erupting from him onto the dried leaves. But Dale just wiped his mouth and told Bradley to carry on, the pink bottle now a permanent fixture in his bag. So many things to go wrong. Any moment, the police. Any moment, Jason. Any moment, Birdie. Any moment, what?

Dale, in a surprisingly effective camouflage t-shirt, paced around the stacks, checking the fruits of Bradley's labor, though there was nothing left to do. He was muttering and agitated, the revolutionary before the coup. Bradley smoked a cigarette, slung deep in the camp chair, and watched the moon (waning crescent) and thought of Van. He just wanted to get through the next few hours peacefully, but that was not an option tonight, he knew. There was something in the air.

Dale eventually settled and grabbed a hot beer from his bag crumpled near the stacks. He plopped into the chair next to Bradley.

"Do we gotta worry about Jason tonight?" Dale asked.

"Probably still drunk." Bradley shifted in his chair and forced a small laugh, but neither of them believed it.

"Boy's acting crazy. Why's he freaking out?"

Bradley wanted to say, "You killed a man, Dale." But instead, he said, "Nerves, I guess," and took another drag off of his cigarette.

"You still nervous?" Dale's hands shook violently again—bizarre spasms that made it hard for him to bring the can to his lips. Bradley wondered what was happening to him. He looked at the ground, praying for Omar's truck to roll up.

"Why are you nervous if nobody knows you're here?" Dale asked. Dale watched him closely, his eyes narrowed. But it didn't seem to be a real question. It was as if he already knew something, and he was daring Bradley to say it.

Bradley didn't speak.

"Is it Birdie?" Dale asked.

Bradley dropped the cigarette. He ran through a million scenarios in which Dale could have known he visited Birdie. Maybe he had seen him there. Maybe he had somehow listened with Onie from the porch.

Bradley eyed Dale's bag behind him, the one with the gun.

"You nervous she gonna find out?" Dale asked. "She won't find out, Dale."

Bradley got up and made some space from Dale, all at once feeling trapped in the maze of the stacks. Suddenly, the line of questioning felt like some elaborate setup to test his loyalty, to catch him in a lie, and Bradley failed. Bradley felt himself unraveling, coming unhinged.

Dale got up, and Bradley flinched.

"What is wrong with you?" Dale said, walking closer.

"Nothing," Bradley said. "Nothing." He took a step back. He needed Dale away from him, to end whatever game he was playing. Bradley wanted to run. He wanted to take off through the woods, but Dale would be after him.

"Why you so skittish? I'm handing you a life on a goddamn silver platter," Dale said, "and you two are freaking out on me." Dale moved closer to Bradley again but Bradley spun away from him.

"Jason and me just—" Bradley said.

"What? Jason and you just what? You and Jason too good for this all of a sudden? Is that it?" Dale jabbed him hard in the chest with his finger. "Jason and you what?" He poked him again, then again. Bradley jumped back, but Dale stayed on him, each jab harder, more agitated, Dale's eyes flashing white.

"Y'all should be grateful," Dale said. "Grateful!"

Bradley swiped at Dale's finger. He crushed Dale's hand in his fist and twisted it to his chest. He leaned over Dale, an inch from his face. "Nobody should have died."

It was an accusation Bradley couldn't rewind. And with it, the instant realization he had put himself in danger. He had admitted to knowing about the dead man. Dale could kill him right there.

Dale ripped his hand free.

Bradley was ready to run; he leaned forward, feet planted firmly on the ground, toes clawing the earth, ready to sprint. Dale leaned in so close that Bradley could smell his breath, sweet with sugar but rotten, an acid bubbling up from below, wine-cooler sick. He looked right at him, eyes unblinking. "Who died, Bradley?"

Bradley shook his head and eyed a route through the woods.

Dale squinted at Bradley, searching his face. "Who died, Bradley? I want you to tell me who died."

Bradley could get to Dale's bag first, get to the gun first. But did Dale have one on him?

"I don't—" Bradley said, but he couldn't finish the sentence. He sounded pathetic, his voice a breathy rattle now.

It was then that Dale's face changed from agitation to bewilderment. "It was you," Dale said. "You shot Tommy."

Bradley shook his head, not sure he heard right. More confusion, more head games.

"You boys shot him," Dale said.

That's when Bradley saw it. A shudder. Dale afraid of him. In that moment, Bradley had transformed into someone very different than Dale had thought, a man capable of killing. Bradley opened his mouth to speak but he fumbled. "No, Dale, I thought—" But he stopped himself before he could finish.

"Did Tommy come up here?" Dale asked. "Was he trapping? Was he messing with you? Is that what happened? You panicked?"

Dale watched Bradley closely, his gaze darting around Bradley's face, trying to make meaning of this new revelation. And Bradley, mystified, fell silent, not knowing what to say, what questions to ask, what to defend against, not sure what was happening. But one thing was clear now: Dale had not killed the hunter.

"Is that why Jason's freaked out?" Dale asked.

Bradley nodded carefully. A lie, of course. But was it? Had Jason somehow…? Everything was reordering, and Bradley's thoughts tried to catch up. If Dale hadn't killed the hunter, who?

"I thought someone was messing with me," Dale said. "But you two—"

Dale stared into the night, as if he could see something, and Bradley thought he might be hallucinating. Dale touched his stomach, but after watching him throw up all day, Bradley couldn't imagine what was left in his belly to let go.

"I owed him a lot of money," Dale said.

The extra money.

Bradley looked at the stacks of plants. Less than they thought, the quality worse, yet more money promised. Dale was able to pay more because the hunter was dead. The months of exhaustion, the days of fear, Dale's paranoia, his hatred for Van and Birdie. Something was starting to crystalize in Bradley's head. He walked closer to Dale.

"What did you owe him for?" Bradley asked. Dale didn't say anything and backed away from Bradley. But now Bradley stepped closer, something waking up in him. "Why'd you owe that hunter?"

Van ratted me out.

Mayhill thinks he's a hitman.

Seventy-five thousand dollars.

"Dale, why'd you owe that hunter so much money?" But Bradley already knew the answer. He knew it in his blood, as if Van whispered the secret to him right there in the woods, as he towered over Dale. Dale had hired Tommy Jones to kill Van.

Bradley thought of Birdie and Onie, their broken hearts. He thought of Randy Mayhill, the loyal best friend he wished he had. He thought of Jimmy Nellums telling him that Van had died, a smirk on his face. He thought of what it felt like in his chest that day, unable to breathe, sobbing so hard in the feed store parking lot he couldn't drive. Bradley thought of the gun just a few feet away.

Then another thought: maybe Dale had sent the hunter to take care of Bradley.

Dale opened his mouth to speak, but his words were interrupted by the loud rumble of a truck. A few moments later, headlights shot through the dark, blinding them, and the two men turned away from the light and covered their eyes.

⠲ ⠌ ⠢ ⠡ ⠌ ⠒ ⠲ ⠡

Dale walked into the bright blast of light. His silhouette looked eerie against the blurry white beams, more telephone pole than man, like he was walking into the belly of a spaceship. (And wouldn't Dale be just the type to be beamed up and represent our kind?) But it was not a spaceship. It was an old Mrs. Baird's Bakery delivery truck driven by the very-tan-but-obviously-Caucasian courier named Omar.

The driver cut the lights. Bradley rubbed his eyes and waited for them to adjust. Omar got out. He was shifty-eyed and moved quickly. Dale trailed behind him, right on his heels. Omar inspected the stacks with a flashlight and nodded his head, and Bradley was surprised to find himself desiring Omar's approval at the work they had done. Omar would drive the plants to a Houston warehouse where they would be cut and dried and packaged and distributed, but Bradley didn't like to think about that part, the dozens of other Bradleys—black, brown, short, tall, urban Bradleys—taking it from there.

Bradley helped Dale and the courier load the bushels into the truck. They piled them in tall stacks like bodies, and Bradley was careful not to touch the truck or say his name to Omar, as if he would remember or care about a man like him. Bradley kept counting down the moments.

Just a few more minutes.

Bradley didn't look at Dale, even at the very end when the man handed Dale a red gym bag full of cash, and Dale gasped audibly upon seeing the money. Then, the man got in the truck and drove away.

Just a few more seconds.

Dale walked over to Bradley, chuckling and swinging the red gym bag. He unzipped it slowly to show Bradley, the light from the almost-full moon illuminating it like pirate's gold in a rusty treasure chest. Bradley stopped breathing. There it was—honest-to-God, stamped by the United States Treasury—mounds upon mounds of tightly wound twenty dollar bills, packed in rolls, and Dale then, as if all were forgiven: "I told you, son. I told you I'd take care of you."

Just like that, after months of boredom and after weeks of agony and after a lifetime of money problems, being a slave to his mother, it was over.

That's it. I'm free.

But that kind of ease, of course, is not for desperate men. Winning the lottery, walking away scot-free. No.

That was when Bradley and Dale heard the hogs begin to root. They were agitated, and Dale swiveled his head quickly left and right, paranoia out of remission. Dale hugged the bag close to his body and pulled a gun from the waist of his jeans. He looked into the dark and squinted. He looked back at the money, trying to choose. "Hold this," he said. He shoved the bag of money into Bradley's chest, then pointed the gun at him. "I swear to God if you move an inch…"

Dale grabbed a flashlight from his bag and edged into the thicket.

It was then, standing in the night with five hundred thousand dollars in cash clenched to his chest, that Bradley Polk, with cat-like vision from weeks of sitting out in the woods in the dark, could see two figures—one large, one small—descending upon Dale from opposite ends of the thicket.

CHAPTER

THIRTY-FIVE

Mayhill gripped the gun. The hogs, impossibly loud, chattered to the left of him and moved through the thicket like a bulldozer. The scrub did not bother them in the least, acting as low tornadoes mowing down branches and vines. He kept his gaze on Bradley and Dale.

Bradley stood in the middle of the woods. After days of looking for him, to see Bradley in the flesh was astounding, the relief immense. He was alive. But Bradley looked scared and small somehow, despite his largeness. Suddenly, Dale shoved Bradley, and then the beam of Dale's flashlight turned toward the trees, toward Mayhill, and bounced through the woods.

Mayhill held up his gun and followed Dale, but there was no straight shot through the trees. *Run*, Mayhill thought. *I should run.* What a cowardly thing to think, but it was all he thought when Dale's sunken face appeared behind the beam. The light narrowed in on a tree ten feet to the left of Mayhill. It settled there for a second and slithered down the trunk. Then, unsatisfied, the beam stalked another tree, closer. More footsteps, louder, slower. Hogs still moving.

"Jason?" Dale yelled, panic in his voice. "Jason, cut it out. You getting paid, boy."

Dale turned, and the light settled on the hogs.

Run. Yes, I could turn to the right and run. But the path was thick with fallen branches and scrub. If Mayhill ran now, he would stumble only a few strides in, and Dale would have seconds of open shots the moment he bolted. Mayhill needed a clear shot. He held his breath and listened. Dale had stopped. No footsteps. The beam settled on a pine far to his left in the opposite direction. *Yes, go there.* Mayhill looked through the sight. Dale's steps waded deeper into the woods, closer to where Mayhill left the hogs, to where he knew Dale could hear them.

Mayhill breathed an uneven breath and crouched down as low as his knees would allow. The trees couldn't hide him but maybe the underbrush would.

Then a second later, Dale spun. Mayhill's shoulder, as if in slow motion, flooded with terrible light. Dale's flashlight pointing at his shoulder. Dale's flashlight pointing between his eyes, burning like a bee sting. Mayhill's eyes closed on instinct, and he turned his head to relieve the shock of the light. He tried to look at Dale, his gun up.

Then a yell.

Out of nowhere, out of the dark, behind Dale, someone Mayhill didn't immediately recognize. A man behind Bradley, shoving Bradley to the ground, ripping the bag from his hands. Dale's light whirled toward the commotion. Dale ran at them.

That boy. That boy who drove the Datsun.

Mayhill ran to the right and stumbled over a branch and onto the ground. He grabbed his gun and looked to Bradley, then back at Dale for his shot.

The light bounced on the two men rolling on the ground. Bradley grabbed at the boy, who was struggling free. The lantern fell to the forest floor, still half illuminating the scene in stop-motion pictures. The glint of gunmetal in the light. Dale on his feet. Dale firing his gun. Dale running and tackling Bradley. One of the boys on the ground, holding his arm, screaming out in pain.

Dale stood with his back to the thicket and to Mayhill, who still crouched on the ground in the woods. Dale's gun was now on Bradley, who had the bag. The boy was in the dirt next to him, trying to sit up but going weak. "Dale, no," Bradley said. "Dale, don't."

Bradley's face twisted in fear, one arm toward the boy, one arm clenching the bag to his chest like a life-preserver. "Dale, please."

Mayhill's heart pulsed through his hands. He pointed his gun right between Dale's shoulder blades. They stuck out so far they looked like wings. It was a straight shot. Dale was going to kill them both, both young men. Dale's bullet had hit one of the boys. His vision flashed to Van. Van on the ground. His killer over him. Is this how it happened? Suddenly, Dale spun toward the woods, and that's when Mayhill could see Birdie, not ten feet away from him, running into the light, the lantern illuminating the long stretch of her white arms, her gun on Dale. Dale's gun right on her.

"Birdie!" Mayhill leapt and pulled the trigger.

Two shots—*two*—blasted through the dark like a string of firecrackers. A scream. Dale dropped backward to the ground, falling hard on Bradley. Bradley scrambled out from under the dead weight of Dale's body, then drug himself out of the light, and disappeared into the woods. The hogs stampeded forward. Confusion everywhere.

Birdie had dropped out of sight.

Mayhill plowed through the thicket, yelling her name, treading through hogs and limbs, his right leg heavy and hot. "Birdie! Birdie!"

Mayhill got almost a hundred yards, weaving through the neat rows of pine, until the adrenaline wore off and pain lanced through him like a fire pick. Something very terrible had happened to his leg. Mayhill fell against a tree and looked at his leg. He had been shot. Thoughts seized him. He should get back to his truck, get back to Birdie's house, somehow get to the hospital two hours away in Houston. But where was Birdie? Had she been hit?

And then, a split-second vision: off in the distance, a flash of white, like the wink of a fawn's tail. He knew it was Birdie—her face, her arms—her paleness a ghostly flare in the dark. He cut the lantern, hoping his eyes would adjust to darkness. He would follow her, but all he got was the glitter of white, and she was gone deep, deep into the woods, but in the thunderstorm of hooves and confusion, Mayhill crumpled to the ground.

Mayhill could see the blood pulsing through his jeans, bleeding everything out of him so fast. He had to get to his truck. He pulled himself up and shifted to his good leg. The woods went black for a second, but he held onto the pine and stayed upright. His energy, his breath, his thoughts—everything was moving out through the apparent hole in his leg. He stared at the impossible amount of blood, and the woods around him came into crystalline focus. Every pine needle, the glinty eye of every hog.

He closed his eyes and tried to map out where he left his truck.

East of here, he thought, not too far. He could make it. He began to walk, tugging his right leg behind him, wincing at every step, stopping every few seconds to lean against a tree and catch his breath. He felt drunk, and the sleep threatened to take him over like a sudden strike to the head, but the thicket ushered him along and eventually he felt like he was floating, slipping above himself into the canopy of the trees, the same words pulsing through him. *I did it, I did it.*

Mayhill understood what was happening.

There is only ever one satisfying conclusion for a hero.

He didn't know how he got there, but Mayhill found himself at his truck. He pressed all of his weight into the door handle and fell into the cab. He braced his forearms into the soft, worn bench and used all of his strength to drag himself in.

In the truck, his senses heightened again: mossy, wet, the smell of dog hair. He had stopped smelling pine a long time ago, having lived here so long, but he could suddenly smell its mintiness, fresh as Christmas. He felt oddly competent all of a sudden, more competent and in control than he ever had in his life. All of his past failures granulated and disappeared before him. *I did it, I did it.*

He understood what was happening.

And he couldn't be here. He had to get off of Birdie's land. He shifted into first gear and gassed it, hogs scattering like mice.

The breeze tore through his truck, and the gush of hot air made him feel like he was swimming, being taken into a current. He stuck his head out the window, willing the crash of air to keep him awake, and as he tore down the road, headlights bouncing wildly, for a moment, he could feel Van beside him, as if he were in the truck—then as if he were swimming through the air alongside him, as if he had surfaced from beneath the pine needles, his voice gasping from the undertow.

He glanced in the rearview mirror, and for a second, the feeling of Van hardened into a person—but it was not Van, of course.

Because it wasn't time for Van yet.

It was Birdie in the rearview mirror—Bradley beside her—and they were running, running, running. Their faces glowing red in his taillights, their arms pumping, their legs sprinting after him. Birdie screaming his name.

There is only ever one satisfying conclusion for a hero.

CHAPTER THIRTY-SIX

T ragedy, Van always said, was simply a matter of ending the
story someplace else.

But where else could it end after all this time, this story
of Randy Mayhill, a man who perfected heroics, whetted it down like
the fine point of a knife, because the only thing better than being a
hero is being a martyr? If she were honest with herself, and all wise
women should be—respectfully disagreeing with Onie that a hero's
only conclusion is death and cheerfully siding with Van that a story
keeps going—Birdie might have found that, even when a life as big as
Randy Mayhill's ended, there were no less than a hundred places for
his story to conclude.

There could be an argument for his story ending the next day,
when Birdie and Bradley inspected the garden and found it remarkably
clean. No cigarette butts or spit cups or barbed wire or anything to
incriminate—just a pair of gloves and a camping lantern with a

surprisingly meticulous picture scratched through the paint on the bottom: a drawing of a hand giving the middle finger.

Near where Dale had fallen, they would find a barely perceptible scrap of a camouflage t-shirt and a shred of a Twizzlers wrapper—but no evidence of Dale's body—because much to their relief and much to their horror, there was no evidence of Dale himself because, lest we forget—Kool-Aid, Twizzlers, Moon Pies, antifreeze, don't matter what—hogs have a sweet tooth.

And also the next day, when Jason limped from his tiny house on his island of stranded people, after he had scrambled away from the scene, terrified, and treated his bullet-grazed arm with tweezers and hydrogen peroxide, he found seventy-five thousand dollars in his glove box. He immediately set to work sketching floor plans for his mama's house on a flattened cigarette carton because it was the only paper he could find.

For seventy-five thousand dollars, I'll forget you and everybody you ever know.

After all of that, the only evidence left would be tucked away neatly next to the gun safe in the back of Van's closet: a red gym bag with a little over four hundred thousand dollars in cash.

Or this conclusion:

Onie at the front of the church, reading Thoreau: "Every blade in the field, every leaf in the forest lays down its life in its season." The tragedy of active voice! Onie's words rising up with the perfume of the peace lilies—with such power, such command—that nobody in that packed church could again doubt her sanity.

Birdie would sit on the front row with Bradley, who, in a sign of a newfound emotional maturity, did not hide in his truck as he had at Van's funeral, but took in life as it was right in front of his face, the two of them passing around the word hero like a collection plate. Afterward, Birdie told him how Mayhill had resurrected now as a kind of Christ in her mind, all dying so she could live and whatnot, that for the rest of her days, when she considered Jesus on the oak-paneled walls of the Methodist church—blue-eyed, pale, gut notably absent— she would only see Randy Mayhill: Mayhill healing the sick, Mayhill pouring the grape juice, Mayhill staring right through her and blessing all she would do for the rest of her days.

When she described the scene to Onie, she would search for the words to describe the way a leaden-legged Randy Mayhill took flight with improbable grace to jump in front of Dale and the bullet meant for her. And Birdie, at a loss for such words, would land only on the unlikely descriptor that Mayhill looked "as triumphant as a cantaloupe ascending through the night air."

And they would all marvel at this: how it was that in his dying moments Randy Mayhill had the foresight to drive away from the plot, off of Birdie's land, into Dale's yard to keep all investigations firmly away from Birdie and fully on Dale Mackey.

The story would be confirmed by a broken down Mrs. Baird's truck caught on the way to Houston, and after finding all the gardening supplies and paraphernalia in Dale's shed, the sheriff would conclude that Dale Mackey was long gone from here—probably to Mexico by now—escaped with the money.

Another nameless man they couldn't identify. Drug deal gone bad. *CRACKED THE CASE!* In the end, they would question Birdie more about the cantaloupe than Randy Mayhill.

Except this: the pink note in Randy Mayhill's back pocket. *I'm sorry, Birdie. I love you.*

"Do you know what this is, Ms. Woods?"

"It belonged to my daddy. May I keep it, please?"

Too tragic, all of it, but luckily, there is another conclusion.

CHAPTER THIRTY-SEVEN

The wet summer turned into an even wetter fall, and the flooding downgraded the hog plague to an inconvenient infestation. The weatherman credited one of the children down south—Niño or Niña—but a name didn't help anyone fathom the hogs' overnight decline any better, and they resented that the direction of equatorial winds could uproot their lives so completely. They could handle their own weather, thank you very much. They didn't need input from the South Americans.

Onie ripped up the crabgrass in the front flowerbeds and put in some purple cabbage for fall. A small wooden sign with white letters bloomed overnight out of the front porch flowerbed: AIN'T NOBODY NOBODY. Bradley didn't know what it meant or why it was there, but he liked it because it sounded like something Van would have said.

With a sudden windfall of money, Birdie hired a crew and was experimenting with a plantation of slash pine, which didn't grow naturally west of the Mississippi, but was a hardy tree and would thrive on her acid-hot soil, and Bradley, the obvious choice for managing the crew—he knew the land intimately, didn't he?—would need a place to live as he and Birdie directed the next phase of her acreage. Birdie offered up Van's room. It was not an unpleasant arrangement, the small house busy with three spoiled dogs (Boo, Atticus, and Vanna), two moody women, and one very large man—a chaos Van and Randy would have adored, though Vanna, Mayhill's stolen dog, did not.

Vanna was still skittish around human females thanks to Bradley's mother's violent outbursts, and so the dog took to hiding in dark spots around the house (closets, corners, under chairs, and whatnot). It was in this daily afternoon APB search for the dog that Birdie found herself in Onie's room looking for Vanna under the bed. She got down on her knees and swept her long arm underneath, but instead of the soft give of dog belly, something hard hit Birdie's hand. She felt around for a moment, trying to discern the object's shape with her fingers, but then dragged it out into the light.

A hunting rifle, beaten up and well-used.

Birdie inspected it closely but did not recognize it immediately as one of Van's or Onie's, then held it up and looked through the sight, as one always does when getting to know a new gun. It was heavy, an old, cheap model, and Birdie turned the gun back and forth in her hands to study the stock. The wood grain was nicked and neglected. The polish had worn off and tiny cracks had started to form in the wood; overall, it was an unexceptional gun except for a design someone had scratched at the bottom of the stock near the butt. She turned the shotgun upright and found that it wasn't a design at all. Initials. T and J scratched lightly into the wood.

Birdie froze—the breath leaving her—then she quickly pushed the gun back under the bed and instinctively held her hands open in front of her, as if to surrender to the imaginary person who had just caught her in possession of what could only be Tommy Jones's gun.

Birdie looked around Onie's room, and all at once, everything smoldered with meaning. An aerial photograph someone had taken of the land. Onie loved it so much she had it printed on canvas and hung it above her bed. The bookshelf. A picture of Van and Mayhill in high school. It stood in a gold frame on the third shelf. Onie's desk where she sat and graded papers. Birdie scanned her brain for anyone else with those initials, but like Onie's television as of late, Birdie's brain had gone suspiciously silent. Of course Tommy Jones's gun was there.

Birdie stuck her head out the door. Onie played a dirge at the piano, a haunting number that sounded like church bells, and Bradley listened from the couch. She smiled at Bradley and he smiled back—all hey-how-ya-doins, dinner's-almost-dones—and Birdie nodded like a jackass—all yeah-that-sounds-great, love-me-some-dirges. She could barely breathe.

Birdie closed the door and slowly slid open Onie's desk drawer. The old wood squeaked like a barn door, and inside was a fat purple marker. The map. She thought of the map Mayhill found in Tommy Jones's truck. How had she not seen it? Those feminine loops that colored in the pasture. No self-respecting hunter would denote a pasture with purple loops.

Next to the marker, a few paperclips and rubber bands, and Onie's Bible curiously puffed in the middle like a fat wallet. Birdie carefully took the Bible from the drawer and placed it on top of the desk, and there, smack-dab in the middle of Matthew, she found: newspaper articles from the past year—*Prayers for Star, Local Woman in Coma, Raises $10,000*, and *Local Woman Unresponsive After Found in Car—*

Tommy Jones's name throughout, the articles edited for grammar because old habits died hard; a glossy flier of hog trapping tips; a thank you note from Mayhill: *If you or Birdie ever need anything at all, I hope you know I will be at your Beck and Call!!! I love you!!!*—the B with pointy flags, the I like a pine tree; a scrap of paper with "Tommy Jones" scribbled on it, his phone number in Onie's handwriting; and Van's obituary, a tea stain like a waning crescent moon. Birdie stared at this blatant scrapbook of revenge and, trying to regain her breath, felt only shame in herself because you would have to be very dim indeed not to realize that she had misread Onie the entire time: she had not been depressed, she had been plotting.

Was Mayhill right that Tommy Jones had been a hitman? Dale, always paranoid, never got his hands dirty so it would make sense he hired Tommy Jones—beater of women, assassin of hogs and men—to take care of Van when he thought he was about to get caught. And there Onie was with a newspaper rap sheet of Tommy Jones's transgressions, his phone number, and a ready excuse to invite him onto her land.

"I gotta hog problem. I need some trapping done, Mr. Jones."

But certainly she had something planned for Dale too.

"Bradley!" Birdie leaned her head out the door, the smell of bacon hitting her in the face. Onie launched into an arpeggio as Bradley hovered outside Onie's room.

"What kind of candy did Dale eat?" Birdie asked.

Bradley looked at her nervously.

"Just tell me," Birdie said. "What kind of candy did Dale eat?"

"Twizzlers mostly, Moon Pies…"

Birdie held the doorframe. She suddenly remembered Onie's trip to the store, memories shaken loose like mulberries from the branch, Onie standing there—bags in hand, teetering like a tight-rope walker—

the bags brimming with Twizzlers and Moon Pies, even though Onie wouldn't let Birdie drink Coke in the house. The look Birdie had given her! The disappointment! The fear Onie was losing her mind!

But there was something else in those bags. In her memory, Birdie zoomed in on the detail. Antifreeze. Antifreeze in the summer. Sweet as sugar, so sweet Mr. Boudreaux used it to kill his hogs. Hog trapping tips: *Choose the right bait. Persistence pays!!!*

"Why are you asking about him?" Bradley asked.

Birdie wanted to say, "Onie hired Tommy Jones and shot him, and I think she was poisoning Dale slowly with Twizzlers."

But instead she said, "Guess I gotta sweet tooth."

Birdie closed the door and hustled back to Onie's desk. She slid the Bible into the drawer and closed it, now acutely aware that her fingerprints stickied everything. She left Onie's room and joined Bradley at the dinner table, guilt and jack-assery firmly affixed to her face. She tried to act normal. "Bacon!" Birdie said. "Haven't had it since lunch!" Onie remained at the piano, and Birdie was glad because she wasn't sure what to say to her yet.

Perhaps it was the dirge or the realization that Bradley could never know this thing about Onie, or maybe it was the stack of bacon for supper—pork for the third meal that day, a pork trifecta, batting a thousand in pork-centric meals—but Birdie Woods felt a sudden crash of loneliness that was almost unbearable.

She wanted desperately to talk to Mayhill right then—more so even than her father, her loss of him so familiar now it barely registered, like a fish feeling water. No, she wanted Mayhill. She wanted Randy Mayhill taking up too much room on the bench, sweating too much, knowing too much about everything. She wanted his too muchness. She wanted to see his too-much reaction the moment the puzzle came together, the realization that Onie—this killer of killers—had executed justice on her own. How satisfying he would have found it! He would have wept like a baby at the beauty of the entire thing, and then hemorrhaged right there on the floor. He would have died then anyway, she decided.

A joy that kills and whatnot.

Tragedy is simply a matter of ending the story someplace else. The mystery solved, Bradley and Birdie safe, Onie sane(ish)—this could be the satisfactory conclusion. But no, even by Van's standards (and he does tell a hell of a story, doesn't he?), such an ending would not suffice either. Because this is the legend of Randy Mayhill, and any story of his cannot stand on two legs.

It must stand on four.

Because she had to, because there was no other way that Birdie could better honor Randy Mayhill than to tamper with evidence (ten-year maximum), as soon as supper was over and Bradley and Onie were yelling at *Wheel of Fortune* (Bradley always painfully wrong; Onie yelling fake answers so he wouldn't feel bad), she marched Tommy Jones's shotgun right out of their house. She put on gloves and wiped the gun clean (alcohol, Rem oil), then drove it like a ticking bomb to Dale's abandoned trailer. She stopped and listened before she got out to make sure no trucks were going down the road and that nobody was there to see her. Then she snuck like a ninja into Dale's shed. She propped the shotgun against the remaining bags of blood meal, and walked quickly back to her truck, ready to tear away as fast as she could.

And that was when it happened. Birdie Woods would remember it for the rest of her life as the moment when, despite the unstoppable torrent of tragedy and betrayals in this world, hope bubbled up from her toes, took fire in her belly, and wouldn't let go.

She opened the truck door to leave, and a tawny cowdog with white ears—much too thin from his low-protein diet of Twizzler scraps and Moon Pies, a sitting duck for hungry hogs—suddenly emerged out of hiding from Dale's shed. He was scratched and bloodied, ribs like sticks. Dale's dog. It had to be Dale's dog, though he had been abandoned for months at this point, hadn't he? How had he survived? Months of deprivation and starvation and loss and hogs and horrors she couldn't imagine. The dog had lived through it.

It was then that the dog, seemingly out of nowhere, stretched his neck and began walking toward her. It was an unnatural lengthening of the scruff, as if he were being pulled gently on a leash, as if someone were honest-to-God leading that dog right to her. The invisible cue still at work, he scrambled up the step and into the truck cab. Then, noticing the plush accommodations of his new situation, the dog turned three times in a circle and plopped down beside Birdie. He nudged his snout at the softness of Birdie's thigh, and looked at her as if to say, "Let's go, Birdie Woods. I've been waiting for you."

AUTHOR'S NOTE AND ACKNOWLEDGEMENTS

This novel is a work of fiction, but several East Texas communities, including my wonderful hometown, inspired the characters and places found in this book. Growing up, I knew an inordinate number of men named Jimmy, and I'd feel guilty if I didn't note that all the Jimmies I knew were kind and generous men. Further, of all my childhood haunts, I still think of the feed store as a magical place. My version of heaven smells like leather, sweet feed, and burnt coffee. And though this is not a political story, I hope it brings attention to our country's history of questionable marijuana laws.

Writing a book requires its own community, and I'm forever grateful to the members of mine. Thank you first to my agent, Josh Getzler at HSG Agency, the best advocate an author could have. You championed this book in a way I could only imagine. Your suggestions made me dig deeper, and your delight in this work continues to inspire me. Also, thanks to Jonathan Cobbe who is always quick with replies, worked weekends on this book, and did a thousand more things I'll never know.

Thank you to Jason Pinter of Polis Books, who celebrates his authors while being a brilliant one himself. May we all have the energy and enthusiasm that you possess. I'm grateful to be in your orbit.

Many thanks also to Stephanie and Stephen Chambers, Apryl Mathes and Adam Shulman for the anecdote about Thoreau, Jon and Linda Caswell, Bryan and Doneita Forrester, Bill and Carolyn Brister,

Mimi Bark, Kristin Cicciarelli, Brandon Boger, Marissa Volsteyn, Dave McCaul, Rick Hynes, Justin Moore, Adam and Amanda Arista, Peter Larsen for the photos and gun knowledge, Tex Thompson, Sally Kemp, Bill Edwards, Mary Ellen Bluntzer, Leska Parker, Daniel Jacob, Jeannie Pierce, Shagit Thakkar, Frank Cohn, Linda Ball, Josh and Adria, Kate and Jamie, and Cathy and Jane.

Extra hugs go to Gina Best, a brilliant writer, editor, and friend, who went well beyond the call of duty for this book.

Many thank yous to my East Texas family for fielding numerous texts about wild hogs and loblolly pines. Thank you for cheering me on. (I feel you too, David, V.B., and Thelma Lea.)

Endless gratitude goes to Suzanne Frank, Dan Hale, and the Writer's Path at SMU for structure, inspiration, long pep talks, and community.

My dad, a character so big he could never be captured in words.

My mother, who is equal parts hilarious and kind. No other mother would have researched guerrilla marijuana growing so tirelessly for her child. You know this book wouldn't have happened without you.

My son Emerson, the silliest, smartest, funniest, fiercest storyteller you'll ever meet. I'm sorry for all the cuss words.

My husband Bryan, for everything. He is not only a brilliant brainstormer, developmental editor, and proofreader, he is a kind, loving, and creative man who always tries. I am a better everything because of you.

Y'all have my heart.

ABOUT THE AUTHOR

Born and raised in in the Piney Woods of East Texas, Heather Harper Ellett is a graduate of SMU and a therapist in private practice. She lives in Dallas with her husband and son. AIN'T NOBODY NOBODY is her debut novel. Follow her at @heatherellett.